wonderfull

DATE DUE

OCT 1 1 2008			
JUN 0 1 2009			
JUL 2 4 2010			

wonderfull

A NOVEL

WILLIAM NEIL SCOTT

NeWest Press

This one's for my family, both immediate and distant, living and dead, who shared with me all their stories, warts and all, in the hope that I might one day find my own. I will never be able to repay that most generous and wonderful of gifts.

HELLO?

Can you hear me?

It's been a while since I've done this, so I'm not sure if you can hear me.

Not that you could respond even if you did.

You might need to turn me up.

Let's try an experiment: If you can hear my voice, flick the lights on and off in the room you're in. Doesn't matter where you are. If you're in a car, then flash the headlights. Or honk your horn. If you're outside and all you've got is a lighter, strike it. And if you don't have any light? Jump up and down. Wave your arms around. Call out. Laugh. Sing a song. Make it loud.

Now. Look outside. See if anyone else is doing it. See if the world is suddenly filled up with cries and car horns and flashing lights and people singing in the streets, flapping their arms like seagulls. Flickering candles that look like ground-bound stars of lighters being struck in wild succession.

Can you see them? Is it wonderful?

CADMUS BRODIE, my father, liked to tell stories. When he was driving and the only other person in the car was me, he'd tell stories to pass the time. He didn't like the radio, for reasons most of you know. Even when we were out of town and the programs started to make sense, he'd still have it off. There was no good music made after 1978, he'd argue. The news didn't hold much hope for him either. Nothing had any relevance to the life he was living. It was all strange and painful, distant and difficult to hear.

So he'd tell stories. And at the beginning of each car ride, he'd tell one story that was different from the rest, but might tie in somewhere along the line of interconnected, far-fetched stories that followed. A warm-up tale, something to get his throat warm, as he put it.

I'm going to follow my father's example. I think that's fitting.

HERE GOES.

ALEXANDER GARFAX, the namesake of our village and the most famous Scottish eccentric, took it upon himself to discover the New World in 1896. He had plans on finding the great lost city of Scotland, Bennogonium. The old man had gotten it into his head that it was somewhere along the east coast of Canada.

He had problems finding a captain. No one wanted to take him. Which makes sense. Garfax was either crazy or tragically misinformed. A pseudo-scientist who cultivated relationships with real scientists, he read out-of-date books with frayed spines and dragons in the margins and used them as the basis for his expedition. The real scientists, who viewed Garfax more as a patron than as a fellow colleague, tried to dissuade him, but Garfax was adamant.

He found a captain in Samuel Townsend, the only man desperate enough to take Garfax on his fool's errand. Townsend had a spotty history, you see. His last two ships sank under strange circumstances. The first sprung multiple leaks in calm water and good weather; the second ran aground while being harried by a massive flock of irate seagulls. No one wanted to give Townsend another shot at captaining. It didn't matter that under regular circumstances, Townsend was the captain you wanted; the man had developed the worst luck.

Then he met Garfax. Listened to the old man's plan. Saw a way out from under his bad luck. A way to wipe clean his ruined reputation in one smooth voyage.

Of course, nothing of the sort happened.

Garfax and Townsend discovered the New World by running into it in the middle of the night. Townsend, a stoic in the classic sense, made his way through the sinking ship to rouse Garfax from his cabin.

"What's happening?" Garfax demanded. "Why have we stopped?"

"We've found the New World," Townsend said. "And we're sinking."

"We can't sink."

"I assure you we can."

And they did. All souls aboard watched the vessel *glug glug glug* its way into settling on the mouth of the bay they had found themselves in, an empty stretch of beach surrounded on all sides by miles and miles of pines.

The next few days were spent making a temporary camp and deciding what to do next. Townsend listened gloomily to the carpenters as they reported that there was no hope in salvaging the vessel. He sighed heavily when his navigator confessed, in between sobs, that he had very little idea of where they were in the New World.

"So where do we go?" Townsend asked quietly. "What happens next?"

"I don't know, sir."

"Well, that's just wonderful."

Not having any practical skill, Garfax kept himself busy by exploring the local environs. While the shipwreck was a noticeable setback, the story that he had built in his mind about his discovery of the great lost city of Scotland could accommodate it. He'd tell this story, rehearsing it out loud as he walked through the pines that surrounded the bay in all directions.

"Shipwrecked," he'd say. "With no chance of rescue. I went into the woods. I cried tears of frustration. I fell to the floor of the forest and found, as I pounded my fists against the dirt, that it was not dirt that I was hitting at all … but smooth stone. A road." As he said this, he searched the ground for his imagined road. "A road," he repeated. "I found a road and I followed it. High into the hills. I came across one building, an ancient watchtower where the auld ones before me watched for the arrival of their cousins from the sea. And then one tower became two. Became a wall. A great wall broken and ruined, covered in vegetation. And then, before I even knew what I was looking at, there it was. Bennogonium. The lost city."

The story gave him hope. Telling it out loud, if only to himself, made him all the more certain of its truth. It didn't matter that there was no road, no towers, no wall, and no city to make it any more than a pleasant diversion.

Back at the beach, while the men waited for Townsend to tell them what to do, they unpacked their belongings and tried to keep themselves occupied. The carpenters made inventories of their tools. The sailors made appeasing gestures to the various personal gods they honoured to carry them through their aquatic life. Some began to gamble. The more educated read. When a domino set and a deck of cards appeared, they all abandoned their previous activities and focused on the games.

"At least there's fish," the men said. "We'd never starve here."

Which was true. There were fish in abundance in the nameless bay.

In 1492, when Christopher Columbus sailed that blue ocean to discover the New World, he took with him four ships. One of those ships, like Townsend's own, ran aground in the discovery. Columbus, already frustrated by the mutinous attitudes of many of his bored crew, decided to solve two problems at once. He gave the men who obeyed him something to do by building a gallows to deal with the men who wouldn't.

When Samuel Townsend's third and final ship sank on the eastern coast of Canada, he made out of the wreckage an elaborate dock. In his arrival, his only thoughts were leaving again, even though there were no boats for him to launch.

Within a month, the men were growing restless. The dock, now lovingly crafted and set, was not enough to keep them in that bay. They left a few at a time, taking what provisions they could carry and setting off through the pines in whatever direction struck them best. Soon more left. Townsend watched them go. He thought about arguing with them, telling them that something was going to happen that would change their situation, but he couldn't come up with a plausible alternative.

Townsend made the decision to die. He realized this only three weeks after the fact. Sitting on the beach, writing in his leather-bound journal, which was almost at the end of paper, it struck him that he would never leave this nameless bay. That this is where he would stay until life left him.

The thought made him angry. The despair that had crept so quietly and completely into his heart set him into a frenzy. He blamed Garfax, the mad eccentric who had come to the New World on a fool's errand. After the last of the forty-three men under his command had disappeared into the pines, Samuel Townsend dressed in his best uniform, loaded his pistol, and walked over to Garfax.

Garfax, in his own way, had come to the same conclusion as the captain. He understood to the very depths of himself that he would never leave the beach. That thought didn't cause him distress, though. Protected by his imagination, it made him smile, granted him a measure of peace. After decades of ranting and raving about possibilities and strange notions, the near-scholar had made a move into the unknown under his own power. Even if he never found Bennogonium in the tangles of pines, that was enough for him.

Townsend found Garfax studying the set of dominoes left behind by the sailors. "What are you doing?" the captain asked tersely.

"My father used to play this game," Garfax said with a small half-smile. "Every day after dinner with his brother, when he came to visit. They played for hours."

"It's not much of a game."

"My father enjoyed it. He never taught me how to play, though. Not exactly. I learned on my own. He'd let me watch, but he never instructed me."

Townsend sighed, gripped the handle of the pistol, and pointed it at the near-scholar.

"I'm going to shoot you now."

Garfax blinked. "Excuse me?"

"I'm going to shoot you now. You've ruined my life. I'm never going to be able to go back home, and even if I could, you've taken from me the only thing I was born to do. I love the sea. And it's all your fault."

"I didn't sink your ship, captain."

"Well, neither did I!" The captain screamed.

They were quiet for a moment. Garfax alternated between contemplating the domino tiles and the barrel of Townsend's pistol. "I don't know what to tell you, then."

Townsend cocked the pistol. "You don't need to tell me anything."

"What are you going to do after I'm gone? Who are you going to talk to?"

"I'm not going to be stuck here with you."

"You'd rather be alone?"

A frown creased Townsend's brow. He hadn't considered the implications of being alone on this desolate bay, with only the dock to mark it as touched by human hands.

"I'd rather not be alone myself," Garfax followed.

"I can't live with you. You'll drive me mad."

"I don't suppose I can live with you either."

"So what do you propose?"

Garfax spread his hands out to the domino tiles before him. "I'll play you for it."

8

"Excuse me? Play me for what?"

"For the pistol," Garfax said. "The rules of the game will be that whoever wins gets to decide who spends the rest of his life in the bay alone. The loser must agree to the winner's decision."

"So if you win—"

"I'll shoot you in the head and spend the rest of my days here alone."

"And if I win—"

"The same but the other way around, I imagine."

Townsend thought for awhile and then, very slowly, crouched down on the other side of the tiles from Garfax. He didn't want to be alone. He didn't want to live with Garfax either. At least this way a decision could be reached. "All right, then. But I've played this game for years. I'm very good."

"Of that," Garfax said. "I have no doubt."

WHAT GARFAX DIDN'T TELL Townsend about the games that his father used to play with his brother when he came to visit, is that his father was a sore loser and a born cheater. For the weeks that Hilbert Garfax entertained his brother, they'd only play a single game. Normally several games can be played in an evening, but Hilbert had manipulated it so that they'd get to a certain point in the game before they'd have to retire for the evening or take care of some urgent household business. He gave strict orders to his servants to be on the lookout for telltale coughs and hand gestures that would instruct them to come to him with sudden events that demanded his attention. Then, when his brother was out on the balcony indulging in an evening cigar, he would come back and rearrange the spider web of ivory tiles so that the already confusing game was more fairly balanced.

Garfax applied the same strategy to his game with Townsend. At first he did this to stall for time. While the prospect of living in the nameless bay didn't appeal to the near-scholar, it was a lot more favourable than being shot by or having to shoot the captain. Townsend, for his part, didn't notice the changes that were made in his absence. After a while, the tiles all looked the same, and each time they finished a nightly session he would pick up his pistol and retire to his own camp on the other side of the bay.

"Tomorrow," he promised. "We will finish the game and one of us will be free of this wretched place."

"Of that," Garfax said. "I have no doubt."

The two of them, the captain and the near-scholar, played every day for the rest of their lives. In time, the settlement of Canada caught up with them. The sailors who had made it to civilization told stories of the shipwreck and drew maps to the best of their remembering to lead people back there. Tales of abundant fish drew fishermen like flies, and they began to build narrow roads and slim paths through the dense pines to get to the nameless bay.

The fishermen found the two men first, still playing their endless game on the beach. They approached slowly, giving the reverence due to characters in a sailor's story. "Sirs?" they said.

The two men looked up from the game.

"Yes?" Townsend said, smoothing his soiled and crumpled tunic.

"Is this your bay?"

"Oh yes," Garfax replied.

The fishermen exchanged looks. "We'd like your permission to settle here, then."

"What for?"

"Well, for the fish, of course. And you have a wonderful dock."

The two men looked at the dock for the first time in over a year. "It is quite nice," Garfax commented.

"Thank you."

"Does that mean yes?"

Garfax nodded. "Of course you can settle here. We'd be glad for the company."

Just as they were about to turn and head back down the road to send for their families, one of the fishermen turned back. "Does the bay have a name? None of the stories mention one."

"It's called Garfax," Townsend said. "This wretched place is called Garfax."

Garfax brushed aside his long and greasy white hair, frowning at the captain. "Is it, now?" The captain smiled through broken and rotted teeth.

"It's what you deserve, you bastard."

Sighing, Garfax shrugged. "Fair enough. It's your move."

ALL RIGHT, throat's warm now.

Can you still hear me?

Good.

I'm not going to start at the beginning, because I don't rightly know where that is anymore. And I'm not going to start at the end and work my way backwards either. That way lies madness. I'm going to start at the part that makes the most sense. I'm going to start with my mother. Because whenever I think of what's happened, I end up coming back to her. All of my stories eventually, in some way or another, come back to her.

So I'm going to start there.

I

Emma Brodie Goes to Water

WHAT YOU HAVE TO UNDERSTAND is that there was something wrong even before Emma Brodie went to water. People just don't suddenly decide to do drastic things. They are driven to it. And even if it isn't immediately apparent what those reasons are—and it may never become apparent—there are always reasons.

People in the village have always tried to dismiss her aquatic sojourn as the whim of a crazy person, a lonely woman acting out in the absence of her husband. I've even thought this. The evidence just doesn't bear this out, though. Because before stealing the boat she had to stock it, and before she stocked it, she had to have the idea.

I've combed back through photo albums, trying to find that idea growing inside her steadily like a flame, something visible that might catch a lens and flare, but nothing appears. The birthday parties for my brother and sister; the pictures she took of the house; the dozens of angles, trying to seduce potential buyers on its eccentricities; the descriptions she wrote and re-wrote detailing its unique and financially appreciable history; the kitchen get togethers she'd have with her few friends from down the hill, bottles of wine and ashtrays piled with stubs on the checkered tablecloth.

Here's a picture.

Someone else has taken it. A friend. My mother has just turned thirty-two, but she looks much younger. She is leaning against the kitchen sink with a glass of raspberry liquid in one hand and a half-finished cigar in the other. Having never habitually smoked cigars, the size of it looks strange in her hand, as if her fingers haven't quite decided how to hold it. The glass, by contrast, is an easy extension of her hand, something she's grown accustomed to without suggesting dependency.

My mother knows she is posing. The sideways tilt of her head, the stray brown hairs that spill free about her shoulders and face, tell me this. She is smiling, enjoying the absurdity of the wine, the too-large cigar in her fingers, and the act of being captured in photograph.

The picture is dated two months before she stole the boat. Is she already starting to get things together? Is she wavering in her decision? Had this plan been built up and torn down many different times over the eleven years she lived in the village? Did it always, among all things, involve the theft of a small, rickety sea vessel?

She looks happy. My mother looks happy in most of the photographs. There she is with Maddox, many years before, holding his sides while he leans forward in his chair to blow out his birthday candles. Here she is with Faith, again an early picture, holding her hand while they take a walk through the pines. They are staring off towards something above them and to the right. Birds in the pines. Faith points and her mouth hangs open in wonder.

WHAT SHE STOCKED the boat with: three rolls of toilet paper, two extra-large and durable black garbage bags, one new toothbrush (green), one half-finished tube of toothpaste, fifteen two-litre bottles of tap water, seven sweaters, three pairs of jeans, eleven t-shirts, twenty pairs of socks, more than two dozen pairs of underwear, ten decks of smokes, three matchbooks, two lighters, a large Bowie knife, a flashlight, a package of AA batteries, three books—which included her mother's copy of *Miss Alexia's Household Book of Common Foretelling*, *Flying with Phantoms: An Account of RAF Pilots during the Second World War*, and one of the last remaining first editions of *A Brief History of Garfax* by the renegade historian Charlie Glenn, three pillows, two sleeping blankets, one turquoise windbreaker, two boxes of beef jerky, two bushels of bananas, seven apples, one loaf of bread, butter, a glass jar of orange marmalade sent over from her family in Glasgow. Finally, she took a revolver she had inherited from her father, a soldier in the Second World War who had survived the miracle of Dunkirk and who, when given the chance, did not steal the gold watch of Franz Emerick, the greatest German composer you've never heard of, during the time he spent in Berlin.

THIS LAST ITEM is what everyone focuses on. That she would take a gun with her on her seven-day exile seems the height of lunacy, proof to everyone that the strain of raising three children by herself, in a country she did not count as her own, had finally pushed this poor woman to desperate measures. To me it says something different. To me it has always suggested that my mother understood herself more completely than anyone else ever did. She knew her stories, her history. She knew that when push came to shove, a Brodie could be in the middle of the most difficult situation and still maintain her composure, that there is always some way off of the beach. She also appreciated the value of time in the way that only a Brodie can.

THERE ARE SO MANY family stories I'm never going to hear. I wonder now, if I ever heard them all, if it all would make any more sense. Or would they in turn just lead back to more stories? People notice different changes at different times, but more often than not, they recognize the most obvious and sudden over the more subtle and constant.

For the people of Garfax, everything turned the day my mother stole the boat and went to water. If pushed, some might allow for the idea that everything had been set into motion the day that Ester Anson had kissed my father on the cheek after they had danced, slipping her keys into his pocket. But for everyone else, all of the blame for what came next was laid at my mother's feet. It was her forsaking of solid ground that brought about everything that followed, the death of that boy and the betrayal of radio signals, the return of Caleb Anson, the prodigal son, and all the unwanted attention he carried home with him. And finally, they blamed her for the great storm that lasted almost four months.

For me, the moment I noticed things were different, that they had changed, was when I came home from one of the last days of school before summer break and found the door to my house locked.

THE DOOR WAS LOCKED. The door was never locked. Back then, no one in Garfax other than businesses and the church locked their doors. It was taken as an unwritten rule that you could walk into a friend's house, take your shoes off, and say hello without bothering to knock at the door. If you did knock, it was received as being somewhat impolite.

So I knocked. Nothing. No sounds. I was eleven years old and still too short to reach the glass by standing on my toes. I walked around the veranda, whose view is still dominated by the large single pine leaning tall and crooked at an almost forty-five degree angle and a commanding view of Garfax Bay, and peered in through the living room windows. Again, nothing. No lights. No movement.

I took my backpack off, left it on the veranda, and went around the side to check the back door. That was locked too. Frustrated, and with the slight need to urinate growing slowly at the back of my scalp, I went to the front steps and sat down, dramatically holding my head in my hands while I waited for Maddox or Faith to get home. They were always late. At least, they were always later than me. While only a few years older, Faith by a year and Maddox by three, their social calendars were already considerably more extensive and demanding than mine. Faith would be at a friend's house. Maddox would be playing basketball.

I spent a lot of my time by myself, mostly out back, wandering through the pines that surround Garfax for miles, making it look sometimes as if the village itself is the only thing keeping the trees from rushing headlong into the cold Atlantic waters.

An hour passed. I went around back and into the woods a little way to piss behind a tree. When I got back, I could see Maddox coming up the hill and past the row of hedges. I walked out to meet him.

"Door's locked," I said.

"Huh?"

I repeated myself. He continued past me and checked the handle. Frowning, he took off his backpack and went around the side. He then proceeded to see if any windows were open, and when he couldn't find any, he returned. "Door's locked," he reported.

"I know. I told you that."

He shrugged.

"Do you have a key?"

"No. Faith has it."

Which made sense. Maddox had a knack for losing keys. Our mother had the habit of not forgiving repetitive mistakes in her offspring.

So we waited for Faith. We sat a few feet apart on the steps. Although he was only three years older than me, Maddox always seemed incredibly grown up and impressive, a perception he often used to get me to do whatever stupid idea that came into his head. One time, when we were both very young and he had just watched Peter Pan, he took me out onto the roof and taught me how to fly. I fell off the roof, thinking of chocolate ice cream and cartoons.

Ever the concerned elder brother, Maddox's first words while simultaneously checking for broken bones and trying to keep me quiet were to say, "You just weren't trying hard enough."

We didn't say much to each other on the steps. When Faith arrived half an hour later, we both stood up and walked out to meet her.

"Door's locked," Maddox said.

"Okay," she said, not sure what it meant to her.

"We don't have a key."

"Oh." She pulled out the key tied to a shoestring that she hung around her neck. Then she let us in the front door.

Of course, a person might not recognize large changes right away. They might miss such a portentous omen as a locked door in a village with a strict open-door policy, instead considering it a frustrating inconvenience.

Oftentimes we'd come home and find our mother gone, off running errands or working at the newspaper office above the grocery store to beat her deadline for the weekly horoscopes and predictions that the superstitious in the village followed with religious devotion.

Emma Brodie had a gift for knowing things that other people didn't know yet, for looking a little way down the road and reporting back what she saw. This frustrated the serious reporters, the college students who had left their degrees midway out of protest and fled to Garfax to achieve some semblance of journalistic credibility. They fashioned themselves as Canadian Hemingways, hard and dangerous men with cultivated tastes let loose in the wilds of the political backwaters of their country, ever determined to sift out and identify the connections between the natural and social spheres governing the world around them. The idea that my mother, with an economy of phrasing, could tell them with precision how things were going to play out in a given situation allowed no space for any sort of friendship or cordial working relationship to develop.

She would leave a note, though. That was how she was. Either taped to a door frame or secured to the fridge by a magnetic pear, our mother would leave a note. First in the house, Maddox did a quick search for a note and came back with a shrug. "She's probably out at the shops," he said, and that didn't seem so impossible either.

We resumed our habits. Maddox sacked out on the living room couch and began to flip through the slim pickings provided by basic cable. Faith headed upstairs, either to read or listen for songs to record off the radio for her latest mix tape. I went for a walk, not noticing as I passed through the kitchen that the eternal game of dominoes played by the ghosts of my father's father, his uncles, and my mother's father, fell silent. So used to their constant presence and ignorance of our daily affairs, I didn't pay any attention to their stares as they craned their necks out of the funeral dress, following me with their eyes until after I closed the door behind.

Our house is bordered on the back, like all Garfaxian dwellings, by the beginning of the treeline of pine that stretches for miles. Twenty steps from the back door and you can easily lose sight of the house and the rest of the village until you get higher up the hill and the tops of buildings and the bay start peeking through gaps in the branches. I picked up sticks and played games, which, admittingly, given my age, was starting to be considered a little childish. My father, before he left for his latest assignment, told me that he wanted me to read more. He directed me to our library, its long shelves filled with books inherited, along with everything else, from Ester Anson.

"You need to start doing something productive," he declared, plucking a book off a shelf and depositing it in my hands with a flourish. The books hadn't helped anything but my imagination. I rarely looked up difficult words. Instead I read sentences over and over until I got the basic meaning of the word and moved on.

Due to my steady diet of books, the pines became filled with adversaries and allies, strange territories and home countries to defend. I threw rocks at trees, delighting in the cracking snap that echoed through the sheltered middle air between treetop and ground. Armed only with branches, I waged war against invisible foes. Days were spent hiding from pursuers bent on my confession or conversion. Weeks were taken to explore every crevice and cleft in the hill face. Every ruined car became evidence of a previous battle. Each new stick of furniture or painting left to rot in the open took on the air of an ancient artifact left behind by some eldritch civilization. A broken nest of cigarette butts on the ground signalled that enemies were nearby, or that my quarry was close.

I forgot all about the locked door and the lack of a note in a total of eight minutes.

After a couple of hours I made my way back, my cheeks red, mumbling imaginary conversations between myself and the cast of characters who inhabited my inner stories in the pines. I was so caught up that even after I broke the treeline, I didn't see Lizzie Parks kneeling in our backyard over a cardboard box until I was only five feet away from her.

I stopped cold. She looked up at me, brushing away the greasy blonde hair from her face with her right hand, which was holding a slightly dented beer can.

"Which one are you?" she asked, squinting.

"I'm Oswald."

She nodded. "Where's your brother? Matthew?"

"Maddox is inside."

"Maddox. Right," she said, nodding to herself. "Look, can you help me pick up these bottles?"

I was no longer looking at her face. My eyes travelled down her neck and shoulder to the plastic and metal appendage fastened to the point where her left arm ended at the elbow.

"Hey," she barked, dropping the beer can and snapping her fingers in front of my face, giving me a whiff of yellow stained nicotine hands.

"Sorry," I mumbled.

Lizzie coughed. "Look, just help me with the bottles."

She had dropped the cardboard box. That was obvious. The handle had ripped and spilled its contents, dented but unbroken, onto our backyard, which was in desperate need of a cut. The alcohol had no order. Each beer was a different brand. The green unlabelled bottles suffered from varying levels of previous consumption.

"Where have you been off to?" she asked, her eyes focused on the task of managing her hand.

"Just walking."

"You go out there a lot."

I shrugged.

"Yeah, you do," she said, a little too forcefully. "I've seen you. Playing games." She laughed a little and I blushed. I knew from hearing people talk that Lizzie went into the pines to drink, but I never saw her. I didn't like the idea that she had seen me without me noticing. She stopped laughing and her eyes started moving very fast before going back down to the bottles. Now that I was closer, other smells began to emerge. There was alcohol, of course, mixed in with sweat and pine sap. And although I couldn't identify it at the time, she also possessed the earthy stink of pot.

To hear her tell it, and she told her story with no great frequency, Lizzie Parks was beautiful for only five short years, between the ages of nineteen and twenty-four. Everything that I know about her I knew from her conversations with my mother, and the talks she and I had many years later, when we found her drifting in the periphery of our home movies.

Before her nineteenth birthday, Lizzie had been overweight, a heavy girl in a town that didn't have an overabundance of obesity or tact. And unlike her younger brother, Sunny, Lizzie lacked the confidence necessary to carry such a burden without letting it control her.

It had taken her a year to lose the weight, a grand total of seventy-one pounds. She didn't starve herself. She didn't break her body on exercise equipment or ruin her knees by suddenly running three miles a day. Lizzie Parks went to the library. She spoke with her family doctor. With an eye to long-term improvement, she implemented a program in small steps until, as if it happened overnight, she looked in the mirror one day and grinned until she laughed. Laughed until she cried.

Lizzie made up for lost time by throwing herself into the social life of the village. She went up with the local kids to Quill Lake for the summer and started attending dances every other week. Boys and men who previously had ignored or teased her started to pay attention. Girls and women did too. Everyone wanted to talk with her. She had a glow, a beauty. A fierce confidence that comes from stepping up to a challenge and overcoming it.

As a village, Garfax has gone through a number of industries. Originally based around fishing, when the fish vanished, the town switched to its other natural resources, lumber and stone. When the economic climate made it impossible to compete with the larger centres of the western provinces, the village switched again to secondary industries. For almost twenty years, nearly 80 percent of the town built airplane parts or produced every plastic bag and associated packaging that you can find in your common grocery store. Not wanting to make plastic bags, Lizzie trained as a machinist in the airplane factory.

Midway through her twenty-fourth year, when anyone and everyone knew her name, Lizzie lost the length of her left arm from her fingertips up to her elbow when her sleeve got caught in a machine that made specialized cuts on metal sheets that when assembled, created the shells of airplane wings.

Cut suddenly into a sharp asymmetrical shape, the woman that Lizzie had become disappeared. She became quiet. She stayed at home and avoided the phone, avoided learning how to properly use the prosthetic appendages she had been given through her company's medical plan. Sharp pains often ran down her arm to the fingers she no longer had. Phantom pain, the doctors informed her. Nothing curbed the sensation, though. No painkillers had an effect. The limited amount of therapy she allowed didn't produce any impact. Lizzie Parks started drinking and spending a lot of time wandering the pines. And just as suddenly as she had appeared at the age of nineteen, she disappeared into the village until the day my mother went to water.

She was not the first Garfaxian to disappear in such a way.

"Can you manage the box?" she asked.

I nodded. "Yeah."

"Good." She stood up and picked up the full green garbage bag laying next to her. "Let's go in, then."

The old men were gone. They had packed up their game of dominoes and left behind the stink of decades stale cigarettes. Lizzie asked me to put the box on the counter and go and get my brother. Struck by the absence at the table, I yelled for Maddox. "No," she said, almost wincing. "I said go get him."

But Maddox was already walking into the kitchen. He stopped at the threshold.

"You're Maddox?"

"Yeah," he replied, uncomfortable.

"I'm Lizzie. Your mother asked me to come and watch you for a bit."

THE TRUTH IS THAT no one other than Lizzie and her three children knew that Emma Brodie had gone to water for the entirety of the first day and most of the second. While we adjusted to the nervous, twitching presence of Lizzie Parks on our living room couch, and the sudden absence of our dead male relatives monopolizing the kitchen table, life in Garfax continued unabated.

No one noticed that a small wooden motorboat, fitted with oars in case of trouble, had been taken. When she recounted the theft to me many years later, my mother still sounded stunned at how easy it had all been.

"They were just floating out there," she said, referring to the small armada of motorboats that had been taken out for the summer in the vain hope that tourists or people passing through Garfax might want to take a quick trip around the bay under their own power. "It was so simple. Untie some rope and climb in. But when I pulled the motor, the sound that made across the water. I was sure someone was going to hear and try and stop me. My heart was just pounding."

To which I would always ask for some more details, try to pry loose more of the story that I had cobbled together elsewhere. She might talk about the books she read, the night the men got together to try and bring her in when Gregory Peck almost drowned, but towards the last day she wouldn't give me anything. Her face would grow still and she'd nod to herself before promptly changing the topic.

"I'm in the mood for tacos," she'd say.

The few fishing boats left in Garfax passed her on their way out and back on their way in. Anyone who noticed the lone motorboat off by itself and the woman leaning against three pillows, her bare feet dangling in the cold Atlantic, didn't think enough of it to mention. An early tourist, perhaps. A bored student from the university, waiting for the summer to start and the exodus to Quill Lake to begin.

That first night, while Lizzie Parks chain-smoked in our living room to the point where our eyes watered even from upstairs, and did the laundry she had brought with her in the garbage bag, my mother laid back and look up at the stars. She had dropped anchor. The waves would pull at her but the boat gave little ground. She smoked only a few cigarettes. She drank a bottle of water. She made her first attempt at urination by leaning over the boat, almost tipping her and her entire stockpile into the bay.

She decided from then on that swimming would provide her only reliable means of relief.

By the second day, people noticed, but even that took time. The fishermen from the day before saw the same boat and the same woman having a cold breakfast of bananas, marmalade, and bread, and decided that if she were still there when they returned, they would say something to their wives. Gregory Peck, who in addition to owning the Two-Stone Bar also ran the business of letting tourists rent his boats, didn't notice when he did his morning inventory. Shivering in his ratty blue dressing gown, he yawned into a cup of coffee, reminding himself for the hundredth time that he needed to remember his glasses in the morning. Satisfied that the collection of blurs on the water were unplundered, he returned back into the Two-Stone to watch the news and some sportscasts on satellite.

Shortly before lunch, about a dozen people were talking. By three a pair of binoculars had been found and were traded between interested parties as they tried to ascertain the meaning of my mother on the bay's surface, happily rereading her favourite parts from *Miss Alexia's*. They talked amongst themselves, passing theories back and forth. How long had she been there? One of them, a teacher on his lunch break, reported that we were in school. She couldn't have been there that long.

We came home from school together. Faith didn't go to a friend's house and Maddox skipped out of basketball practice, claiming that he was needed at home. We had made a pact on the way down the hill that morning that we would return together. Strength in numbers.

Lizzie Parks was upstairs when we got in. She heard the door close and came down to greet us. Her clothes had changed. They were clean. She was clean too, having showered in our parents' bathroom while we were out. Lizzie had tidied up the living room as well, opening the windows to get out the smoke smell that had covered everything from the night before.

"How was school?" she asked, testing the question out on her tongue.

"Fine," Maddox replied, unsure.

"We thought that Mum would be home."

"Oh," Lizzie said, nodding. "She isn't. Yet. She said it would probably be a few days. Maybe a week."

I couldn't help but stare at her prosthetic arm.

"I was thinking," Lizzie said slowly, "that I could make you something.

23

For dinner. Tonight. I didn't last night. I should have. I just, well, I didn't."

"Okay," Faith said.

"What would you like?"

Nothing came to mind.

"Well, let's see what you have."

The four of us explored the kitchen. Apart from where the ingredients for cookies, the boxes of treats, the carrots, and the juices were, the room was largely a mystery to us. Our mother cooked for us, and rarely asked for any help. And when no one was cooking, eating, or entertaining friends, the kitchen was occupied by the dead men playing dominoes. When our mother did cook, it was up to Faith to get her what she needed and maybe do some stirring. Maddox and I did dishes. He washed and I dried. With her right hand, Lizzie opened up all the cupboards, reaching in to push boxes out of the way to get a better idea of the total contents. Maddox accidentally brushed against Lizzie's left arm and shuddered, shuffling away. It was smooth, room temperature, and entirely not a human arm, he told me later. She turned and looked down at him. Her face changed. Her back straightened.

We settled on hamburgers, salad, and ready-to-bake french fries. For the most part, we sat at the table watching Lizzie as she moved through the food preparation process. Her right hand was amazing. I watched it intently. It moved quicker and more nimbly than anyone's hand I'd ever seen. Using her feet, she opened and closed the bottom drawers and cabinets, scooping up bowls for the ground beef and a tray for the fries. When she needed to add the sauce to the beef and separate it into individual patties, she enlisted Maddox and Faith to help her.

Occasionally, though, we'd brush her left arm. It would bump against the side of a counter and resound with a hollow thump that startled the otherwise graceful dance in the kitchen. We'd miss a step, a beat, and we'd drop things. Maddox would tense. Faith would look down. I coughed and Lizzie's back would straighten. Eventually things would get back to normal, the rhythm returning, but we'd stare more and she would hum to herself less.

We ate in the dining room, on the old oak table that had been brought over from Edinburgh in the late fifties, but was far older than all of us added together and multiplied twice. Lizzie looked around at the woodwork along the walls the way everyone who first comes into the house does, but she didn't say anything about it. The burgers were tough, the fries a little crisp, but on the whole not bad.

Lizzie ate exclusively with her right hand. She drank her wine from the bottle and then moved her fork in the same casual motion. She kept her left hand under the table. When Maddox told a joke he heard at school and Faith snorted milk, Lizzie laughed, a sharp shot of a laugh, sounding more like a bark than anything else, and her left arm jutted up and hit the bottom of the table.

Afterwards, Maddox and I did dishes while Faith sat at the table, talking about her day, and Lizzie leaned against the threshold.

"What does it feel like?" Faith asked as we finished.

"What?"

She pointed at the arm. Maddox and I stopped.

"Oh. That. Well. It doesn't really feel like anything."

"It doesn't hurt?"

Lizzie forced a smile. "Not really. Sometimes, I think. But that's not real pain."

"What do you mean?" Maddox asked.

"Sometimes I can feel my fingers," she said. Lizzie laughed a little. Not the bark from before. More like a chuckle, rasped out through years of smoking. "That sounds a bit funny, doesn't it?"

Not sure how to respond, Maddox shrugged.

"Can I touch it?" Faith asked.

Hesitating for a moment, Lizzie lifted up her arm. "Sure."

Standing up from the table, Faith walked over and touched Lizzie Parks' left arm, tracing her finger tentatively across its smooth plastic surface. Lizzie stared at her.

"Does it come off?" she asked.

Lizzie nodded. "Yup."

"Can you take it off?"

"Sure."

Putting down her cigarette, Lizzie rolled up her sleeve to the buckles that attached the prosthetic to her elbow. "Hold my wrist," she told Faith, who did. Undoing the buckles the arm came loose gently, until Faith held it in her hands. Lizzie picked her cigarette back up, her sleeve now empty and dangling against her chest.

"Can I try?" Maddox asked.

Lizzie nodded through a plume of smoke and Faith passed it over. Then it was my turn.

After we had each had our turn, we watched Lizzie reattach the limb, helping her secure it back against the rounded stump that really just looked like an elbow without the arm connected to it.

"There," she said, afterward. "Not so scary now, is it?"

WE CALLED CONNIE MACKENZIE Aunt Connie, even though she was not related to us. "It's what they do here," my mother explained to us once.

"But we have aunts," we told her.

"Not in Canada we don't. And she's a nice woman. Just call her Aunt Connie. You'll see how happy it makes her. The last thing we need is another woman here to call Ms. Mackenzie."

Which was true. There were a lot of Mackenzies in Garfax.

Aunt Connie arrived that night just after nine. The three of us weren't in bed yet, but we were on our way, wrapping up whatever we were doing. Faith had finished her latest mix tape. I was reading towards the end of a chapter. Maddox was flipping back and forth between two mildly interesting programs reaching the end of the hour.

Lizzie met her at the door.

"Ms. Mackenzie."

Aunt Connie opened and closed her mouth. "What are you doing here?"

"Watching the kids."

"Do you know what's happened?"

"No. Emma just asked me to watch the kids for a few days. Told me I could stay here."

"She didn't ask me."

"I don't know anything about that."

"Are they all right?"

"They're fine."

Over Lizzie's shoulder, Aunt Connie saw Maddox walk from the living room over to the stairs.

"Can you come outside for a few minutes?"

"Sure."

While they were gone, we tried to listen from the windows. We couldn't hear words, just tone. Lizzie's voice remained stable, a little bit slurred from the wine, and calm. Aunt Connie's voice went all over the place. High-pitched and loud when she got excited, quiet and whispered when she thought we might have heard her. She was telling Lizzie what she had heard from the people down in the village. The fishermen had come back with their mostly empty nets and confirmed with the small crowd watching from the dock that Emma Brodie had been there for almost two days. Aunt Connie had immediately volunteered to come and check on us.

She left reluctantly. Lizzie watched her go until she was out of sight behind the hedges, whereon she practically broke into a sprint down the hill and back to the village. Lizzie came back inside and locked the door behind her. When she thought we weren't around, that we weren't listening, she leaned her weight against the door.

"Well, fuck," she said.

AFTER THAT we were pretty much doomed. School became a nightmare. Fishermen had told their wives, who told their friends, who told their spouses, who told their children. Suddenly everyone had a pair of binoculars. Everyone was asking us what our mother was doing out on the bay.

Gregory Peck was furious.

"She stole one of my fucking boats," he said, while holding court behind the bar at the Two-Stone, slamming his fist on the counter for effect.

"Come on now, Greg," Denver Brail, sole proprietor of the only movie theatre and legendary ladies' man, cut in. "She didn't steal it. You know exactly where it is. You can see it, for Christ's sake."

"Do you even know the definition of theft, Denver?"

Denver raised an eyebrow. "I know damn well enough that she didn't steal the fucking thing."

"If someone takes something without your permission, even if you know where they are and what they have, even if you can see them with the damn thing, that's theft," he bellowed. A few men muttered their agreement with the bartender's definition.

"Emma borrowed it."

"She didn't ask, Den. And asking makes all the difference."

Denver took a sip of his beer. "It's still not theft. You'll get your boat back."

"When?"

Which is what the question became. When was Emma Brodie going to return to shore? More importantly, why had she left land in the first place? Speculation abounded. The women suggested possible dalliances that Cadmus, my father, might have had. The long business trips away from home. The possibility that they were actually, heaven forbid, divorced and keeping the whole thing secret.

The men put the blame solely on my mother and her lunacy. They brought out copies of her horoscope that they found taped to walls and bathroom mirrors by their girlfriends or wives. "She's obviously a nutter," they said. "Woman thinks she can see the damn future."

College dropouts turned journalists murmured their agreements, took some notes, then scurried back to their hovel-like offices, a hive of collected janitor closets, to pound out article after article detailing Emma Brodie's past and present situation, as well as making some broad guesses at her unlikely future.

On the third day, everything hit the fan. Maddox got into a fight at school when one of the older kids called our mother a lunatic and Maddox responded by knocking out some of his front teeth. Maddox's nose wasn't broken, but it swelled up nicely. The other kid, Tyler Marks, had to be sent to Ms. Temple, the town dentist.

"That," Lizzie said, helping him with some ice when he got home, "wasn't very bright."

"What was I supposed to do?"

Lizzie sighed. "I don't know. What you did, I suppose. Still doesn't make it very bright, though."

Women started coming around to the house. Aunt Connie led the way. The men slowly followed, leaving the comfort of the Two-Stone to get in on the action. Eventually Lizzie had to let them in. They pushed in at all sides and overwhelmed her. Women, old ladies with greying hair who still had their accents from back home. Their Canadian daughters-in-law, who took their orders for food but stayed mostly at the walls, talking amongst themselves, trying to turn invisible. Everyone moved past Lizzie, carelessly brushing past her plastic left arm, and swarmed around Faith and me. The men dragged Maddox out onto the verandah, pushing a pair of binoculars into his hands. The women sat around the kitchen table and smoked, commenting amongst themselves about the beautiful woodwork in the house, how it had looked before we had inherited it. They marvelled at the furniture and fixtures. They eyed the wonderful framework surrounding the mirrors. The men huddled around Maddox and watched through binoculars for the flash of my mother's flashlight as she changed her socks.

Whenever I got the chance, often claiming the need to go to the bathroom, I'd check and see how Maddox was doing. The men were laughing, stooped around him, slapping him on the back. Asking him questions. Telling him jokes. Pointing with their fingers to get him looking in the right place. Eventually he started smiling too.

The living room birthed arguments. Aunt Connie and several of the older women who claimed to be my mother's friends demanded that they be allowed to stay and take care of the children. They began ordering their Canadian daughters-in-law, sending them back to their cars to go collect their things, already packed prior to their arrival, before Lizzie stepped in.

"I'm taking care of the kids. That's already seen to. You don't need to stay."

The older women didn't look at her arm. They were too polite. The mere fact of it made them uncomfortable. "You just might need help. That's all we're saying."

"We're fine."

One of the Canadian daughters-in-law, a Mackenzie, I can't remember which one, spoke up. "Come on, Liz. You can't actually believe you can take care of them, being the way you are."

The room went quiet. The smoke from a hundred cigarettes hung suspended in the air, no longer propelled by the spoken word. All eyes were on Lizzie, whose eyes momentarily darted on the floor before turning to face the Mackenzie by the wall.

"What do you mean?" Lizzie asked.

The Mackenzie was smiling, simultaneously enjoying the rich red wine she had pilfered from my mother's cabinet and the attention and silence of all the women. "You know what I mean, Liz. You're crippled. What if there's an emergency? What are you going to do then?"

"Emma asked me—"

"Emma's not in her right mind. That's fucking plain. Why else would she ask someone like you and not any of us?"

I watched this from the stairs next to Faith, holding her hand. I squeezed her fingers tightly and she squeezed back harder. "It's okay," she said, whispering into my ear. "It'll be over soon. Don't cry."

Lizzie was in the middle of the living room. When I think back to that time, I imagine it as some sort of trial portrait, with Lizzie as the accused standing before a jury of the old women crowded around her, monopolizing every available stick of furniture. Ever looming in the background were the Canadian daughters-in-law.

When she spoke, and it was only after awhile, she spoke slowly. "You all need to leave now," she said. "It's late, and the kids need to get to bed."

She was shaking.

"But—" Aunt Connie said.

Lizzie stared at the Mackenzie on the wall. "We'll be fine. The kids need to get to bed. It's time for you to leave."

As soon as the first woman moved, leaned on her arms to push herself up from a chair to stand, it was over. Motion returned to the room, and like some well-oiled mechanism, the women began to churn out of the house. The blue-grey smoke danced in their wake, spiralling out to the corners of the room. After everyone was out of the living room and moving through the threshold, Lizzie practically ran downstairs into the basement.

Faith pushed my shoulder. "Go see if she's all right."

"But—"

"Now," she said, before hopping down the stairs to make sure everyone got out and into their cars.

Did I mention I was eleven?

I approached the door leading down to the basement in the most roundabout way. I walked through the rooms of the main floor, surveying the destruction and disarray that the concerned citizens of Garfax had left. Their fingerprints on everything.

The door leading down to the basement was closed. I opened it slowly, and felt along the cool wall for the railing. I made my way half-way down the steps, just so that I could see Lizzie before I sat down.

She had taken off her left arm. It was lying on an empty chair. In her right hand she cradled a beer against her collarbone. She wasn't alone. She was sitting in a circle around a table that held a spider web of dominoes spiralling out to the edges.

The dead relatives hadn't stopped playing, but they had slowed down some. My two grandfathers exchanged the occasional look across the table before making their moves. Which was saying something. For as long as I've known them, my grandfathers have always tried to have as little to do with each other as possible.

Jack Brodie, my mother's father, his army jacket off and hung neatly on the back of the chair where he sat, his shirt sleeves rolled up, contemplated the board. William Wilson, my father's father, who was dressed only in his undershirt and shorts, looked to be growing tired of the game. The other two, William's uncles, Hugo and Starling, the men who had raised him, had stopped playing altogether and were watching Lizzie intently.

Hugo and Starling sat on either side of Lizzie. Hugo on the left, Starling on the right. Occasionally Starling would cough, a habit he had picked up during his time in the gas brigades during the First World War. Hugo fingered the keys of his trumpet, a silver masterpiece that had accompanied him since he was fifteen years old. It had been years since I'd heard him play. He didn't look to be playing anytime soon.

Lizzie sat with her back towards the stairs, but every few minutes she'd wipe the back of her hand across her face and I knew she was crying. She'd take a swig, then. Long and deliberate, before settling back and staring at the floor. Up above, the sounds of Garfaxians slowly milling their way through the door and down the steps died out in a flurry of closing car doors.

It wasn't until Lizzie finished her drink, drained the last drop of liquid into her mouth, that I saw her frame begin to shake. All the dead relatives stopped then, their sad, quiet expressions focused squarely on this young crying girl. They looked at each other. Starling, coughing uncomfortably, reached over and took the bottle out of her hand. She let him, and he placed it on the floor beside his seat.

Raking her one good hand through her now clean hair, Lizzie choked back a sob. The grandfathers shushed her gently. Hugo fidgeted with his trumpet and then put it down on the case beside the table. He turned himself towards her in his chair. He reached out and he took her left hand into his own.

Lizzie turned and looked down at the hand that wasn't there, the hand

31

whose fingers she could still feel, even after so many years since the accident, the hand that was being gently caressed by my great uncle Hugo. She looked up at him, her face red and blotchy. Hugo smiled. He entwined his dead fingers through her non-existent ones and squeezed. She squeezed back. He leaned over and kissed her gently on the forehead before whispering something to her I couldn't hear.

Faith came down the stairs then. She touched my shoulder and took my hand, leading me back up the stairs. "I think it's time we called Dad," she told me once we were under the light of the kitchen.

THEY CAME BACK the next day, of course, but this time there were more of them. The excitement brought on by this new and unprecedented event in the village's history spurred it into a frenzied wakefulness. People who congregated to our house moved as a collective, a whirling dervish of laughter, gossip, feigned concern, and drunkenness. Having established her resistance to having anyone else stay to take care of us, Lizzie took to trying to manage the tide. The men opened our refrigerator, plucked our cabinets dry. They emptied their ashtrays off the verandah and the yard quickly sprouted a ripe harvest of empty beer bottles, their last drops mingling with dirt and small stones.

During that second night of siege, Maddox was taken away by the men to the dock. When she found out, Lizzie, furious, got Faith and me together and tore down the small winding road like a woman possessed. She had us wait in the car. She told us to lock the doors.

"Don't let any of the bastards in," she hissed, not looking at us, before she closed the door.

From the back seat we could see the men clustered around my brother, shoving a megaphone into his hands. We could hear his voice, magnified by the horn, push across the water, but couldn't make out the words. I remember wanting so desperately to know what he was saying, but Faith wouldn't let me roll down the windows. It wasn't until years had passed that I realized that I didn't need to hear that night. It was obvious what he was saying, what the men had told him to say. He was the eldest, after all. And with our father gone it was up to him to bring order back to our house.

Lizzie was gone for about five minutes. She snatched the megaphone from Maddox's hand and tossed it at one of the men, hitting him square in the chest. With her left hand waving through the air like some ancient talisman, she tore into them with her voice. Satisfied that she had shamed them to a sufficient degree, she took Maddox by the hand and led him back to the car. Halfway he pulled his hand away.

In the passenger seat on the way back home, he didn't say a word. None of us did.

So we took to hiding. Even at school we hid. The three of us, our shoulders sunk low, our chins down to our chests. Notes passed from desk to desk ended up piled in a heap in front of us. Maddox, humiliated by his night out on the dock, flicked them off one by one, aiming for the kids in front of him. All the sudden attention he had received soured to the point where he wanted nothing more than to be left alone. Faith took out a ballpoint pen and responded to each one, every hateful, poorly spelled missive, biting her lip till it almost bled. She drained that pen dry in expletives and exclamation marks. I read books, ignoring the lessons completely, and whenever I could get my hands on them, I'd scan copies of the latest weekly newspaper that now published daily handbill-sized installments of my mother's solitary excursion.

The excitement reached its peak the day that two of the Franklin boys decided, one night after spending too long at the Two-Stone, to steal one of Gregory Peck's remaining flotilla and go and see what all the fuss was about. Up until then the Franklins had stayed out of the affair. Beside the Ansons, the Franklins are the most famous of Garfax's first families. Joseph Franklin, the family patriarch, had moved his family here all the way from Scotland in the fifties. After the purges brought by the government historians, it was Joseph and his family who kept us together.

The laughter of the two Franklin boys, harsh and loud, punctuated the groan of their motor across the bay. Word spread quickly until Gregory Peck himself came out from behind his altar of the oak bar to stand at the dock. In the dark, all they could see was the intermittent flash of distant flashlights, dim against the black curtain of the water. Bursts of laughter were soon swallowed by the lapping of the waves against the beach and the dock beams. People shivered, complained of being cold.

That Emma Brodie hit one of the Franklin boys with an oar has never been in question. She's admitted that much over the years. The reason why she did so, however, has never been satisfactorily explained. The boys were babbling when they returned to shore, their motor tearing their way across the length of the bay. The pilot was drunk and hit the dock harder than he should have. The other bled from a cut on his scalp.

"She hit me," he said, staring at the slight trickle of blood on his fingers. "That fucking bitch actually hit me."

But their stories never matched up, or when they finally did, it was too late to believe that this final version was actually the truth. In this last draft of their adventure, their intention that night was to bring Emma Brodie home, to end the foolishness that had so consumed the small village of Garfax. They claimed to have brought rope (which they hadn't), to secure her boat and ferry her back in. When it was noted that they had no rope on them upon their return, they promptly explained that she had stolen it, or that it had fallen in the water.

To my mind they tried to get on the boat my mother stole, to steal into that private space she had carved out for herself on that public piece of ocean. And my mother, to her credit, couldn't abide that.

Regardless of their stories, however, Joseph made it publicly clear by the end of that day that they had no business with "that Brodie woman" and that his family was staying out of the whole insane mess.

Either way, the incident changed the tenor of the remaining nights. The situation had turned serious. The men at the Two-Stone, rallying around Gregory Peck, decided to take matters into their own hands. They resolved to go out in force, to bring her back to shore and cease this whole agitating affair.

"She has my property," Gregory declared to his coterie of imbibers. "And when a woman has your property, she has your peace of mind. We cannot rest, the village cannot go back to normal, until everything has been put back into its proper order. An accounting must be made."

Shaking his head, Denver said he would go just to stop them from doing anything truly stupid.

Faith and I searched through every drawer, every book filled with scraps of paper between pages, every written-down note affixed to a surface, to get in contact with our father. Perched on a kitchen chair, Faith called one number after the other. She even called Fetch Books, my father's employer, but they had only the vaguest idea of where he might be.

Eventually, a street magician in Edmonton, whom my father had recently taken a series of photographs of, provided a possible answer. "I think he said he was going to Middle."

My sister, who had been cynical of magicians ever since she had encountered a particularly drunk and incompetent one during one of her birthday parties, wasn't entirely convinced. "That doesn't sound like a real place to me."

"Well, it is," the magician replied curtly. "It's in Saskatchewan."

"Is that a town?"

"Christ, have you never looked at a map? It's a province. Next to Alberta. On the right side."

"All right then. I'll give that a try. Have a nice night." And then, when she was off the phone, she turned to Lizzie. "Is Saskatchewan a real place?"

"I think so," Lizzie replied.

"Cool."

Faith finally got through to my father around midnight, just as the men of the Two-Stone set out to finish what the two boys had started. I sat across from her at the table. She started off talking very loudly, trying to push the urgency of the matter over time zones, provinces, and the chaos going on at the other end of the line. Eventually her voice lowered and she was able to explain the situation calmly. They talked for an hour, and when they were done he was already making his way back. By that time the men had already returned to shore, my mother still floating out in her boat on the bay.

"He's on his way," my sister told me with a yawn.

"Did you tell him I said hi?"

Faith frowned. "No. I didn't. Go to bed."

I WORKED AT DENVER BRAIL'S movie theatre for almost six years. During the third year, he started taking me out on the road with him, in the school bus he converted into a portable movie house, so that the people in the smaller villages, the places like Mantua and other settlements two steps away from becoming ghost towns, could get the occasional bout of entertainment. It became apparent very early on that he always played the same roster of films. I asked him about this, about why he didn't try bringing some of the new movies out on the road with us.

"People like these stories," he replied, shrugging his characteristic shrug.

Which was true. In the field where we set up the projector screen along the side of the school bus, the chairs pulled out from the inside to make up the rows beside the chairs people brought themselves, I watched the same audiences watch the same movies over and over again. They recited the dialogue perfectly. They delighted in the same surprises they had seen every previous summer.

"I tried the new films once," he admitted. "But they didn't take. No one knew what to say. They couldn't follow along. All they could do was watch."

I've wrestled most of the story out of Denver concerning the night the men of the town went in Gregory Peck's boats to rescue my mother from herself. He eventually relented and said he didn't really know what had happened.

"We tried to rope her in," he explained. "Hook her boat so we could tow her back, but she had that damn Bowie knife. Then we got close, tried to pull her onto one of our boats. We thought she'd be screaming, you know? I mean, everyone thought she was absolutely nuts."

She didn't scream at them, though. She spoke in a calm and measured tone, telling them this had nothing to do with them and that they should go back to the village. What she was doing had nothing to do with them.

Handing me a roll of film, Denver leaned against the door frame of the projection booth. "And of course Greg went crazy at that, started yelling about theft of property, about calling in the police to deal with the matter. He was the one who suggested we grab her."

They surrounded her from all sides. Drifting in the bay current until they could almost reach the edge of her boat with their hands.

"And that's when she pulled out that gun of hers. She pointed it right at Greg and told him to go back, to take us with him. She said some other stuff too."

"What did she say?"

He looked at me.

"So what happened then?"

He told me that by then, Gregory was standing up. When my mother drew the gun, he shrieked, declaring the obvious: "She's got a gun!" He then promptly fell out of the boat. Everyone was so close together. When he fell in, the gap of water was filled by wooden hulls brushing together. As Gregory pounded his fists against the bottoms of the boats, the men leaned over and plunged their arms into the water, fishing for a flailing limb. Denver caught him by his collar and pulled him back aboard. With a mixture of gasps, shivers, and tears, the men covered Gregory with their jackets.

Denver shrugged. "We went back. No one said anything. At the dock, we got asked all sorts of questions but couldn't come up with any answers. Everyone was expecting us to bring her back. Greg mumbled something about her having the gun and that we were probably all better off if Emma Brodie never came back to land at all."

FOLLOWING THE FAILED ATTEMPT to bring her back, the second if you believe the first two boys, no one came round to the house. At school no one talked to us. The notes were passed around fast and furious, but none ever reached our desks. When school finally let out for the summer, the usual excitement was muted by whispered wondering and uncomfortable concern. We were being watched. Mum, too. If any of them talked, continued their speculation, they kept it to themselves. They whispered their theories to each other in their beds, in the front seats of cars or the back row of the empty movie theatre.

The journalists wrote page after page, but nothing made it to print. The issues that followed detailed the history of the theft of Garfax's town sign by the government historians back in the seventies, an event that still remained a mark of both shame and pride among local Garfaxians.

It would have been easier if they'd just kept talking, making fun of us, invading our house. In the long run, those few days of silence were probably the most damaging for Maddox, Faith, and me.

This is where the story starts to come undone for us, for me and for the rest of the village. No one noticed my father steal into one of Gregory's boats and row out to the distant point of light that bobbed on the surface of the bay. No one even knew he was back in the village.

No one heard him. Everyone was asleep. That they talked is obvious, but they've never told me what that conversation was about. It could have taken hours or it could have taken minutes. The only thing I know is that they stumbled in at around two in the morning. I heard them fumble with the door, which Lizzie had kept locked ever since the incident with my mother and the gun. My father knocked and I knew they were back. I crept down the stairs and watched them from under the banister.

They were both soaking wet, holding onto each other as if they had swam the whole way back from the bay. Shivering, they both looked incredibly tired.

"Jesus Christ," Lizzie said, letting them in. "What the hell happened to you?"

My father's arm was over my mother's shoulder. She supported his weight. Quietly she whispered some words to Lizzie, who nodded and closed the door behind them. Careful not to stumble, they made their way into the house and up the stairs. I went as quietly as I could to my room and listened to them pass, moving to their bedroom. After they closed the door, there was nothing but silence, and it took me hours to fall back asleep.

THE NEXT DAY the village woke up to an empty bay. Emma Brodie had returned home and only her boat remained. Gregory Peck saw it first, having finally remembered to wear his glasses. Breaking the morning silence, he jumped into one of his motorboats and towed his recovered property back to shore. He retired the vessel that afternoon, getting some of his patrons to help him carry it to his house, where he kept it, and all the remaining stockpiled goods inside, in his garage.

When we woke up, Lizzie Parks was already gone, her garbage bag full of clothes in tow and a counter of empty beer cans and wine bottles left behind. She walked down the hill and through the main row of Garfax's businesses and houses for the first time in years. The few who saw her didn't say hello and she didn't bother either. For the first time since losing her arm to a machine that made the wings of airplanes, Lizzie Parks walked up her front steps and went through her front door instead of escaping into the pines through the sliding glass by her deck.

II

A Mansion in Five Parts

HERE'S ANOTHER PICTURE. It's of my parents together.

They are dancing. My mother and father are dancing, and even though they are not the guests of honour, even though this is another couple's wedding and they have been relegated to the outskirts of the action, out and away from the harsh press of bodies, they hold everyone's attention.

The wedding is for one of the Mackenzies. I don't know which one. The back of the picture just gives says 'Mackenzie Wedding' and the date. Not that it matters. People have stopped looking at them, letting the happy couple occupy the centre of the dance floor, letting them spin soft and slow in circles round each other, happy and drunk in this, the early hours of their matrimony.

There are lights strung up above the crowd, bending arcs of soft illumination that glow warm and soft like candles. The quality of the image is poor. The camera used was not built to capture motion well. All of the couples are dancing fast and intoxicated, clinging to each other as if letting go meant careening off and onto the floor without the possibility of getting up again. There is a desperation to their embraces, a desire to keep the dance going, to follow the screech of the fiddles, the pound of the drums, no matter how fast they go, to their inevitable conclusion. To follow the music till the end.

I imagine a spiral dance, with the newlyweds the central hub in a bike. The further out from the wheel you go, travelling down the spokes of couples old and new, the faster you have to move to keep up.

Nothing is in focus. All features blur together. My father's arms melt into my mother's. Their heads melt into long sweeping curves that

eliminate their necks. Under their bodies, their legs churn like torna-
does, limbic storms keeping them afloat.

When describing how they looked when they returned from the bay,
clutching each other as if each had saved the other from drowning, Lizzie
Parks would say, "The both of them looked like they just went through
five months of bad weather."

BAD WEATHER ASIDE, Cadmus Brodie was up first thing the next morning. He crawled out from bed, away from the prostrate form of my mother,
and made his way to the curtains. They had had the good sense to close
them in the early morning hours.

Peeking through a slit, he winced at the harsh glare of the light.
Cadmus blinked. He looked around the room until he found a lamp. With
dumb hands he fumbled for the switch, clicked it.

The lamp came on.

"Well, then," he sighed. "That's something."

He snuck out of the room, closing the door behind him as quietly as
he could. In the bathroom across the hall, he turned on the light. It came
on. He looked up at it, experimented with it again by switching it off and
on. Off and on.

Cadmus looked in the mirror. His face was scruffy, unshaven. His hair
haystack wild.

"Shower," he said. "Shave."

Over the course of the next hour, my father showered, shaved, and put
on clean clothes. He let his hair drip-dry. Sitting on the toilet, fully dressed
in clothes he hadn't worn in years, he looked around the bathroom. It had
been awhile since he had been home. The room seemed different to his
eyes, although he couldn't put his finger on what exactly stuck out.

His arms and legs ached. He rubbed his eyes.

Opening the door, he walked down the stairs and into the kitchen,
where the dead relatives were clearing away the debris left behind by the
dervish of Garfaxians that had pushed through over the last week.

"Give me that," he said, taking the garbage bag from his father. "I'll do
it. You just sit down."

The dead relatives sat down.

"Did anyone make tea?"

They had.

Dad nodded. "Good." Then he yawned, reaching for the first bit of garbage within reach. "I'll have one, then."

Hugo coughed and then moved to oblige him. Starling signalled that he wouldn't mind a cup himself. Dad smiled.

Once the table was clear of garbage, all five of them sat around and nursed their drinks, poking their fingers through the rising steam. Dad looked around at the wreckage left behind by the Garfaxians, took a quick stock of what was noticeably missing. Tea finished, he stood up from the table and went to work putting his house back in order.

The one thing that can be said about my father is that he was used to picking himself back up after a spell of bad weather.

FAITH WOKE UP NEXT. She heard Dad puttering around downstairs and crossed the door to Maddox's room. Faith knocked, but when she didn't hear anything, she turned the knob and went over to wake up her older brother.

"What is it?"

"Dad's home."

Maddox blinked.

Together they went down the hall to my room. I didn't hear the knock. Sitting on my bed, one on either side, they woke me up. Faith shook my shoulders. Maddox held his hand over my mouth. I have the tendency to talk loudly when I wake.

I must have mumbled something.

"Shut up," Maddox said.

I looked over at Faith.

"Dad's home."

I mumbled something else.

"Yeah. We're going downstairs. Get dressed."

We found Dad in the dining room, standing on the table in his socks. A box was tucked under his arm. With his free hand, he unscrewed the dead bulbs from the glass chandelier and replaced them with fresh ones from the box. The three of us waited at the threshold for him to notice us, but he didn't. He was intent on what he was doing. Dad hummed to himself, a song none of us recognized. He clucked his tongue in time with a fiddle only he could hear, tapped his toes on the smooth oak table along with a drum.

41

It had been over a year since we last saw him. Watching, we waited for him to finish.

POWERFUL FORCES governed Cadmus Brodie's life, even from an early age. The very first instance of this manifested in his childhood somnambulism, a condition that followed him into adulthood and resulted in his utter inability throughout his whole life to separate his waking from his dreaming life.

It's entirely possible that my father's first steps were made unconsciously. He climbed out of his crib and down the stairs to the front door of his small council house in Saltcoats. Only the height of the doorknob prevented him from getting any further. Even his nocturnally governed limbs couldn't circumnavigate a two foot difference in height.

Still, despite this and other odd occurrences, no one really noticed that my father didn't live in two worlds, like everyone else, but in one blended together. They chalked all the happenings, particularly in his youth, to his uniqueness, his special nature.

When he started talking, people began to notice.

For one, he knew things. My father knew things he wasn't supposed to know. If asked about this, he'd tell them that someone had told him, and when pressed to reveal the identity of this informant, he'd tell them that too. But no one knew these people. There was never anyone living on the street that went by that name. Sometimes they did recognize the name, and that was worse.

"He says he's talking to my ma," one of my father's friends would say. "She's been dead for three years."

Not wanting to be outdone or pigeonholed, Cadmus expanded his repertoire to talking to babies that hadn't been born yet, that hadn't even been thought of yet.

"He's a strange one, your son," people would say to his parents.

"He's just a little special," his mother would reply.

"Special my arse."

Cadmus was good with people, though. That's what saved him. He had that unique quality of making whoever he talked to feel like the most important person in the room. A consummate charmer, he found a good number of friends. A good-hearted human being, he kept the friends he found.

In secondary school, girls wanted to be with him. They heard about his sleepwalking, about the walks he'd go for in the middle of the night, walking through buildings that hadn't been built yet or had been torn down for years, buildings that would never be built, that couldn't possibly exist, and want him to take them there. Pulling him into bed with them, they held onto him, hoping to be carried away to that place only he seemed able to go. This never worked, though. It's difficult at the best of times to follow someone into his dreams. The girls left disappointed. They looked for other avenues to escape the long rows of council houses. Not knowing what he had done wrong, Cadmus suffered from bouts of sadness.

Throughout all of this, it was William Wilson, my father's father, who kept him together, who picked him up again. When Cadmus was younger and found himself high in a tree or miles away from home, it was William who climbed up the tree or drove the distance to pick him up. Cadmus never wandered so far that his father couldn't find him and bring him back again.

In my grandfather's house, there were many lights.

An electrician with the heart of an aesthete, William Wilson spent the better part of his adult life constructing an array of illumination throughout the entirety of the government-built council house where he had been born. It had been his mother's house, the house where he had been raised by his uncles when she had abandoned him. But that story comes later.

There was no method to my grandfather's madness, no uniformity that governed the choice of fixtures he fixed to every available surface. Lamps of every conceivable description clustered together like strangers on train station platforms. Chandeliers of the finest crystal hung motionless next to cousins cut from the coarsest glass. Japanese paper lanterns adorned with letters from their unfamiliar language sat next to a desk lamp William had stolen from a hotel on his one and only trip to Rome.

Taken together like that, that strange assortment of fixtures, it could be argued that William had no eye for beauty. That he simply collected what came along, that he had a pack rat's scavenging mentality. It only took a flick of the thirty-seven light switches that dotted the house to prove this argument false.

The most important thing for William Wilson was not the quality of the fixtures. It never had been. It was the quality of the light they produced.

He had started young, even before his apprenticeship, collecting strange bulbs that produced a slightly different illumination than the ones that he saw every day. He collected these bulbs like children collect cards, collect stamps. He moved from bulbs to fixtures, delighting in how the light cast from a bulb changed when it encountered the murky brass of an antique lamp stand. Experimenting with shades, coloured and clear, he played out the glimmers across the wall, watched how they intersected and swirled with the other lights. And slowly, fixture by fixture, William discovered the language of light, its own incandescent grammar.

The small shed behind his house, next to the coal bin, was filled with various lamps and chandeliers that had served their usefulness before being replaced by lights that were more harmonious with his favourites, that changed the feel of a given room more wonderfully than the ones before. Clustered together across the length of the ceiling, hanging upside down, the shed's contents made it look like a bicycle repair shop. There were parts everywhere. The walls teemed with coils of copper wiring and faceplates for switches.

"But what did it look like?" I asked my mother when she told me about the house my father grew up in.

"It's hard to describe," she said. "It was different in different rooms. Some, like the living room, were so bright that it was hard to see the ceiling. It seemed so much taller than it actually was, given that it was a council house. The lights changed the dimensions of things. The bathroom was smaller than it actually was. The kitchen more intimate and welcoming, despite the cold tile floor. And the stairs. Your grandfather had strung naked bulbs around the banister that were dim, like candles or fireflies. So that when you walked up to the bedrooms, in that hallway where he hadn't put a single light, you felt that you were walking away from a party, away from everything that was going on downstairs or outside. A secret place that hadn't been discovered yet."

GROWING UP, it was Dad's responsibility to turn off all the lights on the main floor before going to bed. He'd walk through the rooms and, one by one, flick the switch or turn the knob of each of the thirty-seven fixtures that governed the lights. He did this reverently. He loved his own father deeply, in the quiet way that sons used to love their fathers, or at least in the way that we are told that they did.

William Wilson was beloved, you see. Among friends and family he was beloved. Part charmer, part decent human being, no door in Saltcoats was closed to him, a trait he passed down to his son. The man never walked down the street without stopping several times to talk briefly or at length with a friend or acquaintance who was seeking some momentary diversion or advice on one of the many electrical problems that plagued the government-built division. He danced well, and he played the trumpet as his uncle had taught him passably. He told jokes of every description, different jokes for every occasion, little made-up stories that had everyone rolling in the aisles. But when he worked, he was quiet and calm, and that mix between work and family is ultimately what endeared him to everyone, especially my father.

At nineteen, Cadmus heard through his mother that his father had contracted pneumonia after taking an evening constitutional down to the docks when the weather should have kept him inside. Cadmus was living and working in Glasgow by then, building houses, setting stairs, but he came home to help just the same. Without being asked, he fell back into his childhood routine of dimming the lights.

In his fevered state, William said many things. Sad and painful things. He spoke of lights that were not in the room. Lamps and great congregations of copper wiring that no one had ever seen. These phantom lights pained the older man, and to hear him speak of them pained those around him.

Escaping for the evening, my father went out with friends who had stayed behind after secondary school, boys who couldn't go to university and instead had followed their fathers into the shipyards. A moveable beast, the group of young men shuffled from one pub after another, drinking in liquid heat from dirty glasses in smokey rooms to keep themselves going through periods of rain and harsh winds before they reached their next stop.

Eventually he left, breaking off from his friends, who continued on unabated without him. The weather had died down by then, but my father still had to walk home quickly, his hands buried deep within his pockets.

When he came home, opening the door as quietly as possible, he noticed even through his drunkenness that all of the lights were off. He reached up into the dark confidently and felt the cool glass of a nearby bulb and knew it had been switched off hours ago by his mother.

Given his father's condition, Cadmus's mother had taken his room and given him the couch in the living room. Fumbling his way through the hallway and into the larger room, my father tumbled onto the couch and pulled at the pillows stacked on the neat pile of linens his mother had left for him.

He wasn't tired, though. Now that he was home, all of the shelter provided by the night with his friends faded, and he listened for any sounds coming from William's room upstairs. Sitting on the couch, his fists clenched about the sheets, Cadmus willed himself to sleep.

And when he opened his eyes again, he saw his father slowly lower himself down into his favourite armchair across from him.

"Da," Cadmus said.

"Son."

William looked tired as well, but better than he had done. He was wearing his natty old robe, which in reality was a patchwork of the previous half a dozen robes.

"I didn't hear you come down."

"That's no wonder. You're three sheets to the wind right now."

"That's true," Cadmus chuckled.

William smiled and his only son smiled back.

Sometimes knowledge comes to us in our dreams. We remember things we thought long forgotten, secrets that never make it back to us when we wake. We dream that we can fly. We remember how to breathe underwater. How not to be burnt by fire. How to speak all of the languages ever created.

Cadmus looked at his father. "Jesus," he said.

"What?"

And he knew. In that moment, or maybe the moment before, he knew. He reached over for one of the nearby lamps and pulled the cord. The light didn't come on. It didn't come on and the lights in the Wilson house never burnt out. He was dreaming. He knew he was dreaming because he couldn't turn on the light, that he could never turn on the lights when he dreamed. And he also knew something else. "You're dead, aren't you? You've died?"

His father stared at him. For ten minutes and forty seconds he stared.

"Oh, Dad," Cadmus moaned.

"Don't," William said, stabbing a finger in the air. "Don't you start. If you start, I'll start. And I'm not going to be crying after I'm not even fifteen minutes dead."

But Cadmus couldn't stop. Wilson men cry easy, always have. It's one of the things that makes us easy to like and hard to hate. People go soft on us. And Cadmus, my father, more than three-quarters drunk and talking to his own dead Da, just started misting over, crying whole rivers of tears that ran hot and sticky down his face, down his neck and into his collar, collecting in drops wet and heavy in his lap, staining his pants.

And then William, he starts crying. And that man hates to cry. Absolutely hates it. Even now, dead more than twenty years and sitting on our living room couch, he'll mist over at a commercial for diapers and punch his leg trying to stop the tears, he hates it so much.

That's what he did then, too. Balled his hands into fists and punched his knee, started cursing. "Son of a—"

"Motherfucking—"

"Goddamn—"

"Every time."

And Cadmus gets up, stumbles up, really, and goes over, kneels down and hugs his old man around his middle, wraps his arms around his father's arms so he can't punch his knees no more. Trapped like that, pinned, William's face softened and he started to sob. Silently. His whole frame shook silently. And the two men cried together.

"What the fuck am I supposed to do now?" Cadmus asked.

"You sad bastard," William replied, running his hands through my father's hair. "You live, of course."

When Cadmus woke, which to him was a lot like "walking from one room to another," as he liked to say, his father was gone and his mother was standing over him, her eyes red and puffy, her arms wrapped around herself.

"I have some bad news," she said.

THE FIRST PIECE of published writing my father ever wrote was an obituary.

"You have to write it," his mother told him in between sobs. "I can't do it."

An only child, Cadmus had little option but to follow his mother's wishes. He took a couple of more days off work and bought some paper for his typewriter. Sitting down at the kitchen table in the following morning's early blue, he began to write.

No words came. He wrote and rewrote sentence after sentence. Half an hour later, he fetched himself a wastebasket to manage the pile of crumpled sheets. Two hours later, he had to make another trip to get more paper.

The truth was he didn't really know his father. That everyone loved him was obvious. He was a charmer. He had many friends. But there was a distance there that Cadmus felt needed to be written down.

When he returned home, he called up his relatives, which consisted solely of the two great uncles who had raised his father after his mother, their sister, had died. "I need to know more," he told them. "I need to know where he comes from."

Hugo and Starling sighed. They hummed and hawed. Until eventually they told so many stories that he hadn't heard before that he couldn't stop them even if he wanted to. There is no end to family stories.

William had been illegitimate, born out of wedlock from a union between their sister, Elizabeth Wilson, and a businessman from Aberdeen called Julian Scott, who had stayed briefly in the hotel she worked in as a maid. He had come down on business. One afternoon, after a particularly long and boring set of meetings that largely concerned minute shifts in facts and figures, Julian passed Elizabeth in the hotel hallway and asked her if she liked the pictures.

As it turns out, Elizabeth liked the pictures very much. For the following week they were inseparable. Julian left meetings early to spend time with Elizabeth, taking her to movies, where they spent their time in the dimly lit back rows.

My grandfather's conception had not been something that either party expected or wanted. Elizabeth was horrified, and Julian promptly broke off contact, losing her address and telephone number and never bothering to find her again. The prospect of marriage now impossible, Elizabeth found her only recourse was to have the child and following that, head down to London, leaving William with her brothers.

From the way he tells it, a lot of single mothers went down to London during those times. They had their own families. They took other men's names. They left their children behind in Scotland with brothers and sisters, parents and grandparents.

"So his name should have been Scott," Dad explained to me once, during a time when all the electricity in the house had gone off and we were forced to navigate in the gloom solely by flashlight and miners' helmets. "Same with me. That should be my last name."

"And mine?"

"Yours too, I suppose. Yeah."

Cadmus put down the telephone on his uncles and stumbled back to his mother, informing her of what he discovered. "You can't write that down," she told him, after he was finished. "Don't you dare think you can bring that up now."

The obituary that my father wrote was lifeless. A strict retelling of his father's work history, his personal achievements, and a meditation on the many lives and people he had touched during his too short life. The mourners mourned. The weepers wept. And my father left the church feeling like a liar whose history had been a story that had suddenly become terribly unfamiliar.

Discovery led to curiosity, though. Curiosity led to research. Cadmus took to going through old letters and family records, tracing his family back to the unfortunate meeting of Elizabeth and Julian. The uncles initially refused him access to their own letters, but Cadmus wore them down.

In over forty years, his grandmother had sent them three letters inquiring about her son. The last letter informed them that she was marrying a nice man from Bath who worked as an accountant, and that it would probably be better if they leave it at that.

"Tell everyone I've died," she wrote.

My father tells the story about how William went down to London in his late teens to meet his mother after discovering that she was alive. He found the house she had once lived in and from there was able to discover where she went. William found her at home with her husband and their two children.

"It tore him up," Dad told me. "All his life it tore at him. Not knowing like that. He went to their house but couldn't walk up the steps. He watched them from the street and when her husband noticed and came out to call to him, he ran away."

Everyone loved William Wilson. He took himself into any crowd he came across, all warm and friendly.

"But there was something underneath that."

The research eventually led my father to other researchers interested in their own family histories. Six months after he had buried his father he stumbled across a member of his grandmother's family who was organizing a large family reunion. Initially he didn't speak with her at all. He avoided her letters, her requests for more information. When she phoned him at home, however, he found himself unable to hang up the phone.

The other researcher knew about their shared grandmother's history. Her mother had been told and told her in turn.

"It would mean a lot to me if you'd come."

"Come where?"

"To the reunion. Everyone will be there."

"I don't think that's a good idea."

One thing you can say about the Wilsons is that they are persistent. Coupled with Cadmus's desire to know, he agreed to travel down for the reunion. The next day he bought a camera to capture the event, to finally pin down the areas of his family history that had been like smoke for him over the previous half-year.

He was late, of course. The trains of London confused him, tossed him about, and he ended up two hours behind by the time he got to the hall. He hadn't told his mother where he was going. He lied and told her one of the men at work was having a piss-up to celebrate his brother's upcoming marriage.

Her name was Allison, and she was waiting for him on the front steps. The first thing that struck him was how beautiful she was. She wore fine clothes, a rich wrap around her arms. Everyone mingling outside sharing cigarettes was likewise attired. Dressed in a spotty brown suit that didn't properly fit his tall frame, so that his ankles and wrists pushed out of the fabric, my father felt very out of place.

She noticed him staring at her. She almost smiled before she took in his clothes, his excessive height, with a glance. Crossing her arms, she strode down the steps.

"You're late," she said.

"I'm sorry," he replied. "I got the trains mixed up."

"Did you bring enough film?"

"Excuse me?"

"For the pictures. We were supposed to start pictures an hour ago."

"I'm not sure I understand."

"You're the photographer, aren't you?"

"It was the look on her face," he explained to me. "That look of utter disappointment that couldn't believe that I was related to her. Everyone there was just dressed so nice. They weren't my family."

He took photographs for his grandmother's family for the rest of her night, occasionally looking out at Allison, who kept a vigil on the steps for her long-lost family member. When it started to get late, he felt a hand touch his shoulder.

"You're not the photographer," a voice said.

Cadmus turned and faced the man speaking to him.

"No. I'm not."

"Then what do you think you are doing?"

"I'm sorry. I'll go."

Jordan touched his arm. "No. Don't go. Finish the night and come and see me tomorrow with the film. I'm Jordan Fetch."

JORDAN FETCH, publisher of the famous Fetch line of general interest books, began to feed my father jobs a little bit at a time, primarily in locations that were in or nearby Glasgow, where he lived and worked. At first it was just a fun story to tell, a lark. A short Englishman was paying him to take pictures of buildings and people, something that he might have done on his own. He laughed about it to his friends at work.

He met my mother during this period, while taking photographs of the young men and women who frequented the Barrowland Dance Hall in Glasgow.

My mother, for her part, was always dragged to come out to these dances by her friends, even though from the very first moment they stepped out the door, she knew how it would end.

"Apart from the dancing," she said, "there's no reason for me to go."

"Maybe you'll meet someone, Emma," they replied. "You never know."

"I do."

And she did. When she eventually caved under the external pressure of her friends, she'd find herself having the time of her life dancing, until one man after another came over and flirted with her. She couldn't even pretend to have fun with this. She knew without trying how it would end, and it made the whole conversation part of the evening, the whole social interaction, tiresome and boring.

"I want someone who surprises me," she would say at the end of the night.

One time she went when my father was taking photographs. She had heard about him through her friends, but thought nothing of it. If she was going to meet him, she would know. During the middle of that night, Emma came off the dance floor and into the flashbulb pop of my father's camera.

Emma blinked. Surprised.

"Sorry about that," Cadmus said. "I didn't mean to get you full in the eyes. I thought you were going to turn the other way."

"Um."

Cadmus let his camera hang from his neck. "Hi. I'm Cadmus."

"Um."

"You're Emma, aren't you?"

Now deeply concerned, Emma started looking around. "How do you know my name?"

"I know one of your friends. Jennifer. I've been taking photos of the hall for a couple of weeks now, trying to get some decent shots. I've seen you around a couple of times and got to talking with your friend."

"All right."

"Are you sure you're okay?" Cadmus asked, squinting in the dark light of the dancehall. "You don't look so well."

"I'm fine."

"Come on," he said, taking her gently by the arm. "Let's get you sitting down. Sorry again about the flash. Like I said—"

"You thought I was going to turn the other way."

"Right."

For the rest of that night, Cadmus and Emma sat at the edges of the dance and talked. Well, to be more precise, Cadmus did most of the talking. He always talked when he was nervous, and that night he told story after story, trying to avoid uncomfortable silences with Emma. Emma, for her part, mostly listened. Her eyes wide. Everything he was saying was new. She didn't know, from moment to moment, what he was going to say next. And he had such wonderful stories.

He proposed two weeks later, after a Chinese dinner, while they lay in bed.

"I want to marry you," he said.

"Is that a proposal?"

Cadmus thought about it. "Yes," he replied, nodding. "It is."

Smiling, Emma Brodie traced the curve of his chin with her finger. "Well, I want to marry you as well."

"It's pretty fast."

"It *is* pretty fast."

"I have one condition."

My mother cocked an eyebrow. "Oh?"

Cadmus laughed.

"No, seriously. What is this ominous condition of yours?"

"I don't want you to take my name. I'd like to take yours."

"Why?"

"New beginnings," my father said.

She thought about it. "Is it that important to you?"

"Oh, yes."

"All right. You can have my name."

Even when they were married, my father managed to balance his real work along with the hobby of taking photographs. Living in a small apartment in Glasgow, he installed a darkroom in a closet one evening following a flash of inspiration.

Emma encouraged this side of him. He seemed more alive when he was searching for shots, making everything he looked at appear somehow more than it would have been to the casual eye.

"You make everything wonderful," she told him. "With that camera, you work magic."

"It's just a hobby," he shrugged, but the more assignments he did, the less he believed it. "It's never going to buy us a house."

This weighed heavily on my father's mind. Mum was pregnant with

Maddox, and the need for good carpenters was starting to climb in demand. He told Jordan that he would quit, that he needed to go where the work was.

"Look," Jordan told him. "You're a good photographer. The business is expanding. The books are doing well. How about I give you an assignment, a position, that would give you more financial security?"

"Like what?"

"How would you like to be our man in Canada?"

"What's in Canada?"

"I have no idea. Trees and mountains, I think. There's a real demand for books on Canada right now. No one's writing about it."

"How long would the job be?"

"As long as you want it."

Over a take-away supper that evening, Cadmus told Emma about Jordan's offer, what it might mean.

"How long would you be over there for?"

"A few months," he said. "I'll be back before the baby comes."

Emma thought about it. "Well, I think you should do it, then."

Two weeks later, my father landed in Canada and began the impossible task of capturing the country's landscape through a camera lens. He sent rolls of film back to Jordan by the boxful. He kept his favourite shots for Emma, sending them with long letters inquiring about the pregnancy and how she was managing in university.

Towards the end of those three months, he found his way on the road to Garfax. He couldn't find the town on the map, nor any signposts leading to it. It wasn't until later that he discovered they had been taken during the historical purges the government had implemented ten years before, and that Garfax existed in every single way but on paper.

The road was blocked. Not believing his eyes, he turned off the engine and stepped out onto the asphalt. Framed on both sides by the tall wood of pines, a massive two-storey section of house was being maneuvered down the road. It had stopped as well, and there were men arguing outside, pointing up at where the angles of the second-floor walls had snagged on upper branches of the pines.

Cadmus wandered over, his camera in his hand. He asked what was going on, but no one paid him any attention.

"Road's closed," they said. "You'll have to go back."

"It's a half-hour back to the highway."

They shrugged.

"There wasn't any sign."

"There was supposed to be."

Frustrated, Cadmus circled the section of building. Men were climbing around inside, walking up stairs to get up on the roof. They carried axes. It was obvious to my father that this had only been the latest in a long line of stops this convoy had already been forced to make.

Behind the house he noticed another section a hundred feet away, the men working the truck and the rig sitting in their vehicles or on chairs on top of the elevated verandah. A man came walking up from the truck to see what was going on.

"How's it coming?"

"This is fucking lunacy," was the response.

"Ms. Anson's crying again."

"That's not going to help anyone."

"Can you go talk to her?"

"What the fuck good is that going to do?"

The man shrugged.

"Excuse me," my father interrupted.

"Yeah."

"Do you mind if I take some pictures?"

"You from the paper?"

Cadmus shook his head. "No."

"Ask Ms. Anson."

Ester Anson understood the power and grace that came with decisive action. A child of the Second World War, she learned early on that anything worth having, anything worth achieving, came as a result, as a natural extension, of a decision. She decided to escape her lower middle class lifestyle and she did. She married Simon Anson, an enterprising industrialist who had designs on the Canadian economy. During those first few years, when Simon made poor decision after poor decision, wasting weeks humming and hawing over the most basic of choices, Ester knew that she would need to assert a greater amount of control over their life and affairs.

What followed was a period of incredible prosperity and a marriage blessed with the peace that comes from a clearly understood division of labour. Simon attended the meetings and made the speeches. He talked with the other wealthy husbands of the small elite of the Canadian wealthy and made harmless jokes that everyone thought were the height of wit. Ester stayed in Garfax, made all the financial decisions, met with all the foremen and managers behind their various enterprises. When Ester Anson walked onto the floor of the airplane parts factory, no one had any doubt that she was the true power behind the Anson throne.

Garfaxians fell over themselves in love with her decisiveness. She determined fashion, adjudicated the outcome of gossip, and decided the best possible couplings. Marriages blessed by Ester flourished. Unions that did not heed her warnings were doomed to divorce or exile.

A powerful woman, Ester found herself besieged by suitors raring to replace her husband at her side. While initially finding this amusing, enough soon became enough and she put an end to all speculation.

"I love him," she would say simply.

"But he's not the man for you," they would say. "He's simple. He has no ambition. He tells bad jokes. He's no match for a woman of your quality."

"That's enough," she would interrupt. "There is no other man for me except Simon Anson."

"You wouldn't even consider—"

"No. I've decided."

When Simon Anson finally succumbed to a heart complaint that had ravaged his family throughout the last five generations, the whole of Garfax went into mourning. Ester wore black for a whole year out of respect, barely ever coming out of her mansion on the hill. She tried to contact her only son, Caleb, but they had been estranged for many years already. It would be another few decades before the last remaining Anson finally made his way home.

One day she decided she would leave Garfax for good. The next day she called up the most respected moving company in Canada. "How much would it cost to move a mansion?" she asked.

"Are you kidding me?"

"Do I sound like I'm kidding you?"

Representatives from the moving company travelled all the way to

Garfax to assess the feasibility of moving an entire mansion. They arrived a day late.

"We couldn't find the village on the map," they explained.

"That's because it doesn't exist on paper."

"Excuse me?"

"Long story. Now, what do you think?"

The mansion would need to be cut into five discreet sections. More would be preferable, but after that it would become difficult to maintain structural integrity when it was reassembled. The pressing concern that readily became apparent was the poor quality of the roads that connected Garfax to the rest of the world.

"They're too small," they said. "To be honest, we think it would be a mistake to even attempt this."

"That's unacceptable. I'm leaving Garfax and I'm taking my husband's house with me."

Faced with such naked decisiveness, the representatives resolved to make it happen.

Sometimes a strong decision isn't enough, however. The roads had snagged the house only a few miles out of the village. They cut the trees back but only managed to make another few hundred feet before they got stuck again.

"We should turn back," they explained.

"No."

This is the part of Ester Anson's story where my father appeared.

Cadmus found Ester Anson crying in the driver's seat of her dead husband's car. He knocked on the door and was confronted with the angriest expression he had ever seen on a woman's face.

"I'm sorry," he said. "I'll come back later."

As he was walking away, she rolled down the window and called out to him. "Who are you?"

Cadmus turned around. "I'm Cadmus Brodie," he said.

"All right. But who are you?"

"I'm a photographer. I wanted to ask you if I could take some photographs of your house."

"Why?"

"Because," he said with a shrug. "It's beautiful."

Ester nodded and looked at the steering wheel, stunned into silence. My father approached the car and pulled out his handkerchief from his pocket and handed it to her.

"Thank you," Ester said.

Cadmus nodded.

"Your accent," she said. "Where are you from?"

"Glasgow. I'm here taking pictures for a line of books about Canada."

"I see. You're a tall one, though. I didn't know they grew them that tall in Glasgow."

"Little-known secret," Cadmus said with a smile. "Can I ask you a question?"

"Of course."

"Your house wasn't designed by Ethan Bramble, was it?"

Ester blinked. "Yes. As a matter of fact it was."

"I thought so."

"You know Bramble's work?"

"I interviewed him a few weeks ago in Alberta while I was taking photographs for some articles on contemporary Canadian architecture. I love his work."

Ester wiped the last tear from her red face. "So do I."

"Would you mind showing me around your house?" Cadmus asked.

For the next forty-five minutes, that's exactly what she did, leading Cadmus by the arm through the various rooms of the two sections of her house that were being transported. He spent several rolls of film capturing the various angles, the odd juxtaposition of grand bay window looking out at a sea of pine trees a few feet away, of Ester Anson walking upstairs leading to open air. She laughed as she told stories about her husband, about the time they had spent in Garfax.

Running her hand across the mantelpiece of one of the fireplaces, she became quiet.

"Is anything wrong?" Cadmus asked.

She nodded. "Simon loved it here."

"It's a lovely home."

"That's not what I meant. He loved it here. In Garfax. He's buried here."

"So why do you want to leave?"

"Because," she explained, "I have to. I can't stay here without him.

I don't want to die here. There are just too many memories. Little ghosts. I cannot abide that. And there's so much left to do."

"So why are you taking the house with you?"

Ester Anson opened and closed her mouth. "You know," she said. "I have absolutely no idea."

Eventually the men were ready to move again, the pines cut back to make way for another few hundred feet of progress. "We're good to go, Ms. Anson," they said, finding the two of them in her parlour.

Ester Anson drew herself to her full height and tilted her jaw forward. "We're not going anywhere."

"I don't understand."

"I've decided not to take my mansion with me."

"But—"

"You'll still get paid. That's not a concern."

"So we're going back?"

Ester shook her head. "No. We'll drag these two sections into the woods."

"Excuse me?"

"We Garfaxians have a history of leaving things behind us," she explained.

Which was true. The pines surrounding Garfax are filled with artifacts of the past that the previous inhabitants have left behind. The number of vehicles that end up wrapped around trees or left to rust in clearings is staggering. The remains of old houses, a makeshift shantytown, still stand from when the whole village moved two miles into the pines to avoid the attention of the government-appointed historians. While Ester Anson's decision to move a large portion of her dissected mansion into the pines made absolutely no sense to the men charged with moving it, when Garfaxians heard about it less than an hour later, they nodded and said with a smile, "That woman has always had an abundance of class."

Ropes and axes were distributed among the men. Within two hours' time, almost the entire population of Garfax had come out to help, their parked cars lining the small winding road for over a mile. Sections of wall were torn apart and dragged through the pines. Men chopped a path for whole rooms to move through. Furniture worth a small fortune was unpacked and carried in with them.

Alcohol was brought out by the caseful. Musicians carried their instruments. When the final stick of furniture, the last corner of architecture, was safely surrounded by the pines, the party began. Elaborate oak tables were crowded by laughing men and smiling women. Small fires were constructed. Lamps were lighted. Doors were taken off their hinges and danced on.

Cadmus was awestruck. He walked around the festivities in a daze, raising his camera to his eye periodically to take a quick snapshot of the unbelievable proceedings. As the night grew later, he came across Ester Anson sitting a little ways away from the dancing, watching with a satisfied smile on her face.

"This is amazing," he confided.

"It is," she agreed. "It truly is. I should have done this from the beginning."

"Would you like to dance? It's not right that you're off by your own here."

She looked up at him. "I'm a little bit old for dancing."

"Nonsense," he said, extending his arm.

Laughing, Ester Anson reached up and took my father's arm.

For the rest of the evening, the people of Garfax laughed and danced, drank and told stories. When the morning blue came, they extinguished the fires, turned off the lights, and moved through the silent pines back to their cars. One of the men from the moving company had been left to drive Ester to Benning. They found him asleep in the front seat.

"I want you to have my house," Ester told Cadmus in the blue.

"That's extremely generous," my father said, a little drunk.

"I'm serious. I'm leaving it behind me, Cadmus. The rest of it is yours."

"Are you sure?"

"I've decided."

Cadmus opened the door for her and woke up the driver. Before getting in, she stood on her tiptoes and pulled him down to kiss him on the cheek. "Thank you," she said.

"You're absolutely welcome."

Ester Anson left Garfax, never to return. Within the span of twenty-four hours, my father had inherited the three remaining sections of her mansion. Just like that, Cadmus Brodie had the house that he had wanted for his family since even before he had met Emma.

HAVING EXCHANGED the final bulb, Dad climbed down off the dining room table and turned around. I think we startled him, because he jumped.

We stood there for a moment. Him holding the box of dead and live light bulbs and us clustered together on the threshold.

"Hey guys," he said at last.

"Hey Dad," we said.

"It's been a while."

Which was true.

III

Radio Drama

AFTER SHE WENT TO WATER, and after she returned, my mother spent five weeks on the top floor of our house, shuffling between the rooms. We didn't see her. Our father made it perfectly clear that she wasn't to be disturbed.

"Your mother, well, she's been through a lot," he explained to us, gathering us into the living room his second day back in the village. "And right now what she needs is time. It's important that you all behave. I don't want to see you fighting. I don't want to hear you yelling. We just need to leave her alone for a bit. Let her figure things out."

And we did. We left her alone. Most of the time we weren't even in the house at all. We'd stay outside for hours on end. Faith and Maddox tried initially to spend time with their friends after school, but ever since Emma went to water, the parents kept their kids inside.

"I don't want you hanging around those Brodie kids," they'd say.

When I wasn't in school, I was out walking in the pines, like I always did. But I didn't play games. I didn't invent stories in my head based on books I read. Instead I'd stare out at the bay, watch the fishing boats come back in the evening and leave again in the morning. I made sure to look out for Lizzie, but she never showed. I wondered if she was out there anyway.

Only my father saw our mother. The only time he left the house was to get groceries. Other than that, he was always there. He'd cook her meals, change the sheets on the bed, wash her clothes, and bring them all up to her.

We didn't see her, but we all heard her. The toilet would flush. The shower would run. When she wandered around or paced in long lines in her bedroom, we'd hear the creak of the wood floor overhead.

"When is she coming down?" Faith would ask.

"Any day now," Dad would always say. "She's getting better all the time."

After the second week, we stopped asking. At first we were afraid to ask, but we soon became accustomed to the new rhythm in the house. Maddox turned the television on again. Faith tuned the radio and prepped a new tape for her latest mix. I pushed open the double sliding doors to the library and didn't flinch at the sound it made.

It was almost disturbing to see her again, suddenly standing there in the threshold of the kitchen while the rest of us were eating breakfast. She was fully dressed. She was even wearing her long overcoat, her hands pushed deep into the pockets. Maddox saw her first. He was in the middle of talking with Dad about the test he had that day when he stopped in mid- bite and just stared. Dad turned around in his seat.

"Are you hungry?" he asked.

Mum looked at him. Shook her head. "No. I'm fine."

"Is there anything I can get you? Tea?"

"I'm fine, really. Thanks."

Five weeks is a long time for children, especially five weeks that are full of all sorts of stories and upsets. I remember looking at my mother then and being slightly disappointed. I remembered her being taller, somehow. Larger. Someone capable of stealing a boat and turning the town upside down. I was disappointed that she was just my Mum again and not this mythical figure the village had made her out to be.

"Hi Mum," Faith said.

Mum smiled. "Hi Faith. How are you?"

Faith shrugged. "Fine."

"All right. Maddox? Oswald?"

"Maddie's got a test today."

Maddox glared at me.

"All ready for it?"

"I'll be fine."

"Good."

Dad stood up then, went over to stand in front of her. "How are you feeling?" he asked, touching her elbow.

"A lot better," Mum said. "Yeah. A lot better. I was actually thinking about going down to the village today. Stopping by the paper, I have an idea for an article that I'd like to write."

Dad frowned. "Are you sure that's a good idea?"

"Yes," Mum said, but she said it too quickly.

"You're sure?"

"I'm sure. I need to go down. Start getting back into the swing of things. Put everything behind us."

"Do you need me to drive you?"

"No. Thanks. I'll be fine. The walk'll do me good. I'll be back in a little while. Good luck on your test, Maddie."

Mum kissed Dad and then left. We watched her go. When Dad turned back, he shepherded us through the rest of our morning routine before sending us off to school.

EMMA BRODIE WROTE the horoscopes for the village paper. Even those who didn't like her very much, who didn't believe in such superstitious nonsense, made it a point to check her foretellings each and every issue. Just in case, you understand.

The morning she came downstairs and went down into the village, she had in her possession a small addition to the next issue, a short horoscope. She kept it in her pocket. On the walk down, she twirled it around her fingers, folding and unfolding it.

The Canadian-styled Hemingways, the ex-students turned journalists, were less than impressed with her sudden reappearance. They all went quiet when she entered the office. The publisher, Barton Hen, was likewise cold.

"I'm not running that," he said, without even looking at it. "We're cutting the horoscopes from the paper."

"But it needs to go in," she said.

"No. It doesn't. I'm sorry, Emma, but that's all I've got. You got people all upset with your stunt, got them a little worried. Upset people don't read newspapers."

Mum frowned. "What do upset people do, then?"

"They talk. They gossip. They don't read newspapers."

"It needs to go in, Bar."

"I'm sorry."

Mum pulled out the slip of paper from her pocket when she was back on the street. She unfolded it and looked at it.

This whole business of seeing the future is actually a big misconception. You don't see the future; you know it, and even the stuff you do know you don't know a lot of. It's like memory. That's how my mother talked about it. Seeing the future was like remembering it. You don't see your memories; you know them.

The only thing she knew about the message in her hand was that it was important for it to be published. She went back to the paper the following morning, and the morning after that, and one more time the morning after that. Each time she got more agitated, more nervous, raising her voice in increments.

"It's important," she said. "You have to publish this."

"Go home," Barton said. "We're done with the future. I'm only publishing stuff on the present now. The future is bad news."

In the evenings, my parents would argue. Mum would get upset and start yelling, and my father, who thought that things in the village were just going back to normal, would get angry.

"People are going to forget," he said. "They will. And everything will go back to normal. But you can't keep doing this. You can't keep acting this way. It's not fair. Not to me or the kids. It's not fair to you. You need to calm down."

"I can't," she said. "It needs to be published."

Dad sighed, slumped his shoulders. "What's so important about it?"

"I don't know."

"You don't know?"

"No. I don't."

"Can I read it?"

Mum dug into her pocket and retrieved the scrap of paper, handing it to him. He was quiet for a moment.

"What does this even mean?"

"I don't know."

"What do you mean you don't know? I don't understand that. Explain it to me."

"I don't know."

"But you wrote it."

"I know. I can't explain it."

"I don't want you going down to that paper again. I don't want you causing a scene. We're going to let things settle down. We're going to let things get back to normal."

THAT EVENING, when everyone was in the living room watching some movie on the television, I snuck out to the cloakroom and rifled through my mother's pockets. I found the scrap of paper there, pulled it out, and went into the kitchen to read it.

The dead relatives were there, playing their eternal game of dominoes, but they didn't pay much attention to me. Over the click-clacking of tiles, I read my mother's message. Here's what it said:

Don't. Do not. Stop. Do not proceed. This will pass and when it does you will be better for it passing. This is not the end of the world. You have nothing to prove. Everything will work out. I promise. Just don't. Please. Begin again.

I only noticed that I was shaking when I put the folded scrap of paper back in the pocket of my mother's coat. Dad, hearing me shuffling around, called me into the living room. I went in, joined them. We watched the rest of the movie. I don't remember what it was. Some Western flick. Cowboys and Indians. An endless sky rendered in black and white. Good guys and bad guys. Black hats and white.

It took forever to get to sleep. I kept turning it over in my head, what she'd written. I wondered what it meant, and knew, in that horrible way that you know things, that it wouldn't be too long before I found out.

IT TOOK FOUR DAYS.

During that time, my mother grew more and more restless. She stood at the window for hours, staring out at the village, out at the bay. When Dad came home, she'd ask him question after question, what had happened in the village, what were people saying, had anything happened.

"Nothing has happened. Nothing's going to happen. Everything's fine."

But she knew better, and each day she asked again. I knew too. I could feel it. I'd go for walks and I'd feel it. A heaviness in my gut. A twisting and growing dread.

One morning, it was the weekend, I heard my mother calling for my Dad. I was upstairs, in my room, reading a book. There was a tone in her voice. Her voice was higher. Scared. I ran downstairs, and by that time she was calling for Maddox and Faith.

I found her by the front door, pulling on her coat and driving her feet into her boots. "Oswald, where's Dad? Where is everyone?"

"They went out for a walk. About an hour ago."

"Where? Where did they go?"

"I don't know."

Mum was pacing frantically. When she got scared, her fingers danced, as if tapping out music on an invisible keyboard. I'd only ever seen this once before.

"I need you to come with me," she said.

"Where?"

"Honey, I just need you to come with me, okay?"

"All right."

She put her hand on my head. "Good boy. I need to get the keys." And then she ran into the kitchen while I pulled on my coat and shoes.

"Hurry up," she said, rushing down the stairs and towards the car.

She fumbled the keys in the lock, cursed several times. The door finally open, she jumped in, simultaneously jamming the keys into the ignition while leaning over to unlock my door. "Get in."

My mother never did much driving. When the radio came on, she practically punched it with her fist to get it to shut off. After the fourth hit, it went quiet and she reversed out of the drive and into the road.

"Where are we going? What's happening?"

"I don't know," my mother said. And I believed her.

People think that when you see the future, you get everything all at once, the whole picture in booming audio and crystal clarity. That's not the way it works. It's like knowing. And sometimes you can know things years in advance. Almost whole lifetimes.

"Other times," my mother would say, years after, "you only get a few minutes. Sometimes less. Sometimes you only get to know ten feet in front of you."

This was one of those times.

Mum drove fast, faster than I'd ever gone before. She made me buckle my seatbelt but didn't fasten her own. Through the window she squinted, looking for whatever it was we were rushing towards.

We left Garfax and drove up the hill into the pines. I'd never been there, but we were going in the direction of Quill Lake, which was half an hour away. We stopped twenty minutes later, pulling hard into the meager shoulder. Mum got out of the car and looked around. I followed her.

"Where are we going?" I asked.

Mum didn't answer. She was looking for something familiar. "There," she said, pointing. Then she started to run into the woods.

"Mum."

"Come on, Oz. We've got to hurry."

I ran after my mother but she was faster than I was. I kept tripping over roots. I called out to her when she disappeared. "Mum."

"Over here. Come on. Hurry."

I ran, my heart pounding. Our voices echoed in that empty space between forest floor and pine top. We passed by broken-down hulls of cars. Remnants of furniture and house frames. All the detritus that Garfax had accumulated and discarded over its century-and-a-half-long history.

Mum stopped returning my calls. She went quiet and I got louder. "Mum. Mum."

I kept running forward. Pushing my way when the pines got denser and then breaking into a dead sprint when they opened up into a clearing. My lungs ached. "I can't," I said. "I can't."

"Oswald," she said, suddenly closer, just up ahead.

"Mum."

"Oz. Don't. Don't come over here. Stay where you are."

But I didn't. I was terrified. I ran over to her.

She was crouching down. She had stopped. My mother was crouching down over something and she had stopped running. She was out of breath, breathing hard. She was looking at something. She was mumbling something.

"Mum."

She turned to me, broke off her conversation, this sad and scared look on her face. "Oz," she barked. "Stay right there. Don't come any closer."

But I was walking forward. "Mum."

"Stop."

Even now I remember that the colour of the boy's arm was whiter than it was supposed to be. And my mother was whispering to him. She had her hand on his face, brushing something away from his eyes. Maybe his hair. And she was alternating between whispering to him and yelling at me.

"It's all right," she said to the boy. "It's all right. You're fine. You're fine, honey. It's okay. I'm here. I'm here. You're okay. You're going to be fine."

"Mum."

"Oswald, stop."

I remember next thinking that the boy's body was bent at a funny angle. That legs don't bend that way. That he was looking away from me and he shouldn't be able to look away from me. I didn't understand how he could look away from me.

My mother grabbed me hard and by the shoulders. She put her body between me and the boy. She pushed me into her chest. "Mum," I said. And it's all I could say. I just kept saying it over and over again. "Mum. Mum. Mummy. Mum."

"Oswald," she said, pulling me away and looking at me, forcing me to look at her. "Look at me."

"Mum."

"Oz, it's all right. I need you to do something for me. I need you to do something."

"But—" And I pointed to the boy.

"Don't look at it," she said. "Don't. Honey, it's important that you listen to me. Can you do that? Can you listen to me? Look at me."

I looked. I looked and I listened. I nodded.

"That's a good boy. Good boy. I need you to do something. I need you to go back to the car."

I started shaking. I didn't want to go back to the car. I didn't want to go back the way I came. "Honey, it's important. I need you to go back to the car and get me the blanket from the back seat. Can you do that? Can you do that for me?"

And she was shaking too. I noticed that. My shoulders were shaking because her hands were shaking and she was holding me there.

"Oswald? Can you do that for me? I need you to get me the blanket from the back seat. Can you do that?"

I swallowed. I nodded again.

"Good. That's great. You're a good boy. You're a brave, good boy. I need you to run, sweetheart. Okay? As fast as you can, I need you to run. Can you do that? Can you run to the car and back, as fast as you can?"

I nodded.

"Good. Go. Run."

And I ran.

DURING THE FOUR-MONTH storm that raged along the coast and through Garfax, I had the opportunity to sit with Barton Hen for a number of hours and talk about my mother. We were in his offices, moving pots and pans around to collect the rainwater that streamed down through the numerous holes opening up in the ceiling. The electricity gone, we were reduced to moving around with miners' helmets on.

At first nothing but silence passed between us. We were so obsessed with the emptying and refilling of the pots. But when a moment of calm came, he'd pull me into his office, which was bleeding water from the walls and ruining all his papers, hand me a soggy cigarette, and tell me a little bit more about my mother and the Franklin boy.

"In my experience," he began, sitting down in his slippery leather chair, "a tragedy, especially a sudden tragedy, is a story gone backwards. It's very different than a victory. A victory is a story working the right way. It moves from beginning to end, passing through the usual trials and tribulations, little celebrations and minor setbacks. So that when you reach the moment of victory, you know what's come before, you know about how hard it was, how much work went into it. That's how you can appreciate a victory."

My cigarette went out. I hadn't noticed. Hen leaned over and lit it again.

"A tragedy is backwards. Like I said. You get the climax at the beginning, but it doesn't make any sense. A car rolls on the road and kills four kids going for a joyride. You get an idea of what the story is. It's terrible, but you get it. The basic outline. But then it starts to unravel. You get a better idea of what those kids were like, what their stories were, and the tragedy just gets worse. You find out that two of the kids were in love. You find out that one got the other one pregnant. You find out that they were going to keep the child. And on and on."

I nodded. I smoked my cigarette. Hen looked out the window into sheet after sheet of my mother's storm, and breathed out his own plume of cigar smoke.

"Tell me about the Franklin boy," I asked.

Even then, almost fifteen years after I had run up with my mother, who was following her ten-foot premonition, into the pines, I didn't know the whole story. I only knew that the boy was dead. That my mother was blamed for it. That if she had set herself in the coffin of public opinion by going to water, then finding the boy like that, bringing him to town and into the screaming arms of his mother, were the nails that made it final.

GARFAX DOESN'T EXIST on paper. That's the first thing you have to understand. When the government historians went through the provinces in the seventies to make the nation's story easier to comprehend, they erased whole communities from the maps and textbooks. Garfax was one of those villages. Having no real industry, having never birthed a hero or been part of any important historical moment, it was an easy decision to make. This country is filled with such villages. For the most part, people move away. No one lives there anymore. They're ghost towns. Old fishing villages that lost their fish and now stand with their roofs ripped off. You drive long enough and you'll find them.

After the historians came, though, people stayed in Garfax. I've heard that there are people in the prairies that did the same thing. But since it didn't exist on paper, Garfax had to make its own way. The village had to find a way to support itself, get itself electricity, heat, radio, all the necessities of life that are usually government provided.

Enter Joseph Franklin, who, when he came over from Scotland, brought his whole family with him. An electrician and mechanic, a homegrown scientist, Joseph Franklin instilled his love for machines, for currents and wavelengths, into each and every member of his family. When the historians came and took all the road signs leading to Garfax away, when they erased the village from the map and cut off the power, it was Franklin everyone turned to.

He's the one that figured out how to draw power from the main lines that cut this way and that through the pines, the one who constructed our very own series of radio antennas and small relay towers out of abandoned railway tracks. He organized the businesses, suggested improvements and plans of action.

Since that time, the Franklins as a whole have taken care of Garfax, tending to the roads that no longer get serviced by the province, caring for the stitched-together power lines and makeshift antennas.

The boy my mother found was Joseph's youngest, Timothy. He was already dead when she found him. He had died some time in the night, having fallen from one of the taller pines and broken several bones in his body, the more important of these residing in his neck. In his hand he held a makeshift antenna, twisted out of its regular shape to resemble a long spiralling cord.

WHEN TIMOTHY FRANKLIN was thirteen, he went down into the basement of his uncle's house to fetch a length of wire that his father needed for some repairs at the library. That was the job of the younger Franklins. Helping their parents, their older siblings and cousins, until they were old enough to take part in it themselves.

Tim walked down the stairs, which were carpeted, and stepped onto the cold stone floor of the basement. There were a few lights already on, but that didn't bother him. He was listening to music on his headphones, mouthing the words quietly to himself.

"Maybe if he had those damn things off," Hen said, "it would have saved his life."

To get to the storage room in the basement, you have to walk past the washer and dryer, which are separated in their own distinct section. Walking carefully through the debris of boxes filled with taped coils of wires, fixtures, and tubes, Tim turned his head for a moment just in time to see his cousin Jessica, her back turned to him, take off her t-shirt and throw it into the washer.

She was in her underwear.

Older than Tim by about four years, Jess was growing into a beautiful woman. Long days spent working with cables and wires, on building and repairing, had made her body lean and taut. Franklin men appreciate muscles on their women; they like the ripple of hard tissue across arms and backs. A few years ago, when one of the Franklin boys brought home a girl from Benning, the family spent the better part of the evening making fun of her chicken arms, her skinny legs.

Jess didn't notice that Tim was there with her in the basement. He ducked back behind the wall, watching her through a split in the wood. She was in between loads. Putting in the clothes she was wearing along with some sheets, she started hauling out the load from the dryer. He watched her bend and lift, fold and put away.

She was beautiful. The most beautiful thing that he had ever seen. At thirteen years old, Tim knew about women only in the most general sense. He understood sex, the mechanics of it, but he didn't recognize the churning in his stomach, the pounding in his chest, the sudden erection.

He watched her until she was done folding. Took in all her details. How her brown hair came out of her ponytail and played out against her back, sticking in some places and drifting in others. He noted her eyes, focused and calm. Her poise was utterly confident and self-assured, as if being half-naked was the most normal thing in the world for her.

When the older Franklin finally threw on a clean shirt, pulled on a new, snug-fitting pair of jeans, Tim crept back the way he came and ran out of his house into the pines.

And that's the story of how Tim fell in love with his cousin.

Of course it doesn't end there. Tim knew he couldn't tell her how he felt. He couldn't tell anyone. That didn't stop him from spending as much time with her as he could, talking to her, helping her with her own repairs. Thirteen years old, inexperienced, in love—people started to notice. Jess didn't. She had babysat Tim when they were younger. She had watched him grow up. She had never conceived of him in any way other than her cousin.

The older Franklins started to talk amongst themselves. They didn't want to bring the matter up with Tim. Not directly. None of them could bear to hear what the boy would say if they were right.

So, when Jess was old enough, they started sending her out into the pines to check on the radio antennas.

When the historians came through the provinces during the seventies, intent on erasing all traces of extraneous history, they were followed by bulldozers. Buildings and radio towers were taken down. Railroad tracks were pulled up. You can still find roads, though. You drive long enough in this country and you'll find roads that curve and bend into cul-de-sacs surrounded by nothing but trees and grass, holes in the ground.

To solve the problem of the radio tower, Joseph Franklin constructed a series of radio relays attached to the tallest pine trees. In this way the village could pull a lingering signal from Benning, a town that actually existed on the official maps.

Joseph charged Jess with the maintenance of these antennas. She started spending more and more time in the pines, pushing out further to check the most distant stations. Sometimes she'd be gone for weeks, the only trace of her the hum of her voice or pop of a song she sang through the radio programs that drifted in from civilization.

Frustrated by his uncle's decision, Tim locked himself in his room and turned the radio up loud, waiting and listening for any trace of Jess's voice. He pulled together broken sentences, flashes of consonants and vowels, and made out of the wreckage of sound a love song sung only for him.

The next time she went out into the pines, Tim followed her. After climbing down from one of the antennas, she found him there, waiting for him at the bottom.

"Hey," Jess said. "What are you doing out here?"

"I was just out walking." He couldn't look at her. He was shaking too hard.

"We're out pretty far."

"I wanted to see you."

Jess noticed he was shaking. She stepped towards him. "Everything all right?"

Words build up inside a person, and if you're not of the kind who can open their mouth once and a while and let those out, they explode, coming out all broken, loud and wrong. Tim wasn't good with words. Like his siblings, Tim was good with wires.

"I love you," he blurted out, looking up.

Jess frowned. "What's happened?"

"Nothing," he said, quickly. "Nothing's wrong. Everything's fine. I love you. I came out to tell you I love you."

People say things all the time that we don't understand. Jess walked over to him, thinking that something had happened, something at school, something at home. She put one hand on his shoulder, one hand on his face. He was almost crying. "I love you too, Tim. Now what's wrong?"

Tim kissed her. He grabbed her neck and kissed her, stepping up on his toes to kiss her. She pulled away but he held on. She would be the first and last girl Tim ever kissed, and she pushed him off.

"What the fuck?"

"I'm sorry," he said.

"What the fuck was that?"

"I love you," he repeated. "And I needed to tell you that."

Jess stared at her cousin, stunned, still tasting his saliva on her mouth. Her stomach wretched, her mind furiously putting together all the accidental run-ins and hanging-arounds over the last few weeks until it all made sense.

"You're sick," she said.

"What?"

"You're sick. What are you thinking? You can't love me. I'm your fucking cousin."

Tim frowned. "No. That's not—"

"You can't love me."

"But I do. I feel it."

"Just shut up," she said, moving away from him. "Stop talking. Stop."

Tim followed her, doggedly. "Jess."

"Stop. Don't."

He tried to reach for her again, but she moved away from him. He reached again and she shoved him, hard, in the chest, forcing him down onto the floor of the pines. As he lay prone like that, Jess kicked him in the side. "Don't fucking touch me," she screamed, kicking him again.

"But—"

"You're sick." And again.

"Jess—"

"And if you ever tell anyone about this." One more kick.

"I wouldn't."

Breathing hard, her heart pounding and stomach tight in knots, Jess backed off. Tim leaned to sit up. "Stay the fuck down," Jess said. "Just stay there. I've got antennas to check."

"I'll come with you."

"Go home, Tim. Don't tell anyone about this."

"But—"

Jess was already gone, heading up the hill and into the pines.

Tim went home and locked himself back up in his bedroom. When Jess returned, he tried to go out and see her, but she ignored him. If they were in a group of family and he asked a question, she'd pretend she hadn't heard it. The elder Franklins looked on, tried to keep Tim busy with other things.

"Stop bothering your cousin," they said. "She's got important work to do."

And then, all of a sudden, Tim stopped bothering her altogether. He left his room and started spending more time doing work around with his other family. The Franklins breathed a sigh of relief. His crush had passed. He seemed to be getting back into the swing of things. Sure, they thought, he was spending more and more time out in the pines, but that was probably what he needed right now. He didn't talk much. He needed time to figure things out.

No one noticed the tools he took with him on those trips.

I SHOULD HAVE PUBLISHED your mother's horoscope," Hen admitted.

"Huh?"

"That horoscope. The one she wanted printed. I think it was for Tim. And I think if he'd read it he might have stopped."

I pulled a final drag off the soggy cigarette, then extinguished it in a puddle forming on a side table, listened to it fizzle.

"That boy was always so good with antennas," he finished, moving to stand up from his rain-soaked desk. "Too bad he couldn't climb a tree to save his life."

DURING THAT SUMMER, it seemed like my parents only had one voice between them. If my mother talked, my father went silent. The same was true in reverse.

Getting us ready for the funeral, Emma moved through picking the right clothes for us, instructing us on what we could and could not do at the service. It was our first funeral. Even for Maddox, the oldest, it was the first.

We didn't talk much. We let Mum do all the talking. She described what the service would be like, how long it would be. "You won't be expected to take part," she said, smoothing out Maddie's tie and shirt. "But if you do, you should know how to do it right."

She paid particular attention to Maddox. If she was talking to anyone, even when she was directing her comments to Faith or me, she was talking to him. Explaining his responsibilities, making sure he understood. I can't help but wonder now if a lot of that had to do with the Franklin boy and how close he and Maddox were in age.

We all came down the stairs together. Dad was in the living room, already dressed, sitting with the dead relatives, who were also clad in their funeral attire. With no game between them, the dead men stared at their hands, let their eyes linger on the wallpaper patterns and the grain of the mantle's wood.

"We're ready," Emma said.

Cadmus nodded.

All of us walked down to the village. We were joined on the road by other families. No one spoke. All dressed up and heading down the hill, no one said anything to anyone. The night was warmer than most. The humidity made the clothes uncomfortable. Kids pulled at the necklines of their shirts, the tightness of their jackets. The older men and women, the parents, kept their eyes straight ahead.

The shops were closed. We passed them on the way. All the boats were docked and floating quietly in the harbour. Rough men who spent hard days out far from home, plumbing the depths of the ocean for the rare catch of fish, had pulled on suits that they had worn for their weddings. Their hands still cut up and raw from their work, their beards unkempt and bushy, they all tried their best to appear sombre, civilized.

Many were already drunk. Through the haze of expensive perfume that was bought years before and only used for special occasions, you could smell it. Flasks appeared and disappeared between people like silver coins in a magic trick. No one seemed to run out. They passed and passed the flasks between them until they could stomach the walk to the funeral.

Lizzie was there but she wasn't drunk. She appeared behind us silently, just a few steps back. I was surprised to see her there. Wearing a plain black dress, her left sleeve hanging loose instead of pinned to her chest, she smiled at me a little smile. Dressed like that, her hair clean and the stench of alcohol no longer present, she seemed years younger. I smiled back.

Before Ester Anson left Garfax, she had the largest house in the village. Since it had been broken apart, two parts left to the pines and three parts stitched together to make up our own home, the honour of largest dwelling fell to the Franklins. Out of all the houses in Garfax, the Franklin home commands the best view. Set up a little ways up from the main road, it looks out from the centre of the mouth of Garfax Bay. From its long, wraparound verandahs, you can see all the houses littering the sides of the bay. You can hear the sound of the seagulls and the docks below. The traffic, what little there is, gets muffled by the pines and surrounding houses, the accompanying hedgerows. Nowhere in Garfax are the roads so well maintained, preserved as best as possible since the historians came and took our town sign away.

Many weddings are held at the Franklin home. Many celebrations and funerals, as well. The house front is dominated by two large pine trees that no longer produce needles, having been struck by lightning during the first year of the village's existence. It was the twin trees, struck like that, that ultimately convinced Joseph Franklin to settle his family there and build their great house.

We weren't the last to arrive, nor were we the first. We walked up the stone steps and into the garden. Long strings of white lights were strung from the trees to the house, producing a warm halo of dancing illumination on the grounds. Families milled around, talking amongst themselves. Off in the distance, the children played.

The Franklins, all of them, were stationed by the front door on the verandah. They greeted guests, pointed out where refreshments would be, accepted condolences.

Looking back, it strikes me as odd that there were no pictures of Timothy, no large rendition of him for us to look at. There was, in point of fact, nothing of him at all to look at. He was gone. Utterly erased by his passing. The service would be closed casket. People barely even mentioned his name.

We got looks, of course. As soon as we stepped onto the grass, we got looks. The mood of the funeral changed. People talked lower, crowded a little closer together. Emma squeezed her husband's hand. Cadmus squeezed back, looked over at her.

"Here we go," he said, the first thing out of his mouth since the boy's passing.

The three of us kids were left in the garden while our parents ascended the stairs up to the front door. Maddox had his hands in his pockets. He watched them carefully. Faith looked to me but I was looking elsewhere, at the people gathering in groups who were also intent on the action on the stairs.

Dad had his hand on the small of Mum's back. I remember this because when I turned to look back, I thought it looked large, like a giant spider, fingers spread wide. They went forward together. Mum spoke. She spoke to Bethany Franklin, the mother of Timothy and wife of Joseph. She was sitting down. In a chair larger than all of the others present on the verandah. Joseph stood behind her, touching her shoulder.

Bethany's lip quivered. She stared at my mother though hard eyes that were done with crying. Halfway through whatever Emma was saying, she stood up, brought herself up to full height, and stepped forward. She didn't say anything. Joseph stepped forward.

Then Bethany Franklin slapped my mother. Hard and loud. And my father's hand on the small of her back turned into a fist.

Everybody stopped. Bethany didn't say anything. She didn't back down, didn't offer any kind of explanation or scream or do anything. She just stood there and stared at my mother, lip quivering. To her credit, Mum barely flinched. Finishing what she had come there to say, she nodded to Joseph and walked back down the stairs to join the rest of us.

My mother shook. Both her face and Dad's face were crimson.

Maddox opened his mouth. His hands were balled into fists.

"No," Cadmus said, holding out his hand. "Don't."

Maddox looked up at him. Looked to Mum. She looked down, shook her head.

"It'll be over soon," Dad said, turning back to the garden, to the people staring and whispering. "It'll all be over soon."

I remember then hoping that he would be right, knowing that he was wrong.

THE CHURCH IN GARFAX has very few parishioners. We don't even have a priest. About a decade back, the last priest died. He was an older gentleman when he came here, and although he served faithfully, he soon expired from heart troubles. Word was sent for a replacement, but the story is that the replacement got lost trying to find the village and now runs his services out of the back of his van, travelling along the coast, healing the hearts and minds of people not yet ready to give up the ghosts of their dying villages. I've never met the man. It's been said that he's still looking for Garfax.

Even without a priest, the church remains open. The religious among us still come in and pray. They bring their own bibles. They read by themselves or to each other, and if they come across a spiritual crisis, they only have to turn to the person next to them to seek comfort.

Funerals and weddings, as you can understand, become problematic without a priest. They become illegal without a justice of the peace or government official. Yet for almost thirty years now, we've managed, married our partners and buried our dead as a criminal act.

It is up to each family how to go about the proceedings. Fishermen get buried at sea. For a while, workers at the factory that made airplane parts were cremated and a fund was set up so that their ashes could be released in mid-air from an Air Canada passenger jet. When a Franklin died, the service was held at home amid the spiderweb of light bulbs that had become synonymous with the family over the years.

If there was a service, we didn't see it. At one point in the evening, everyone congregated into the Franklin house, into the living room and dining room, to sit around, talk, drink, and eat. The place filled with smoke. Faith and I hung out on the verandah with Lizzie, who nursed her way through a few beers. She kept us company for most of that night, her back turned away from the garden and facing the windows.

Without looking at us, she told us stories about her life before the accident, and some stories of her life since. Faith sat next to her, on her right side, and occasionally Lizzie would run her hand through my sister's hair.

Maddox was inside. So were Mum and Dad.

I didn't see Jessica that night. Not once. I heard she was there, or that she might have been there. It depends on who was telling the story. I didn't know to look for her that night, though. I didn't know the story. I drifted at the outskirts of conversations, listening to snatches of gossip and speculation.

Isn't that what I've been doing all along?

The topics ranged. People talked about work, about babies on the way or children they were raising. They talked about problems with electricity, problems with roads. Someone mentioned that their radio was acting strange.

If anyone brought up the Franklin boy, they did it quickly and then dropped it. There were just so many questions. He was so young, they said. Too young. To break his bones from a fall in the middle of the pines. What was he doing? And the woman who found him. What was she doing? How did she know?

"You ever read her horoscopes? The ones in the paper?"

Of course they did. Everyone did.

Towards the end of the night, when children started getting grumpy and tired, the parents emerged. One at a time, then in groups, they came out onto the verandah and breathed deep the saltwater air coming from the bay. Some had been crying. Some were far too drunk.

And before they left, each and every one, they twisted off a white bulb light from the strings that hung above their heads and placed it in their pocket. They pulled the bulbs from everywhere. From the dead, lightning-struck trees where they hung coiled around, from the verandah railings, from the very air in places. In small chunks and bits, the light began to fade. Bulbs disappeared into pockets, into handbags, and then the people left, carrying away the cooling glass.

Mum emerged. She saw us. "Come with me," she said. "You need to do something now."

Leading the way, with Lizzie behind us, herding us, we walked towards one of the burnt-out trees.

"Pick a light," she said. "Any light."

"Why?" Faith pointed.

"To say goodbye to the Franklin boy," she explained.

Faith pointed to one just above my mother's head. "All right," she said, and pulled a cloth out of her handbag, folded it, and handed it to Faith. "Twist it off," she said, holding Faith up so she could reach it, grunting slightly under her twelve-year-old weight.

Then it was my turn. I picked one closer to the ground.

"Good boy," she said.

The bulb was hot in my hand. The cloth insulated some of the heat, but not all. The light extinguished, Mum took the bulb from me, wrapped it up, and handed it back. "Keep it somewhere safe," she told us.

We nodded.

Satisfied, Mum and Lizzie walked off and away from the tree to find their own lights.

"Where's Dad?" I asked.

Faith shrugged, yawned. "Inside, I guess."

"I'm going to go get him. Maddie, too."

"Don't," Faith said.

"Why not?"

"They'll be out when they're out."

"But I want to go home."

"What did Mum say?" Faith asked. "She said not to whine. We'll be going soon anyway. All the lights are going out."

"I'll just be a minute."

"Oswald."

But I was already heading across the garden and up the stairs.

The lights outside weren't the only ones people were taking away with them, stuffing in their pockets and handbags. Unscrewing the decorative glass from chandeliers, drunk fishermen with handkerchiefs or discarded ties in their hands unscrewed lights and twisted off the bulbs.

Lamps had already been taken out. Whole rooms were darkened.

In the dark it became hard to see. People still shuffled out of the house, and without any light, they pushed passed me. Apologies and gruff rejoinders murmured in the smokey middle air. I found myself hands outstretched, pushing deeper into the house, navigating my way through an ever-changing topography of legs and torsos, mourning skirts and dress pants.

A few conversations were still going on. A small group of Franklins in their twenties clustered around the kitchen table, smoking cigarettes, drinking beer, and playing cards. Only a single light glowed above them, making the room seem almost candlelit. I left the kitchen and proceeded upstairs, occasionally calling for my father.

"He's outside," someone told me.

"I saw him upstairs," another one said.

"He left hours ago."

I found him in one of the bedrooms. I found him from his voice. He was talking to someone.

"Dad?" I called him from the threshold.

"Be quiet," someone else, Maddox, told me.

"We need to go," I whispered.

"Give him a minute."

Dad didn't notice us. He continued talking without interruption.

In the dark, Maddox came up alongside me, dipping down low enough so he could talk softly into my ear. "He's dreaming again," he told me.

"Who's he talking to?"

"Dunno."

But we listened. It didn't make much sense. Little Dad said while he was sleepwalking made much sense. "You only ever tell half-stories," Emma had told him once, pointing this out in the middle of a party. "You never finish telling a story; you always break off and go onto something new."

"Is that true?" he asked.

She nodded. "Yup. I only get the other half when you're sleeping."

Whatever half this conversation this story belonged to, I couldn't piece it together.

Mum came in a few minutes later, brandishing the flashlight she always took with her. She caught Maddox and me in the beam. Then Cadmus. "What are you doing here?" she asked me.

"I came looking for them."

Mum frowned and shooed us outside. Through the door we heard her whisper to our father. She pushed the flashlight into his hands, made his thumb flick the switch on and off. "You're awake," she said. "You're awake. You're awake. And it's time to go."

They came out a few minutes later, Dad holding the flashlight and a spent light bulb.

We found Lizzie and Faith waiting for us at the garden's edge. Together we walked down the stone steps and onto the street. Lighting our way with the flashlight, the six of us walked until we stopped by Lizzie's house.

The two women hugged and then Lizzie was gone, through the door and into her house. We walked back up the hill and into the house in silence. Lights were coming on in small bursts all over the village. Living rooms that had been left dark during the funeral erupted into lights muted by curtains. Cars started up and their headlights danced along the curves and bends of the rows, fluttering through the hedges.

Within moments of being home, we were already getting our coats off. Dad disappeared into the sitting room while Faith and Maddox stumbled upstairs. Despite my complaints of being tired, I found myself awake. I followed my mother into the kitchen, where she was making some tea for the dead relatives, who had resumed their game of dominoes, smoking stale cigarettes.

The tap hissed water into the kettle. I placed my hand on the back of my father's father's chair and looked over his dusty shoulder to the game stretched out below. They had only recently started again.

"What's on your mind?" Mum asked, back still turned, focused on the kettle, on the tumbling water.

I pulled out the bulb from my pocket and rolled it in my hand.

"Oswald."

I was thinking about the Franklin boy again. Since we found him there, my mother and I, in the woods, I hadn't had much time to think about him. Too pale arms. Open eyes. Leaves in his hair, and body bent in strange angles. I tapped the bulb in the palm of my hand and looked at her, and then to the game my ancestors were playing.

"What if he comes back?" I asked.

Mum had turned around now, leaning against the kitchen counter. "Who?"

"The Franklin boy. What if he comes back?"

She followed my gaze to her own father, who looked back at her. "He won't," Mum said, looking at him.

"But what if he does?"

Mum came over to me and placed her hand, cool from the kettle, on my forehead, smoothing out the hair that drifted across my eyes. "If you ever see that Franklin boy again, if he ever bothers you, I want you to tell him to come talk to me."

I looked up at her. Her eyes were fierce. Cold and determined. I nodded, looking down. She hooked my chin with her thumb and forced my eyes up again.

"I'm serious. If you ever see him again, if he even says a word to you. Tell me. I'll take care of it."

"All right."

"All right. Now, it's time for you to go to bed. It's been a long day."

THE NEXT MORNING the radios changed. The first person who noticed, the first person who listened long enough to realize that the radio was saying something different than it had for all the years before, was Aunt Connie.

She was doing her crosswords. She was sitting at the kitchen table.

Spread out in front of her was the week's worth of crosswords produced by Barton Hen's newspaper. Each puzzle had been cut out and sat in chronological order next to its cousins. Dressed in her bathrobe, munching on a bowl of cereal, Aunt Connie pulled her legs up onto the chair and sat cross-legged.

Aunt Connie had never been anyone's wife. She had never been anyone's girlfriend. She had never had any children or any real friends with whom she could spend much time. When she came home, she came home alone, and for the first thirty years of her life, this bothered her immensely. She felt the lack, the emptiness, that others supposed she should feel.

"You poor thing," they'd say, looking at the solitariness of her life.

And Connie would look at her own life and wonder what was so terrible that everyone around her saw. So many people said it, however, that she started to believe it herself. Until one day, in her mid-thirties, when she crawled out of bed on a Saturday morning and ate breakfast stark naked on her living room couch, curtains drawn wide with a good view of the bay.

It was the most liberating moment of her life. Instead of a series of empty, interconnecting rooms, which was how most people described her home, the house filled up with her own personal quirks and eccentricities.

"I have enough life in me," she said, "to fill up all these rooms. I don't need anyone else to do it for me." So resolved, Aunt Connie settled blissfully into an old-maidhood of her own delirious and joyful choosing.

A husband would have ruined all that. A husband wouldn't have understood how much pleasure it gave her to sit cross-legged in a natty old robe in the early hours of the morning and meditate on the crosswords of the last week. A husband would wonder why she didn't ever use a dictionary. Why she didn't stop if a question plagued her. Why she didn't just pick up a respectable and useful pastime. It was for all of these reasons that Aunt Connie frequently said, "Husbands are bullshit," whenever she listened to one of her friends talk about their married woes.

She was acutely attuned to the rooms of her house. So much so that when the radio stopped playing music, she noticed almost immediately. She placed her pen down on the table. She listened.

Sometimes the reception dipped in Garfax. It went hand in hand with having a jury-rigged system of metal trees stealing the lingering signals from civilization. Weather played havoc with the signals, oftentimes leaving empty days of mindless static while storms raged along the coast.

This wasn't static, though. This was groaning.

Aunt Connie frowned.

Adjusting her robe tighter across her chest, she stood up and went over to the kitchen counter where the radio sat. She bent down, leaned closer. She listened. Through the gargle and hiss of ambient radio noise, she heard the sound again. The huffing and grunting.

"Oh God," the radio said. "Oh my Jesus."

Aunt Connie's eyebrows raised.

It was a man's voice, but whose voice she couldn't tell. The ambient noise distorted the tenor and depth of the sound, making it deeper in places, higher in others. Stretching the voice out so it sounded distant, strained. But it was most certainly a man's voice. He grunted again. Cursed some more. His breathing came hard.

"That's it," the radio said, this time in a woman's voice. "That's it, that's it, that's it. Come on, come on, come on."

Aunt Connie looked around the kitchen, suddenly aware that she was listening to something very private, something she shouldn't be able to hear. Her face flushed red, but she reached over and turned up the dial.

The groaning and moaning of the radio, the staccato exclamations, continued for several minutes. She heard the crush of leather seats. The banging of feet against a dashboard. The moment-to-moment repositioning of bodies in a cramped space.

"Here it comes," the male voice said.

"Wait. Not yet. Not yet."

"Sorry."

"No. Wait, you bastard. I'm not there yet."

"Sorry."

"Wait!"

"Sorry. Sorry. Sorry."

"Don't you fucking dare."

"Fuck!"

There was a moment of silence, of settling leather and relaxing limbs. Then a smack of skin on skin, of bones colliding. "I told you to wait," the woman said.

"Sorry," the other voice replied. "I couldn't help it."

"That's bullshit."

"Sorry," the voice repeated, suddenly farther away, falling away. "I'm sorry."

"Sorry my ass."

And then the radio died altogether, only to return to a different brand of music entirely from what she was listening to before. It was piano music now. Classical. One of Franz Emerick's more famous compositions, the "Calling of Wings."

Aunt Connie exhaled. Her heart raced. Her face burned. She didn't realize that she had been holding her breath.

OF COURSE, AUNT CONNIE didn't tell anyone right away that the radios had begun to speak, had begun to listen and report back what they heard. She was too embarrassed. But by mid-afternoon, people all over the village were starting to realize that something was going on with the signals.

A group of older Garfaxians gathered together to play dominoes and listen to a game of cricket on the verandah of one of their neighbours. The game was playing. The anticipated teams were represented. But the players were different.

It wasn't that the older Garfaxian men didn't recognize the names. It was just that the names were so old. They were the heroes they had grown up with. Players from fifty years ago who they had listened to in their younger incarnations.

"This has happened before," one of the men intoned.

"He's going to foul this shot," another prophesized, only to be proved right a second later.

Unsettled by this déjà vu, this repeating and folding of history, the men put down the tiles to their game, folded their hands in their laps, and waited fearfully for the game to finish and for history to catch up with them again.

More and more reports followed. Along with the repeating histories, the old broadcasts that were being passed off as new, people heard their own voices turned back on them, coming out strange and alien through the radio speakers. They heard their wives, or who they thought were their wives, singing songs to their children, talking about them to their friends at the kitchen table. They heard their husbands boast about their sexual prowess, their imagined romantic adventures. They listened to furious couplings, chilled arguments, hasty arguments, and the tender mundanities of daily conversation.

Everyone listened.

The men, as they did with each and every crisis, flocked to the Two-Stone. With Gregory Peck behind the bar, they lined up their portable radios and listened to their histories and secrets spoken back to them by the rebellious technology. People postulated about the voices they heard. Some claimed to recognize the cadence and tenor of a particular speaker, but others stepped up to claim the opposite. Theories abounded.

Even though he despised the chaos of strange events, Gregory Peck couldn't argue with the influx of customers, the increasing demand on his stores. He kept a series of radios playing at all times. He even placed a few in the bathroom, although these he quickly replaced when it was discovered that the sounds of urination and drunken speculation could be heard halfway across the bay in Aunt Connie's living room.

Teenagers crammed into cars, whether they were borrowed from their parents or lying rotting in the middle of the pines, and listened to the secrets of the adults. They giggled, made jokes. Virgin couples held sweaty hands and tried to decipher the gasps, groans, and laughs that accompanied that strange territory they saw soon approaching. Older couples languished through cigarettes, made crude comments, traced the outlines of their lover's jaw or the bends of strands of each other's hair.

The dead relatives gathered together, clumped in tight groups around small radios, hoping to hear word from their wives. The occasional missive came through. Gentle words followed harsh recriminations. They opened and closed their lifeless mouths, trying to force out words that came out in hoarse whispers. Ghosts choked back tears. William Wilson, having heard his wife's voice (or what he hoped was his wife's voice) for the first time in almost forty years, balled his hand into his fist, hit his leg, and then left the room as the sobbing overtook him. And at night, Garfaxians could tune in at almost any hour and hear Starling blast away on his silver trumpet.

At home, our kitchen suddenly empty of dead relatives, Maddox, Faith, and I sat around Faith's stereo. Maddox fiddled with the dial, playing through the frequencies, shifting through secrets and histories.

"Cut it out," Faith said.

"I want to find something good."

Dad caught us in the middle of listening to a woman sing a lullaby to her child. We only noticed when he flicked the light on and off. "I don't want you listening to that garbage," he said.

"But—"

"No. That's people's private lives you're listening to."

"Then why's it on the radio?" Maddox wanted to know.

Why indeed?

THE WHYS AND HOWS were debated endlessly at the Franklin house. The older Franklins piled into the living room and pulled apart one of their radios, pulled its guts and laid it out on the table to divine the reason.

"It must be the signal," one of them said. "There's nothing wrong with the set."

"Well, nothing that could be wrong with *all* the sets."

"So it must be the signal."

"That makes sense."

"What's wrong with the signal, then?"

Jessica shrugged. "All of the towers were fine when I checked last."

"Why don't you check them again? See if one of them got knocked over or damaged. That might explain it."

"Sure."

"Now, please."

And she left.

"Do you honestly think it's the tower?"

Silence.

"I think it's because of Emma," a woman said.

"Why do you think that?"

"Because of everything that's happened. She started it. All of it. Taking that boat."

"She didn't make Tim—"

"Don't."

"I'm just saying—"

"I know what you're saying, and you're wrong. I feel it. She started it. All of this is happening because of her."

"What if it isn't?"

"What else could it be?"

"What if it's something Tim did?"

Again, silence.

"Do you think it can still hear us?"

"What?"

"The radio. Do you think it's still listening?"

"No, of course not. We took it apart."

Even mangled and dissected as it was, the radio was still listening. And within minutes everyone was wondering if my mother had caused all of this trouble when she had decided to go to water.

AFTER HEARING THE FRANKLINS, things got worse. There seemed to be radios everywhere. We couldn't escape it. The signal grew agitated.

Walking through the village, through the classrooms, through the stores, we heard people talking about our mother over the PA. We heard them call her horrible names, accuse her of killing the Franklin boy.

"Don't listen," Dad said, herding us through the aisles of the grocery store. "Just don't listen."

But during the week and a half the radios spoke, it was impossible to do anything else.

The elusiveness of the signal frustrated Maddox to no end. It was worse than when the kids at school whispered rumours about our mother during that week she went to water. One afternoon, during the weekend, he handed me a baseball bat and told me to follow him.

"Where are we going?"

He didn't tell me.

We went into the pines, and when we found an abandoned hulk of a car, we bashed in the radio, shattered it into pieces. That sound carried. Even many years later, people still talk about hearing cursing and crashing during those last few days the radio spoke. Holding the baseball bat limply by my side, I watched my older brother smash face plates and destroy tape decks.

Faith turned the radio off entirely. She unscrewed the aerial. She plugged in her headphones and listened to old mix tapes. She listened to CDs. She read.

"You don't have to listen," she told me.

But I did. Whenever I got the chance, I listened. I walked out into the pines with a small radio that I smuggled out of the house and listened to the village talk about my mother for hours. I heard the crashes of Maddox's baseball bat fall hard against the offending devices. I marvelled at the sounds of history repeating itself as reports of wars long past played out in serialized offerings. I hummed along to the trill of Starling's trumpet.

"Sometimes I can feel my fingers—"

"Fucking bitch couldn't mind her own business."

"I love you."

"Come on, come on, come on."

The final thuds of wood on plastic. Over and over again.

"Bombs fall in the heart of London."

"Peace!"

"Can anyone hear me?"

"I should have brought her up on charges."

"Hush little baby, don't say a word—"

"I see you. I know you don't see me, but I see you. You're so beautiful. Do you know how beautiful you are?"

"Damn woman thinks she can see the future."

"When are you going to tell your wife—"

"—your husband—"

"—your boyfriend—"

"—girlfriend—"

"—about us."

"—about me."

"We can leave this place."

"And what about her husband? He's a strange one."

"I need another drink."

"War is declared."

"Sometimes he doesn't even know you're in the room with him."

"I miss you, love."

"And there are such beautiful lights."

"They're not even from here."

"I can hear you."

"Will wonders never fucking cease?"

My mouth went dry. I wanted to speak but couldn't. Wanted to say something, scream it into the radio, have it travel through the air and reach everyone. Wanted to set the record straight, tell the true story. It occurred to me, though, that I didn't even know what that was.

I asked my mother for the first time what drove her to go to water that night. She was on the verandah, smoking cigarettes, her feet up on the railing, staring out at the bay.

"What did you say?" she asked.

"Why did you do it?"

"Do what?"

"Steal the boat."

Mum considered her cigarette, rolled it between her fingers. "I saw this television program once, about this woman caught in a flood. It was sudden. The water just broke over the edge and within minutes she was caught in the height of a tree with her two children, holding the high branches, trying to keep them all from being washed away. The water was strong. The current, I mean. So strong. And she had one of them on each arm. She knew if they were going to survive, then she would have to grab the branch fully. That was the only way they were going to make it. Of course, that would mean letting go of one of her children."

She exhaled a thin stream of smoke. Shook her head.

"I couldn't imagine making that kind of decision. There's no right choice, and no matter what you decide, you can't live with it after. There's no going on for a mother after that."

"So what did she do?"

Mum shrugged. "She kissed her daughter and then let her go. And once she was gone, swallowed by that flood, she hauled herself onto the branch with her son."

"Why did she let the daughter go?"

Mum looked at me. "Because she was older. When she was interviewed, the interviewer, a man, asked her why she had chosen to save her son. He thought it had something to do with the culture, about how men were always more prized than women. But that wasn't it. She simply replied that the daughter was older. By six years. And the son hadn't had those six years, that he deserved them as much as his sister had."

We both went quiet.

"So why'd you steal the boat?" I asked again.

Mum stood up, extinguished her cigarette. "I just told you," she said, and then went inside.

THE MORE PEOPLE talked, the more the radios listened. The more they listened, the more we said. Until the radios blared secrets and histories and whispers and screams and trumpet calls all hours of the day. The sounds blended together, forming a horrible wailing mix. Groaning and grunting turned to weeping and sighing. Confessions became humiliations. Masked by the radio static, the stretching of voices, people became bolder and said almost anything that came into their heads. All the painful events of the past came back on us. You could hear it at all hours. Somewhere a radio was turned up loud. The pines echoed with car stereos pounding out hurtful missives, and even though Maddox hunted ceaselessly, he couldn't silence them all. There was always another radio, always more people who wanted to listen, who wanted to speak.

When Jessica returned from checking the metal tree towers, she brought with her a curled antenna twisted into a spiralling cord. She had found it in one of the pines. It was identical to the one found in Timothy's pale, dead hand.

She came back into Garfax from the main road, holding the antenna. It almost looked like a sword. The roads were littered with radio sets that had been thrown from car windows, brought out from houses and smashed on the sidewalk. We heard her approach from all sides, the crunching of her heavy work boots on the guts of the speakers echoing through our rooms.

"I found at least three more like this," she told Joseph. "In the highest pines. But there has to be more. A lot more."

"And you think that's what's twisting the signal?"

"I do."

Because out in the pines, up in the treetop heights of needles and sap stink, she had climbed into an atmosphere of ambient noise and chatter. It had hurt her teeth to be up that high, to hear everything in her bones, the signal rattling her ribcage.

"We're never going to find them all," Joseph said.

"I don't think we will, no." Jess agreed. "So what do we do now?"

Joseph didn't reply. It was obvious what had to be done.

FEW RESISTED THE PURGE. Garfax has only ever had the slighted tolerance for wonders. They are like bad house guests. They always wear out their welcome.

Garfaxians opened their doors to the Franklins, who scoured the rooms for every offending radio set. They gathered them together in the flatbeds of trucks and drove them down in screaming piles to the dock. Gregory Peck lent out his boats free of charge, and soon small armadas of Franklins were launched, loaded down with humming devices.

They drowned the sound, throwing the offending sets overboard in the middle of the bay, waited for them to get waterlogged and silent. It took almost five days for all of the sets to be rounded up. Even Faith's stereo was taken, much to her dismay. We were told to wait in the living room. The five of us sat while the Franklins roamed through our house, checking for anything that might tell secrets in the middle of the night.

And then it was over. There were no more radios. Cars and trucks had been gutted. The grocery store ceiling went quiet. Antennas were torn off houses, off businesses, off everything. And all of it thrown into the bay.

Of course, there were always going to be some radios that evaded the purge. Even now, many years later, it isn't uncommon to come across a car in the pines that has a radio set still in it. Some people, like yourselves, even brought them into your houses, tentatively turned them on after years of silence, curious to see if they were still listening, still receiving.

And they are. If you're listening to me now, if you can hear me, then they are.

IV

Intermission

WHEN THE LAST RADIO SET found by the Franklins was tossed into Garfax bay and the village was plunged into silence, when we couldn't leave the house without getting stared at by friends and neighbours, people we had grown up with, who blamed my mother for all the strangeness, my father said, in a tone that I believed, "This isn't the end of the world."

He was sitting out with my mother on the deck when he said it. She had her legs up and resting on his knees. With the tips of his fingers, he stroked her ankles, tickled her feet. Mum's arms were folded, her head buried in the thick sweater she wore to stave off the morning chill.

We were all out that morning. Having breakfast. My father had made the meal, and even the dead relatives were there, leaning against the verandah rails, holding onto their saucers and cups, sipping their tea loudly.

"It sure feels like it," Maddox said.

Cadmus looked over at his eldest son and gave him a sympathetic look. "I know it feels like that now, but it'll be fine. We're all going to be fine. This is not the end of the world. Look," he said, gesturing to the world beyond the verandah. "The end of the world wouldn't look so lovely."

We all looked out at the bay, at the village that hugged the coast and the pines that surrounded us on all sides. Birds sang in the tree branches. Fishing boats puttered back and forth, navigating around the few tourists who travelled through from distant western provinces to get some Maritime flavour.

He was right. The end of the world wouldn't look so lovely.

GARFAXIANS ARE SLOW to forget and even slower to forgive, but finally my father wore them down. He was our face in the village, and a week after the radios were drowned in the bay, he walked down the hill and into the Two-Stone, walked right up to the bar, right across from Gregory Peck, and asked him how business was.

Gregory blinked. "What?"

Cadmus smiled. "I asked you how business was going, Greg."

"Oh. Well. It's fine. Actually—"

Easy as that, Dad began the healing process. Like his father before him, he had a way with people, of making them feel important and cared for. He stretched this ability to the limit, and when sheer charm wasn't enough to convince people to let us back into their lives, he began killing them with kindness.

He unpacked his camera, set up his old darkroom in the closet, and began to advertise his services for anyone who would pay. He even did free jobs. He got in contact with the schools and got them to agree for him to take all the class and graduation pictures. He offered large discounts for newly married couples to have their wedding photographs done as long as our whole family was allowed to attend the ceremony. He approached the vain with the promise of portraits.

With each snap of the camera, each frozen second of wonder, he bought our way back into Garfax. It helped immensely that until Cadmus Brodie returned, Garfax had been without a professional photographer.

IT'S STRANGE HOW THINGS HAPPEN. I wonder now if my mother knew it all along, if she knew everything that would follow when she took to water at the beginning of that summer, of the series of events that occurred as a result of her decision. I think she did.

One of my father's earliest attempts to win his family's way back into the hearts of the village was to hold free child portrait sessions at our house, for anyone who was interested. It was, in retrospect, a bold move, and more than a little blatant. Only a few months after the Franklin boy's death and the radio drama, it was an overt ploy to make our stitched-together house seem less mythic, less dire in the eyes of the village.

It was no surprise then that few people took him up on his offer. Only his best friends brought their children, who were more than reluctant themselves to enter into a house that was already growing in stature as a local legend.

Sara Lonnie was one of those children.

She was the same age as me. She was in my class. We didn't talk much, but we had grown up together. Sara came to Garfax late, only a few years before, and had some difficulty fitting in to the already tightly knit community. It didn't help matters much that she came from a single-parent home, that there was only her father taking care of her.

Sara's father, Thomas, frequented the Two-Stone. He was a handyman, an expert in all things general. He often worked hand in hand with the Franklins. When they needed a wall torn down to expose some wires and then built back up again, it was Thomas that they called. The man read. He read constantly. Within two years of living in Garfax, he had read every book in the village library. He hardly slept. Between running around doing odd jobs in the afternoon and taking care of Sara in the evening, his nights were spent reading.

I have to think now that the library we had inherited from Ester Anson had a lot to do with his decision to bring his daughter to have her photograph taken that day. As soon as he was in the house, as soon as he had introduced himself and Sara to Dad, he asked about the library.

"If you'd like," Cadmus said, "you can take a look while I take your daughter's photograph."

And that was the end of that story. The man vanished, passing by my mother, who was sitting on the stairs, watching her husband take pictures.

HERE'S THAT FIRST PHOTOGRAPH of Sara, age eleven.

It's a full-on portrait. The picture is dominated primarily with her face and terminates just below her shoulders. She is looking directly into the camera. She isn't smiling, but she isn't frowning. The look on her face isn't blank, either. Her eyes, a light brown, are open. Her lips are together but not clenched. Her nose, it is fair to say, is slightly larger than most girls' noses. I know this because she told me, that she always thought it was too big for her face.

How can I describe it? She is simply looking at the camera.

Her hair is longer here than it will be for the rest of her life. Her father believes at this point that all girls should have long hair. Her hair is brown and wet. It has been permanently wet, rain soaked, for almost six years now, ever since her parents divorced and her mother left her to pursue a better life. It hangs down just below her shoulders, the strands curling at the bottom.

She is wearing a polo shirt. One of her father's, I think. It is big on her. A white shirt with blue stripes, blue collar. The collar is open and reveals her collarbone.

It is a beautiful picture, the one I love the most. I think I love it the most because it's so naked, because it's the person she is when she isn't around anyone else. She isn't being teased by the kids at school or plagued by Tyler Marks or Deborah Cunning. She isn't being crushed under the weight of the braces that are a year away. She isn't taking care of me or worrying about what she's going to be when she grows up or any of that. She is simply an eleven-year-old girl looking into my father's camera.

I WAS JUST COMING IN when Sara was leaving, her father's hands brimming with books that my father lent him from our library. As I reached for the door, she opened it and stepped out onto the verandah.

"Hey, Oz," she said.

"Hey," I said. "What are you doing here?"

"Getting my picture taken. Dad wanted to look at your library."

"Oh."

"It's nice."

"Thanks."

Tom came out then, talking with my father. They pushed passed us and that was the end of our conversation. She mouthed goodbye and I waved as I backed into the house. Dad walked them to the car. When I went inside, my mother looked at me through the banister railings.

"Hey," she said.

"Hey."

"Did you have fun?"

"Sure. I guess."

"Do you know Sara? The Lonnie girl?"

I looked over at the Lonnies getting into the car. "Yeah. She's in my class."

Emma smiled at me. A small, sad little smile.

Yeah, I think she knew. Even then she knew. Sometimes my mother could see for miles.

IT'S A TRADITION for the older kids in Garfax to pilgrimage their way to Quill Lake at the beginning of each summer. It is in no way an official campground, so there are no roads that lead to the lake. You have to park on the degenerating road that leads out from Garfax and eventually joins up with the main highway to Benning. From there you have to carry your gear, your tent and your provisions, through a few miles of pine.

There are signposts in the pines, arrows and names from people who have come before, carved out in bark. Far enough away from the village, there is no refuse here, only a few abandoned cars. No evidence of Ester Anson's mansion or her belongings. No paintings hanging and rotting in the treetops. No furniture left to ruin in the open air.

Like the ocean, the pines are so close to the lake that it looks like the forest will swallow it whole. It's easy to imagine that the trees have actually breached the surface of the water, that underneath there is an aquatic patch of trees reaching up to brush against young, swimming legs.

In the summer, Quill Lake is never empty. All the older kids and younger adults camp around the water's edge, their tents dotting its outside. Music plays constantly, either from a stereo or handmade from self-brought instruments. It's an excuse, is what it is. An excuse to be loud, to party, to have all kinds of fun that is difficult in the village. No one is watching. Everyone is.

You walk from campsite to campsite, beer in hand, and the stories constantly change. Relationships spark and explode in the night, only to fizzle out in the morning. Naked night swimming in groups leads to solitary dips in the morning blue, floating on your back while you watch the sky change colour and birds fly past, abandoning their nightly nests.

The year following my mother's going to water, it was Maddie's time to head to Quill Lake. He was just old enough.

In the months leading up to it, he didn't talk about it. Older kids don't talk about Quill Lake to their parents, but everyone knows what goes on. There's always a move among the old ones to stop the kids from heading out there. So far away from help, from home, anything can happen.

Accidents abound in the minds of the families, but everyone remembers what it was like when they went there. It's impossible to fight against that sort of nostalgia. Even better, there hasn't been a serious accident at the lake for years.

Maddox didn't have to talk about it, but it was obvious he was excited. He jittered around the house when he was there. He bought some new clothes. He spent more and more time with his friends, the few who had remained after my mother went to water and the others he picked up over the course of the year.

"Just be careful," my father said to him.

"Just be careful about what?"

"You know what."

And my older brother would grin. Ear to ear.

Faith and I pestered him, asking him questions that just had him laughing. "It's no big deal," he'd shrug. "It probably won't be that fun anyway."

"Bullshit," Faith said.

"Yeah, bullshit," I repeated.

And that grin just got larger.

School let out and cars all over the village were prepped for the exodus to the lake. That night Maddox didn't sleep. Neither did I. I could hear him pacing around, packing and repacking. He stole down onto the verandah and chain-smoked through a pack of stale cigarettes he had lifted off our mother a month ago.

Somewhere along the night I must have dozed off. I woke to hear Maddox trip over some clothes littered on his bedroom floor. Blinking, I looked outside and saw the sky had turned from black to deep grey.

When he went downstairs, I followed him. He had packed all of his stuff for the eighth time, left a note on the fridge saying how long he'd be gone for and when he would call to check in.

Maddox waited outside for almost an hour before Deborah Cunning's car drove by. It passed right by our house and stopped a few houses down, where it picked up one of the Mackenzie girls. Maddox coughed. I watched him from the partings of the blinds in the living room.

Making a U-turn, the car came back past our house and stopped out on the road. Even from the window I could see the other kids crowded in the back seat, staring out at our house and Maddox on the verandah. Maddox frowned. He didn't move. He clenched his jaw.

There was music spilling out of the car. The car sat there for five minutes, not moving up our driveway an inch.

Finally, Maddox picked up his bags and took a step down the front stairs. I heard laughing and the car peeled down the road. Maddox stopped.

To his credit, he didn't run after them. He stayed on that verandah for another twenty minutes, until it became too cold and he returned inside.

Later that morning, when Dad discovered that Maddox had been left behind by his classmates, he pulled on his jacket and searched for his keys.

"Come on," he told him.

"Where?"

"I'll take you to the lake. We can leave right now."

"No. I'm not going."

Dad sighed. "Yes you are. It's important."

"No one wants me there."

"Yes, they do. You can't let one person ruin things for you like this."

"It's not just Deborah fault."

"I'm taking you to the lake."

Maddox slammed his fist on the table. "No. You're not. I'm staying. I'm not going anyway." He went upstairs and closed the door to his bedroom behind him.

My father just stood there, holding the car keys in his hand. He saw me watching him. "I'm going for a drive," he told me. "I'll be back later."

The house was silent again. I watched some cartoons, wandered through the now empty library. When I got hungry, I went into the kitchen to make myself a sandwich and found my mother standing in the middle of the room. She looked thinner that she had been. She was staring out the back window.

"Mum?"

"Hey Oswald," she said softly, not turning around.

"Are you okay?"

"I'm fine."

We didn't say anything for awhile.

"I was just about to make you a sandwich," she said at last.

BETWEEN THE TIME my mother went to water and the prodigal son of Garfax, Caleb Anson, returned after his thirty-year absence, intent on bringing us all into the future and back on the maps, there were five years of peace.

It would be the last peace that Garfax would ever enjoy.

Even now, with my mother's storm raging down the coast, tearing roofs off buildings and turning the roads into rivers, carrying away pavement stones and depositing them into the bay, people look back on that time with a desperate nostalgia. Nothing of note happened during that time. Nothing at all. After listening to a person, relative or friend, explain for hours about how those five years were the best of his or her life, how at least during that time you knew where you stood, you would come away with a few images, maybe a memory, but no stories to tie them altogether.

I've asked Faith this question, if she remembers anything about that time. She started talking about music, about bands she had gone to Benning to see, about times she had spent out at Quill Lake when she was old enough to go, but nothing stands out. She remembers campfires and getting drunk, peeing in an alley and screaming at the top of her lungs. But nothing specific, nothing that separates one year from the next.

"But what about boyfriends?" I asked, hoping to pick up a chronology of boys to tie her memory together. "Don't you remember them?"

She shrugged. "Not really. I didn't have that many."

"What were there names?"

And for the life of her she couldn't answer. She had to go and look it up.

My own memory of that time is equally spotty. I remember the flash-bulb popping of my father's camera, the strained smiles of friends and neighbours, and the instinctive blink that follows the photographic lightning strike. I remember dimly that he did this less and less as time slowed. Photography wouldn't pay the bills in the long term, and coupled with my mother's inability to sell her horoscopes to the village paper, Cadmus had to go back to his old job of carpenter. Thomas helped him out. The exchange of books and drinks down at the Two-Stone made them fast friends, enough so that soon he was working almost exclusively with Thomas. There was only going to be more work in the years ahead. Without government money, the village was always going to need repairs as it got older. Soon Dad had enough work that he didn't know what to do with it all, and the sounds of his camera were replaced by the thudding of hammers into walls, of nails being pounded into floorboards.

SOMETHING IN THAT FIFTH YEAR changed. It was the middle of summer and it was like the winds shifted. There was something in the air. We all woke up in the morning wide awake and anxious. We walked through our daily routines of work and school holding our breath, afraid to talk about it but too nervous to let it go.

A vicious restlessness descended on Garfax. Conversations in the Two-Stone over a game of dominoes degenerated into arguments, descended into the occasional brawl. Husbands and wives, having grown complacent with their partners, started looking elsewhere, fluttering around the periphery of the younger dances, taking the first, stuttering steps into adultery. The parties at Quill Lake grew louder and more daring. The usual back and forth of teenage love affairs and rivalries exploded into miniature epics and tragedies. Hearts were broken then reformed over night. We ran from the fires into the lake, into that sudden burst of shocking cold, hoping to rid ourselves of this boundless energy.

"Something is going to happen," I said to my mother one afternoon in the kitchen.

"Something's always going to happen," she replied.

"What is it?"

She looked over at me, smiled that sad little smile of hers. "You'll see."

I didn't have to wait long, although like everything else before or after, I didn't realize what that something was until it had already happened. I should have been paying closer attention. If I had, I would have noticed the importance of the sound of my father's hammer changing into the hammering of keys on a typewriter. I would have picked it out as odd that there was a sudden screeching of tires on Garfax's main road. I would have acknowledged the significance of a knock at the door.

V

The Magic Show

WHAT ARE YOU DOING?" my mother wanted to know, finding my father in the dining room one evening, pecking away at the keys of the typewriter that he had used to write his own father's eulogy, surrounded by crumpled pages.

"Working," Dad replied.

Mum frowned. "Doesn't look like working. You usually have a hammer in your hand. Nails in your teeth."

Dad smiled, looked up. "This," he declared, "is a special kind of work."

Mum smoothed her hands across his shoulders, leaned her chin on his head, looked down at the page in progress. Dad covered it with his hands.

"Is it a secret?"

Reaching behind him, Dad stroked her cheek. "Don't you already know?"

It was Mum's turn to smile. She kissed his forehead. "I don't know everything."

"Could have fooled me."

"So how long are you going to keep me in the dark?"

"It's almost done. A few more days. Maybe a week. Tops."

"All right," she said, patting his shoulders. "Keep your secrets."

"It won't be secret much longer."

A week and a half later, Dad presented her with the fruits of his labour at the kitchen table over dinner. It was eleven pages of tight, narrow script, bound together by three staples driven hastily through its upper left-hand corner.

"Is it a story?" I asked.

"No," he smiled, handing it to Mum. "It's not a story."

Mum wore a puzzled expression on her face, an expression she rarely showed to anyone other than Dad. She read the title, *Cadmus Brodie's Solution for the Modern Man*, followed by a small *and Woman* in brackets.

"Why is the woman in brackets?" she asked.

"I didn't know you wrote," Faith said, fiddling with her macaroni.

Dad smiled and winked at her. "I'm a university man, Faith. You don't go to university without learning something about the written word."

"You studied photography," my mother said, flipping through the eleven pages.

"Emma," he said, "if a picture's worth a thousand words, just imagine what I can do with a blank page."

"So what am I looking at?"

"You are looking at the sum total of all my experience and wisdom, everything that I've learned to be true over the past few decades."

"That doesn't answer my question."

"It's a self-help package."

"Oh."

Mum continued to flip through the pages.

"Why'd you write a self-help book?" Maddox asked.

"First, it's not a book, Maddie. It's a package. And second, because," Cadmus explained, "I think I can help people. Everyone's always telling me that I'm a good listener. Aren't they?"

"Yeah."

"And when they have problems they come to me, and after we talk they usually feel better. I thought I'd share that with the rest of the world."

"Oh."

"I still don't see why the woman is in brackets."

"The woman is in brackets," Cadmus sighed, as if it were self-evident, "because men need more help than women in getting their priorities straight, their lives together."

Mum frowned. "I still don't like the brackets."

"I'll take them out," he said, smiling, throwing up his hands in a flourish. "This is a first draft, after all. Not the final piece by any stretch of the imagination."

Everyone was quiet for a time, watching Mum scan through the pages. "Well," Dad said. "What do you think?"

Mum looked up. "Where'd you get the idea to do this?"

IT HAD BEEN THOMAS LONNIE'S IDEA. Since returning back to Garfax and his work in carpentry, my father had spent more time with Tom than he did apart. If he wasn't working on staircases or walls, hand in hand with the Franklins, he was often at the Two-Stone or Tom's house walking through rooms filled with books that the other man had borrowed, bought, stolen or rescued since coming to the village.

Thomas Lonnie was a man beset by problems, all of them from his past. After the first year of working with Cadmus, he started talking about them, about how his ex-wife left him, all of a sudden, one rainy afternoon, abandoning both him and their only daughter, Sara. He worried about Sara, about how her hair wouldn't dry after that day. He talked about finding her at the front gate, eight years old, when he came back home from work. Standing in the rain like that, looking down the road for her mother, who had left and was never coming back.

"Her hair just won't dry," he would mumble. "I've tried everything, but it doesn't take."

Cadmus was a good listener. People liked him because of it. They liked him more because he always took their side, took the long view. After listening to all of your stories, my father had the unique ability to string them together with what was happening to you in the present and make it all okay. They were just stories, the way my father told it. Your life, your troubles, all the frustrations, were just stories, little tales leading somewhere else, somewhere better. He made people feel important, their lives filled with wonder.

"You should write a book," Thomas said to him, three months prior to Dad's sitting down at the dining room table and pecking out those first, hesitant sentences. "I'd like to read that book. I think a lot of other people would, too."

From such a dedicated reader as Tom, Cadmus took that as a winning endorsement.

He started writing at first to satisfy his friend. That was what he told himself when he sat down in front of the typewriter he hadn't used since his own father's funeral. It was all for his friend. Then, as he kept pecking away, trimming some sentences, expanding others, he found himself caught up in something he hadn't felt in years, ever since my mother had gone to water.

"It was like motion," he explained to me during a long afternoon of my mother's four-month-long storm. We were sitting in the basement, surrounded by the wreckage of so many broken clocks that he had smashed the night before with a baseball bat. In the dark, together like that, the only light the glare from the miners' helmets we wore, it felt very much like being miles underground. As if we were in an abandoned mine or tomb.

"What is?" I asked, fighting off sleep.

For his entire life, my father was governed by forces greater than himself. Appetites and desires, twists of chance and the rigours of his somnambulism. "It's like being caught up in a wind. Or maybe a wave. It was like how it used to be. Like something was starting again. As if I were going somewhere."

The five-year peace between the Franklin boy's death and the return of Caleb Anson had been difficult for my father. After running around Canada with his camera, having adventures, taking pictures, meeting amazing people, he had been suddenly fixed to a single location, a permanent spot. Even his sleep patterns evened out for a bit. He rarely sleepwalked, almost to the point where we stopped checking in the middle of a conversation to see if he was actually speaking to us or someone he was dreaming.

That sense of restlessness had hit Cadmus in the same way that it had hit everyone else. That feeling that there was something more, something coming on the horizon, coupled with Tom's suggestion, is what made him see his composition through to the end, caused him to dance in the hallways of our house with my mother again, to laugh in the middle of a walk with one of us, pointing at something almost out of sight.

THAT NIGHT, AFTER DAD had presented his self-help package at the kitchen table, Mum found him on the verandah, smoking a cigar, singing to himself. She flicked the lights on and off before she came out.

"I'm awake," he said, grinning.

Mum smiled, stepping out on the verandah. "Just checking."

She was holding the eleven pages in her hands.

"Did you read it?" he asked.

"Every last word."

"And?"

Mum sat down, flipped through the pages. "There's some typos. Some spelling mistakes. And I'm not sure about some of the words you chose. I think there are better ones. I marked them down," she said, showing him the blue ink notations.

"That impressive, huh?"

My mother looked up at her husband and sighed. "It's also really good."

"Are you just saying that?"

"No. I don't just say things like that."

"That's true," Dad said, nodding, taking a puff. "So you really like it?"

"I do," Mum said, standing up. "I think it's wonderful."

I watched them from the living room window. Dad leaned down and wrapped his arms around her after extinguishing the cigar in the ashtray. "You're always surprising me," she said. "Why do you have to do that?"

Dad laughed. "Because you wouldn't have married me otherwise."

AFTER HE HAD MADE all the spelling corrections, all the line edits that my mother had advised, and after he had received Tom's endorsement, Dad went down to the photocopier at the local paper that used to print my mother's horoscopes and made three dozen copies of *Cadmus Brodie's Solution for the Modern Man and Woman*. It was the most excitement the Canadian-styled Hemingways had seen in years.

"What have you got there, Brodie?"

"What's that for?"

"Why do you need so many copies?"

And Dad just smiled. "You'll have to buy one to find out, gentlemen," he replied.

"But what is it?"

"A solution," he said.

He sold five of the copies right then and there, the pages still warm from the machine.

I was recruited early on to help him go door to door. It was my job to sit in the car and hand him copies from the pile in the back seat. To appear more professional, Dad rifled through the old Anson attic until he found one of Simon Anson's old briefcases. Blowing the dust off the leather, he polished it up nice until it looked every part the accessory of a man in command over his own destiny.

"Why'd you buy that?" fishermen would say upon coming home and finding their wives or girlfriends flipping through the pages of my father's writing.

"He just looked so professional," the women would reply. "He had a briefcase and everything."

Word started to spread as more and more people started buying and reading his self-help package. He started getting asked about it when he was down in the Two-Stone with Tom. "That's an amazing book you've got there, Brodie," someone would say.

"It's not a book," Dad would reply. "It's a package."

"What's the difference?"

"A package is more a tool kit," he philosophized. "Something to get you started."

Tom leaned back in his chair and grinned through his buzz. "I know an author," he said to himself.

"I really like what you've got here, Cadmus," someone would say.

"Where are you going to take it from here?" Another would ask.

And for the life of him, my father had no idea.

THERE ARE PEOPLE who wait and people who are waited for. My family, for the most part, were people who were waited for. People waited to see what we would do. They waited for us to return, to start, to do anything. While my father gallivanted across the country taking pictures, my mother waited for him to return so that they could start their life together properly. When my mother went to water, the whole village waited to see what would happen next.

Maddox, in his own way, had this same quality. Even from a very young age, people were waiting for him to surprise them, to do something truly extraordinary.

The earliest memory I have of my brother is when he is seven and our father has just returned for a month in between projects. He is talking constantly on the phone, speaking with Fetch about possible layouts, prints that he wants included in the next book. There are photographs laid out over all the wood floors, tables, and chairs. None of us are allowed to go in when he is working, and since he's been home he is always working, walking through the avenues and streets of his own photographic maze.

It is the day of the last firework display ever to be seen in Garfax. Over breakfast Mum tells him this, and Dad looks up, looks at us as if seeing us for the first time in weeks.

"The last?" he asks.

Mum nods. "Yes. The last."

For sixteen years prior to this, Denver Brail has held the most elaborate fireworks display at the beginning of each winter. It takes him weeks to prepare, to get the combinations and positions of the cannons just right. He is working with a constantly dwindling supply, a finite amount of decorative explosives. The story goes that he salvaged them from a train he found in the pines, a train that has no tracks before or in front of it.

There are other stories that surround this train.

This is the last year, though. After this all the fireworks will be gone and Denver will dismantle the cannons. This is the last year and Mum wants us all to go and see them.

"That," my father says, "is a great idea. Exactly what we need."

And it's like we're a real family again, like the ones you read about, see on television. He helps us all get dressed, navigates our way through difficult sleeves and pants that are made treacherous because they are so large and meant to protect us from the cold. I am four and need help with everything. Faith is six and wants to do everything herself. Maddox is seven. He is a big boy.

We, all of us, the whole village, come out to see the last fireworks. We stand on the edge of the bay, shivering, clustered together in small and large groups, watching our breath fade away from us in grey vapour. Denver walks the perimeter of the beach, checking the cannons, making some final calculations.

There is no speech. There is never a speech before the fireworks. They don't commemorate anything. They don't celebrate anything. There is no reason that Denver has ever given that he chose that particular day every year to set the sky alight. It's just habit. Something he fell into.

The fuses are set and the explosions go off, cracking like whips across the length of the bay, disappearing across the endless stretch of ocean. The rockets hurtle skyward, whistling and screaming. People flinch, they gasp, they hold their breath.

Then everything explodes. There are so many colours. And we are, all of us, looking up at the sky. We all look so surprised. It takes our breath away. Even Denver. There are rockets of every description. They scream and shatter into multicoloured shrapnel, mushroom clouds of luminescent splendour.

The display lasts fifteen minutes, and throughout all that time no one moves. Some people start shouting, singing further along the coast. The song, I can't remember what it is, gets picked up and tossed down through the groups in verse and refrain, chorus and bridge. We are all singing the same song, just not at the same time.

My mother starts laughing, delighted at the chaos. Dad smiles.

And then, after the big finale, the sky darkens and doesn't light again. We wait just in case it decides to explode again, but it doesn't. "Sorry folks," Denver says to us, walking down the beach. "That's all there is. Show's over."

Pats on the shoulder, shakes of the hand, and people start to wander away from the beach and back into the village. On the way home, Maddox makes exploding noises, throwing his hands up into the air.

"I want to be fireworks," he declares.

Emma rustles his hat. "Honey, you can't be fireworks," she tells him. "People can't fly and they don't explode."

He seems disappointed, and when my mother heads off in front of us with Faith, Dad leans down and whispers in his ear. "That's not exactly true," he tells him. "You can be fireworks."

"I can?"

"Sure you can. You're destined for wonderful things, Maddie. We all are."

And my brother smiles so wide.

Being the eldest, after my mother went to water, and maybe even a little before then, people were waiting for Maddox to display some sort of gift, some level of prowess that would elevate him above them, make him special. He came from a storied family, particularly if you listened to my father tell the tale.

The truth of it was he was well on his way to being just that before my mother changed things. People liked Maddox in the same way that people liked Dad, or how people had liked his father before him. He was popular, easy to talk to. Charming. I should point out that I did not inherit this particular gift from my father. In fact, there are times when I don't see much of anything of him in me. My father is loud, full of motion and excitement. Even when he sleeps, he's doing something, moving around, off on adventures. He seems given to motion and discovering new things in a way that I could never approach.

I am much more like my mother, I think.

Maddox is his father's son, but after the village turned against us, he faltered a bit. His gestures, the way he walked, everything changed. A lot of that had to do with being left waiting on the verandah by Deborah Cunning that summer when he was supposed to go to Quill Lake. He had never been rejected like that before, something most children by that time would have experienced at least a little of. When the radios spoke and told secrets, said things about our family that made his face turn crimson, things only became worse. At school he was sure people were talking about him. A hesitancy crept into everything he did. Every hand-shake, every expression, every word. He started holding something back, hiding pieces of himself. He didn't go out as much.

Still, people waited for my brother. They continued to pay him the same level of attention. They watched him, biding their time for the day that my brother would surprise them all and do something spectacular. But after all of that, Maddox had little interest in doing anything special, anything wonderful, anything that would draw attention to himself. He didn't want to be talked about anymore. He didn't want to be laughed at or ignored. He wanted very much to just go away, even though there was no place for him to go.

We spent a lot of time together during those empty five years. Maddox kept me company in the library, walking through the rows of book-shelves, looking for something that would pique his interest. He didn't like novels, couldn't abide stories. He much more preferred non-fiction, paying particular attention to the books my father had pictures in. He read the entire Fetch line of Canadian books and most of the British ones too. He became an expert in general interest, shooting off facts, figures, and interesting tidbits at the drop of a hat. In the summers, he worked a little with Tom and Dad, doing whatever gopher work they needed. And if he wasn't doing that, he took me with him when he went walking in the pines.

The pines changed for me as I grew older, or at least the way I related to them changed. When I was a kid, my head boiling over with stories, I brought those stories out with me amidst the trees. Tight congregations of bark became fortresses. Small caves or clefts in the hill became deep caverns with monsters inside. Husks of cars and furniture left abandoned turned into props for me to continue on stories after they had ended on the page. The older I got, the less I took with me into the pines. I started, I suppose, to see them as they actually were.

Maddox helped with that. He took me to broken-down cars and explained to me that they were wrecks from drunk drivers who had gone off the narrow roads and who didn't want the trouble of trying to pull them back up the hill, so they drove them deeper in, leaving them to rust and rot. He showed me the two remaining ruined sections of Ester Anson's mansion. We walked up a staircase that terminated into empty air, forming a railess balcony surrounded on all sides by trees. The rooms, all of them missing walls, none of them closed from the pines, were covered in graffiti, alcohol stains, and smears from cigarette butts. Kids came out here to party sometimes, he said. We'd come across furniture that had been stolen from the house or pictures that had been taken and hung in the high trees, the canvases destroyed by the elements to reveal only the barest frames, their centres left empty.

We'd find other buildings, or the remains of buildings, in the pines, much deeper in. We'd find a wall leaning against a line of trees that had bent under the initial weight but had grown around it over the years, branches bursting through the skin. Maddox didn't know where these had come from.

One day, during the fourth year of peace, Maddox took me to a car he had found and we climbed into the back seat, the leather creaking beneath us. The windshield had been smashed, along with most of the front end. There was a little blood on the dashboard.

"It's amazing they got it this far in," he said.

We sat there for awhile, listening to nothing. I noticed the radio was still intact. I thought about reaching for it, but didn't. I stared out the window at the trees, some of them only a foot away from the glass, their branches scratching against its smooth surface.

"When they find this, maybe in a few days, they'll strip it for parts. Bring them back in town and leave the rest to just rust out here."

I didn't ask who they were.

"But that's in a few days."

This was how we talked back then. Maddox would speak and I would listen, occasionally asking questions. I sank into the leather, pushed my knees against the front seat.

"I don't think this was a local car," he continued. "I don't recognize it. So it might be longer before someone comes out here for it."

I thought about that. I thought about the car just lying out here, abandoned in the middle of the woods, imagining what it would be like sitting out here in the middle of the night. For now, no one in the world apart from the driver knew it was here but us.

"Do you want to see something?" Maddox said, reaching into his jacket pocket.

I nodded.

He looked at me for a hard second. It was strange to see him so serious and still. "All right," he said, finally, and pulled out a large metal ball from his pocket.

The metal ball was smooth and shiny, half the size of a man's fist.

"What's that?" I asked.

"Watch."

He started to move the ball around his palm, rolling it from side to side in slow, concentric circles. The warped mirror surface of the ball reminded me of the burnished bronze plates we had inherited from Ester Anson. It reflected light dimly, sending off sunbeams that came in through the broken car windows and moved lazily up to the ceiling, where they twirled and danced in mismatched silvery-white triangles and cubes.

Maddox started working the sphere more with his fingers then, at times flicking his wrist so that it hung suspended in air for a moment before gently returning to the safety of his palm. Then he'd turn his hand entirely so that the sphere rattled along the length of his knuckles. Again he'd flick the wrist and the sphere hurtled effortlessly from one hand to the next.

"Keep watching," he told me.

His hands moved faster. I was entranced. The play of light on the sphere's surface, the liquid flow of my brother's hands. I didn't know what he was doing until, all of a sudden, the sphere was gone and his fists were closed. He looked at me.

I looked at him.

He opened his fists, and in each one sat a sphere identical to the one from before, but half the size. Maddox smiled a little smile, pleased with himself.

"What did you just do?" I asked.

"Magic," he told me.

"Where'd you learn how to do that?"

He had found the trick, which he told me was called the Dancing Spheres, in a book in the library. From the Fetch line of British general interest books. He had come across it during his systematic exploration of everything our father had contributed to. Through Cadmus's black-and-white photographs and the author's accompanying descriptions, he started to learn the tricks, bit by bit, slowly over the course of a year. He didn't show anyone. He practiced when no one was looking. He knew almost every trick in the book. Card tricks and hat tricks. Sleight of hand gags that pulled objects out of thin air and inserted them into people's ears.

"Can I see more?" I asked.

Maddox nodded. Over the next few weeks, we'd come out to the pines and he'd perform tricks for me. He'd create sparks out of a warm night's air, letting them jump and shudder in the palm of his hand, illuminating his face in a warm candlelight. He'd read my mind and guess the card I was holding in my hand. He'd throw a rock that I had written my initials on into the deep pines and then let me find it again in my shirt pocket.

"You're really good," I told him, one night when we were wandering back home.

"Thanks," he said, genuinely pleased.

"You should show Mum and Dad."

He shook his head.

"Why not?"

He shrugged.

"I think they'd really like it. It's pretty cool."

"I don't know."

"Think about it," I said.

"Sure. I'll think about it," he said, as we passed by the rotted frame of an ancient sofa.

It wasn't just the tricks, either. Maddox knew all sorts of stories from the book that he had read, magic stories. He told me about turning water into wine, coal into gold. He talked about the mystical properties of stones and crystals, the various curses and blessings used by the world's magic men and women.

"There's a way to turn invisible," he told me once.

"How's that?"

"You steal a raven's egg from its nest and boil it. Then you put it back in. A few days later, the nest will be abandoned and the egg will be gone. There'll be a crystal in its place. You put the crystal in your mouth and you disappear."

"Have you tried it?"

"No," he laughed. "That's just a story."

A LOT OF PEOPLE DISAPPEAR in Garfax. Few ever come back.

After Lizzie Parks accompanied our family to the funeral for the Franklin boy, I didn't see her again for the five quiet years that followed. There are some people in your life who you see only once in a great while, and each time they appear, they seem so remarkably changed. Lizzie was one of those people, because the next time I saw her, she was screaming down the narrow roads of the pines in a cab she had purchased second-hand out of Benning.

She had only learned how to drive the year before, at the age of thirty-one. It was her way of dealing with the restlessness that had accumulated in the village.

"What you have to understand about my sister," Sunny, her younger brother, told me once while sacked out on the couch, waiting for Faith to finish getting ready upstairs, "is that she's stubborn. All of us are. That's the way we were raised. Push us down for a while and we'll stay there for a time, sure. But we get back up."

Taking care of us for those seven days, being given that responsibility by Emma, had caused a change in Lizzie. She wasn't going to remain invisible, fading away from view entirely. She needed a job, though, and in classic Parks fashion, she picked a job that was as ill-suited and far from her experience as possible.

"Teach me how to drive," she asked Denver.

"Why?" the sole proprietor of the only movie theatre in Garfax wanted to know.

"Because I need to work."

"There are plenty of jobs. You could work here with me."

Lizzie shook her head. "Thanks, but no. I don't want to run projectors or stand behind a counter."

"What do you want to do, then?"

"I want to drive a cab."

Denver raised an eyebrow.

"But your arm? I don't mean to be rude, but—"

"I'll drive automatic," she cut him off.

"Fair enough. When do you want to get started?"

"Now, if that's all right?"

"Sure. Okay. Yeah, let's go."

When I worked with Denver, running projectors, he could laugh about the experience, but back then it terrified him. "We crashed five and a half cars getting her comfortable behind the wheel. The first one was the worst. Always is. That shook her. She didn't come back for a whole month after that."

"But she did?"

"Course she did. And then promptly crashed a second car. She was only away a week after that one," Denver laughed. "Teaching a thirty-year-old how to drive is a very different creature than teaching a kid. It takes longer. But she got it."

I never got around to asking him what a half a car crash looks like. That's another story.

Few people like driving the narrow roads that lead in and out of Garfax. Many go to great lengths to avoid making those trips. Some don't learn how to drive at all. Almost no one makes it their business to drive, but those who do tend to make good money. Lizzie was interested in good money as much as she was interested in mobility, in talking with people and taking them from place to place. She wanted to be seen again. Wanted to be a part of things.

It took her about six months before she was comfortable enough behind the wheel to actually take the bus to Benning and purchase her first and only cab. She brought back her first customer with her. They had a lot in common, they quickly discovered. They had both vanished from the village for a time and were interested in getting back into things.

He was middle-aged, but still quite handsome. He kept himself fit, dressed well. His hair was immaculate, except in the back where he let it grow purposefully wild and curly. The man could smile, too. Laugh. Driving back, Lizzie found herself laughing along with his jokes, telling him all sorts of stories she hadn't told in years. So caught up in the conversation, the rolling from one story to the next, she barely noticed that the two-and-a-half-hour drive into Benning was over until they crested the hill and saw Garfax Bay.

"That takes me back," the man sighed. "Oh yes. Most certainly."

"How long have you been gone?"

"Almost thirty years, now. I left when I was seventeen."

"Is it like coming home?" Lizzie asked.

The man's smile faltered a little. "Not really. It's been awhile."

"Where did you live? What house?"

"It's not there anymore."

"What happened to it?"

He told her the story. "Oh," she said, after he was done. "Well it's still here. Most of it. It's just not where you left it."

The man opened and closed his mouth. "Really? Could we go there?"

"Of course we could."

And in this way did Caleb Anson, the village's prodigal son and only child born to Ester and Simon Anson, return home to Garfax.

AND WHILE ALL THIS WAS HAPPENING, while Lizzie Parks was returning back from Benning with Caleb Anson in tow, my father sat at the Two-Stone Bar, at the centre of a group of men, figuring out what to do about his book.

"It's not a book," he corrected.

"Sorry," one of the men said. "The package. The tool kit. There's just so much there."

"Yeah," another man piped in. "It really, what's the word?"

"Spoke?" someone said.

"Yeah. It spoke to me. Got me where I live, you know?"

Cadmus nodded his head, trying to piece together all the feedback through the haze of cigarette smoke and alcohol. "But where does it go from here, guys?"

"You don't know?"

He shook his head, shrugged his shoulders. "No. I don't."

"Well, you need to print more. That's the first thing."

"Then what?"

"Keep selling them."

"Well, sure. There's that. But what then?"

The group was at a loss.

"What the package is trying to do," Cadmus said after a time. "I mean, what I think I'm trying to say with it, is that what we've got to do is deal with our problems now."

"Yeah."

"I don't know about you guys, but the best times of my life have been when I've been dealing with what's in front of me."

More nods of agreement.

"But it's been awhile since I've done that."

"What do you mean?"

Cadmus shrugged again. "I don't know. Things have been different for awhile. We've all felt it."

No one said anything. They stared into their drinks. Took drags of their cigarettes.

"Exactly. That. We've all felt that. We remember the good days, though. I mean, who doesn't? Who doesn't sit and think about everything wonderful that's happened and how that doesn't happen to them anymore."

"Times are different," the men shrugged.

"That's bullshit," he said. "We're different. Times are always the same. We're the ones who aren't like we used to be."

"I don't get it."

"Neither do I," Cadmus confessed. "Not really. I just know that writing that package, actually doing something instead of the usual stuff, made me feel the way I used to feel. And I want to keep doing that."

"So what are you going to do?"

Cadmus took a drink from his beer. "I don't know."

"I know what you're talking about," Tom said. "When I read your package, what you said about living in the past, I kept thinking about my wife."

"Ex-wife," Cadmus said.

"Yeah, exactly. I kept thinking about her. I mean, it's been years and I'm still thinking about her."

"Yeah."

"And it's safe, you know? Thinking like that. That's what you said on page seven. About things being safe."

"Yeah."

"And that got me thinking," Tom continued, sounding out his thoughts as he was thinking them. "Fuck safety."

Cadmus blinked. "Fuck safety?"

"Yeah. Fuck it. I don't know what my wife's doing now."

"Ex-wife."

"Yeah. I don't know what she's doing, but I'm sure she's not sitting around thinking about me. Maybe she's got a whole new family. Maybe she hasn't. But she's living. She's out there actually doing it, you know."

"You don't know that."

Tom nodded. "Sure, but that's how it feels. And when I figured that out, I thought, you know, maybe it's time I got a move on. Began again. Like you said."

"That's a hard thing to do," someone muttered.

The men were silent, everyone looking at Tom, then Cadmus, then Tom again. The restlessness that had grown in them over the last year was bubbling to the surface, coming out in fidgeting legs and twitchy fingers. They smoked copiously, gulped their drinks continually.

"I'm just tired of waiting," one of the men said.

"So don't," Cadmus said, looking at him. "I mean, what the hell are you waiting for?"

And then the man told him. And then after him another man started talking. Then another. And then another. Until all of the men were telling their stories, puzzling out where their lives had gone wrong and when things had stopped making sense. They talked about wives they had grown bored of, about children who no longer made sense to them. But when they talked about them in the Two-Stone that afternoon, sitting across the tables from each other, they spoke about their families and their lives the way they hadn't done in years. To Cadmus it almost seemed like pride, mixed with a deep sadness and a desire to return.

"But there's no going back," one of the men told him after he finished his story. "You've got to keep going with this, Cadmus. See where it goes."

"It's helping," another said.

"I still don't know what that means, though."

"Just keep talking," Tom said, looking down at the wedding ring he still had around his finger. "Eventually you'll figure it out."

Stumbling back home a few hours later, off by himself for the first time in hours, my father figured out what he was going to do with the book. He picked up his pace, quickening his drunken gait until he was practically barreling this way and that down the gravel side road that let to our house.

"Emma," he said, as soon he crossed the threshold.

"What's wrong?" Faith said, stopping in mid-stride as she descended the stairs.

"Where's your mother?"

"Upstairs."

Dad ran upstairs, passed my sister, and found my mother in the bedroom, tidying up her bookshelves. "Emma."

"What is it?"

"I figured it out. I know what I'm going to do next."

"With what?"

"The book."

"You mean the package?"

Cadmus shook his head. "Right. That. I figured it out."

"What are you going to do?"

"I'm going to hold meetings. I'm going to get people talking."

Emma raised an eyebrow. "Meetings?"

"Right. Meetings. Here at the house to start. Then, later, if there's enough interest, we'll figure something else out."

"But why?"

Cadmus grinned. "To keep people talking."

THE ANNOUNCEMENT OF the first meeting to discuss the contents of Cadmus Brodie's self-help package was met with a flood of requests. There were so many, in fact, that they could not all be accommodated.

"Twelve is a good number," Mum told him, as he puzzled over the list.

"Twelve?"

Mum nodded. "Twelve. We have enough chairs. We can all sit comfortably in the sitting room. There's not too many. Everyone will get a chance to talk. And there's not too few, so people won't feel intimidated if they don't want to speak right away."

Dad considered this. "Twelve does sound like a good number."

Mum smiled, kissed him on the forehead. "I'm very proud of you," she said.

"Thank you."

Dad was still nervous, though. He had never held a meeting like this before, never called together any sort of formal gathering with him at the head. He spoke about it endlessly over the kitchen table, wondering aloud if he should wear a suit for the occasion or if he should play music. Should he provide food or maybe put up a sign?

"What about entertainment?" he asked. "Will people expect entertainment?"

Mum shrugged her shoulders. "That I can't help you with."

"You should talk to him," I told Maddox, while we were walking through the pines the next day.

"Talk to who?"

"Dad. About the meeting. You could do your magic tricks. For the entertainment."

Maddox gave me a stern look. "I don't think so."

"Come on. It'll be great. You're really good."

"No. I'm not ready for that. And I don't want you talking to Mum or Dad about it either. I want you to promise me."

"I promise."

And I kept my promise. I didn't tell Mum or Dad. I told Faith.

"He's really good," I said.

Faith raised an eyebrow. "Maddie? Can do magic tricks?"

"They're amazing."

"But he says he doesn't want to show them. You can't make him."

"He just needs some convincing," I assured her.

Faith thought for a moment, then nodded. "I'll see what I can do."

She never told me exactly what she said to Dad, but the following day, when Maddox came through the library, he found Dad there looking through books.

"Hey, Dad."

Dad gave a quick nod.

"What are you looking for?"

Sighing, Dad placed his hands on his hips. "I'm looking for that Fetch book about magic I did the photographs for," he explained.

Maddox stopped. "What for?"

"I was thinking of trying to do some of the sleight of hand tricks for the meeting. Your mother thought it would be a good idea. She says everyone likes a good magic show. You haven't seen it anywhere, have you?"

Maddox made a performance of looking through the shelves for a couple of minutes before putting his hand on the book, handing it over to Dad. "That the one?"

Snapping his fingers, Dad smiled. "That's the one. Thanks, son. I'm going to go and work on something right now."

And Maddox watched him go. He came to find me a half-hour later. "You didn't talk to Dad, did you?"

"About what?"

Maddox looked at me, all innocent, then shook his head. "Forget it." He found Dad in the dining room, trying to make one billiard ball turn into two smaller ones. The sound of the ball slipping from his fingers, plunking on the ground, and then rolling across the hardwood, rattled through the house.

"How's it going?" Maddox asked, peeking his head inside.

Dad sighed. "It's not as easy as I thought," he confessed. "Although I think I've got the handle on one of the card tricks. Want to see?"

"Sure."

For the next few minutes, Dad went through all the card tricks in the books, getting them all wrong. He guessed the wrong cards that Maddox held in his hands. When he shuffled the deck, the cards exploded in his hands, forcing him to curse and pick them up one by one. Maddox took pity on him, watching him pick up the cards on his hands and knees, and knowing that he was still intent on trying anyway, even though he might look utterly stupid.

"I think I've figured it out," Maddox said, pretending to read the book.

"Give it a shot then, son," Dad said, pushing the piles of mismatched cards into his hands.

Maddox shuffled them quickly and efficiently and then, slowly at first, he went through the card tricks. He paused for effect at the beginning, looking at the book for reference, but each time the trick worked. And when each trick worked, Dad gave out a laugh, or a breath of astonishment.

"Have you done this before?" he asked. "Because I've been working at this and it just doesn't make any sense to me."

"No," Maddox shrugged.

"Natural gift, then," Dad noted. "It's quite a thing to have. Why don't you try some of the other tricks."

And slowly, trick by trick, Dad led Maddox through an entire routine. As each trick passed, Maddox moved quicker and quicker, more confident and less concerned that he would be discovered.

"You've convinced me," Dad said, after the last trick.

"Convinced you of what?"

"You should be the entertainment for the meeting."

Maddox looked at Dad. "I'm not that good."

"No, you're not. You're great," Dad corrected. "It's so good to see you doing things again." And with that he placed his hand on his eldest son's shoulder and smiled at him.

Maddox, despite his better judgment, smiled back.

EVERYONE ARRIVED PROMPTLY for the first meeting, each carrying some tray of food that they put towards the potluck. That had been Mum's idea.

"You can't go wrong with potluck. At least you know everyone will have at least one dish they like."

Among the people who arrived for that first meeting were Denver Brail, Thomas Lonnie, Lizzie Parks, and Aunt Connie. Although Lizzie was late, she was on her way back from a trip to Benning and would be arriving shortly.

Everyone was excited. They chattered amongst themselves for a good hour before Dad began herding them into the living room and into their chairs. He began the meeting by telling his own story, about his motivation for writing the package. Most of this everyone had heard before, but this time he strung all the stories together so that they led somewhere. Specifically, he told the stories together so that they led into the room he was now in.

"And that's what I'm talking about," he concluded. "That's what, I hope, I'm trying to say with the package. We're all just a collection of stories. Some of them are good. Some of them aren't so good. Oftentimes we get bogged down by stories in our life that we think we can't change. We get stuck there. They're always on our mind. We tell ourselves that life was better during this time, or things were brighter during that time. And we build up the future so that we'll get to someplace good, but in the meantime we're stuck in between the two, dealing with not being able to go back or go forward."

He opened the floor after that, inviting everyone to tell their own stories. We listened as Thomas Lonnie talked about his wife, about how she left him and their daughter and went off to pursue her own life. Tom spoke about how that moment changed his life forever, and how he was unable to move beyond that point.

Then Aunt Connie spoke. She talked about how she thought everyone in the village perceived her a certain way, and what she thought was expected of her while she was growing up. Whose business should it be if she decided to live alone, without a husband or a family? Why was that such a bad thing? Why should she have to be like everyone else?

And then Denver spoke. And then everyone began to speak.

And then the doorbell rang.

Not wanting to break up the meeting, Mum went to go answer the door. I was looking over my shoulder at the time, and saw her open it. I saw Lizzie standing in the threshold, smiling, and behind her, a taller man, wearing a decent suit, who I had never met before.

"Hey Emma," Lizzie said. "Sorry I'm late. I brought someone."

"Hi," Caleb said, extending his hand. "I'm Caleb—"

"I know who you are," Mum finished for him.

Caleb frowned. Let his hand drop.

By this time, everyone was squirming in their seats to see who was at the door. Dad, too. He excused himself, inviting everyone to take a break, stretch their legs, and have some of the food, while he went to the door.

"I've been telling him all about what we're doing here," Lizzie was saying. "And he's really interested."

"I am," Caleb said. "It sounds really intriguing."

"So I didn't think it would be a problem if he came along. Both to see the house and to come and meet some people. He says he might be staying for a bit. Coming home and all that."

"Right," Caleb added.

But Mum didn't say anything. She just stood and stared daggers at Caleb. When Dad came up behind her, placing a hand on her shoulder, she practically jumped. All three of them noticed. Mum excused herself and went into the dining room.

"Hi," Caleb tried again, this time with Dad. "I'm Caleb Anson."

"Anson?"

Caleb nodded. "Yes. Ester and Simon's son."

Dad smiled, slightly bewildered. "Ms. Anson never mentioned a son."

Caleb nodded again. "We were estranged for quite sometime."

"Can we come in yet, Cadmus?" Lizzie asked.

Nodding his head, Dad laughed and shook Caleb's hand. "Of course. My manners. Forgive me. Come on in. Sit down. There's food on the side there."

"Thanks."

After Lizzie and Caleb were settled, Dad went into the dining room to check on Mum, who was pacing around the table.

"What's wrong?" he asked.

"I don't want that man in my house," Mum said, shaking.

"Why not?"

"I just don't want him in my house, Cadmus. Get him to leave."

"He's Lizzie's guest. And he says he's Ms. Anson's son."

"He is."

Dad frowned. "How do you know that?"

"I know."

"It would be rude to kick him out."

"I don't fucking care. Get him out of here."

Dad walked over to her, around the table, and grabbed her lightly by the shoulders. "You have to give me a lot more than that."

"There's nothing more than that."

"Emma."

Mum was still shaking. Dad pulled her in and held her. "Christ, what's wrong? Come on. Tell me."

"Twelve's a good number. You need to keep it at twelve."

"You can't be serious."

Mum grunted, pushing him away. "Fine. You're going to do what you want. Like you always do. But I'm not going to sit around and watch this time."

"What are you talking about?"

"I'll be upstairs."

"Emma."

But by that time she was already out the door and up the stairs.

To break up the rest of the meeting, Dad followed Caleb's entrance with the entertainment portion that he had promised them all at the beginning. Maddox stood up, arranged a table with several different props, and began, trick by trick, to work through them.

He started off easy, with tricks that most people recognized. The card tricks were first, of course. He guessed the suit and number of all the cards that each of the people in the room had all at once. He made them disappear and then reappear in shirt pockets and sleeves, which was followed by much applause.

Dad relaxed a little, sinking back into his seat. He clapped and gave Maddox encouragement as he went. Caleb, by contrast, was on the edge of his seat, his mouth open in wonder as the tricks became more and more daring.

Maddox juggled the metal balls and made them go from being two to one. He let them dance on his hand, over his knuckles, spiral in his palm, and then disappear altogether.

"Amazing," Caleb said.

My brother grinned.

Sparks flew from his hand and he managed a brief levitation that had everyone standing up in excitement. Aunt Connie, ever the skeptic, waved her hands around his floating body to see if there were any strings attached. "I'd believe it better," she said, after Maddox had landed, "if there were strings involved."

Caleb couldn't contain his appreciation and awe at my brother's skills. With each trick, he heaped more and more praise on him, saying that this was the best version of this particular trick or the most innovative use of that particular trick he had seen since he had been to India or Russia.

When it was all over, everyone clapped, and it took a while for the group to get settled and continue on with the meeting. Dad began again by reiterating for Lizzie and Caleb's benefit what he had said about stories at the start of the meeting. Caleb listened intently. When Lizzie spoke, she told her own story about the brief years she had been pretty, the accident at the airplane factory, and how taking care of Maddox, Faith, and me, five years ago had helped her realize that she could be useful again.

Dad encouraged her to speak. He pointed out to her during and afterwards the stories she had told herself. About how when she was overweight she probably had a very different perception of the world and herself than she did before. Just as the accident had changed her perception further.

"I get that," Lizzie said. "I see it all differently now, since I started going out more. I'm not hiding from my arm anymore." She tapped it against the chair for emphasis.

And finally, after Lizzie spoke, it was Caleb's turn to talk.

"If you want to," Dad said. "You don't have to if you don't want to."

"No," Caleb said. "I'd like to."

Caleb had been born in Garfax. When Ester and Simon Anson came here from Britain, they came with the express desire to start a family here. Ester had chosen Garfax, chosen it as the place to build their home and raise their children.

"Which just turned out to be me," Caleb said.

After seeing so much during the war, they found it hard to live in a place that wasn't in some way touched by its presence. Everywhere there was history History in everything. In walls. In buildings. In streets. People seemed temporary and almost pointless up next to that much historical weight.

"So we came here."

They had Ethan Bramble, that famous Canadian architect, build the house for them. And when they were done, they integrated themselves within the village's social life. They were beloved. Denver gave his agreement to this. Ester and Simon Anson were truly beloved by the village. After the historians had come and taken away their sign, the village's very existence from all the official records, it had been the Ansons who convinced everyone that they were worth something again.

"But I didn't see it that way," Caleb said. "I guess I didn't truly appreciate this place my whole life. I left as soon as I could. It was just too small, Garfax. Nothing ever happened here. We had all these books that talked about so many places, and I would never get to see them if I stayed where I was. So I left."

And he stayed gone. Travelling for most of his life. It wasn't until Ester finally died, a year before he arrived again in Garfax, that he even considered coming back.

"I've travelled a lot," Caleb admitted. "And I've seen a lot. But there was never any place I found that I could call home. I never thought that place would be Garfax, but after my mother died, I thought it would be a good place to start."

Dad, nodding along to Caleb's story, agreed. "It's never to late to build yourself a better future," he said.

Caleb looked at him then. He frowned a little. Almost confused. "What did you say?"

"You can build your future. That's what we've been talking about tonight. Most people separate their past and their future away from the present stories that they're living in. The future has to be built. It doesn't arrive. It's something that you work towards, that you build out of where you've come from."

Caleb nodded, but he wasn't really paying attention anymore. His eyes opened wide. He stared at the floor. And when Dad finished the meeting, Caleb shook his hand and then promptly went out onto the verandah to smoke a trail of cigarettes. He remained there after everyone else had left, only barely mumbling a goodbye to each of them, he was so engrossed in his thoughts.

Dad came out during Caleb's sixth cigarette.

"Some meeting," Caleb mumbled, excited. "That was some meeting, Cadmus."

"Thank you, Mr. Anson."

"Call me Cal," he said.

"All right."

They stayed there for a while. They looked out at the bay. It was Caleb who broke the moment. "I'm going to build a hotel," he said. The words came out hesitantly, as if he weren't sure of what he was going to say, but after he said them, a smile crept across his face. He nodded to himself, took another drag from his cigarette. "Yes. That's exactly what I'm going to do. I'm going to build a hotel."

Dad just stared at him. Dumbfounded.

VI

Wunderkammer

THE BARROWLAND is a dance hall in the city of Glasgow. I've never been there, but I've heard stories about it. It was the place my grandfather, Jack Brodie, took the woman who would later become his wife, Mary, on their first date. That particular date was just short of a disaster; he hardly spoke or looked at her, he was so nervous. In the cyclic nature of fate, it was also the place my father met my mother. Unlike Jack, Cadmus had no problem speaking or looking at my mother that night. In fact, as she points out each time this story comes up, her difficulty came in getting a word in; he was so talkative.

Everybody gets nervous, just in different ways.

Next to the dance hall is one of the most famous marketplaces in Scotland, the Barras. On weekends, when my mother was seven years old, her father would take her down there to see all the strange and wonderful objects that were up for sale. They had everything you could possibly imagine. Next to the ordinary goods, the foods and the linens, you'd find stalls set up that sold music that nobody had ever heard of, from across the globe, like the compositions of Franz Emerick. You'd find books written in strange languages, intricate toy boxes, and mechanisms that had to be puzzled over before their function become clear. Mechanical birds sang next to cages of live ones. Street magicians and jugglers darted amidst the crowd. Chalk artists sketched a whole new city on the floor of the already existent one.

Jack Brodie, my mother's father, was a man consumed with a desire to see amazing things. After coming home from the war, everything seemed slightly less real to him. He had seen so much, done so much, that the normal day-to-day affairs bored him. Until he had a daughter. My mother. And he started to see the world again through her eyes, saw the wonder that she was seeing for the first time. He delighted in her ability to know things, to see a little further down the road when other people couldn't.

While growing up, people often commented to my grandparents that my mother wasn't right, that she was strange in some way. Jack's reply to this was to simply say, "She's my daughter."

He took to taking long walks with her when she was older. He'd follow her directions. When they'd come up to a museum and my mother might say, without ever having stepped inside, she didn't want to see any boring paintings of lifeless statues, he'd nod his head and ask her where she wanted to go. And she'd lead him. My mother led her father through the city he had grown up in and she'd take him, holding his hand, through it as if it were the first time.

When she was seven years old, she took Jack to the Barras. There was always something new to be seen there. No matter how many times they had been there, they always managed to find something new to delight in. On one particular trip, they came across a man selling what looked like boxes, steamer trunks, in a remote corner of the market.

"You wanted to come here?" Jack asked. "All he's selling is boxes."

Emma shook her head. "There's things inside the boxes," she said.

The salesman, an older gentlemen with long, thinning hair, nodded when he heard my mother's assessment and ambled over. "You're most certainly right about that, lovely. These are not just boxes."

"What are they?" Jack asked.

"Museums," the man replied.

Emma smiled. My grandfather frowned.

The salesman explained that, before people had actual museums, large buildings dedicated to housing all the artifacts they had collected from around the world, they had these. Wonder cabinets, he called them, although he used a German word. "Here," he said. "Let me show you."

"That one has a mermaid inside it," Emma blurted out.

The salesman stopped fiddling with the lock on one of the trunks and turned around. "And how did you know that?"

"My daughter knows all kinds of things," Jack said.

"Does she?"

"She does. But a mermaid?"

"Yes," the salesman said, and opened up the box to show the curled-up skeleton of what looked like a mermaid. "Found off the coast of Ireland almost a hundred years ago," he continued. "Preserved perfectly with a unique combination of herbs and oils."

Jack looked at the bones, crouched down low so he could almost touch them. "She's beautiful," he said.

"However," the salesman went on, moving to another box, "if you're looking for something a bit more exotic—"

"That one has a dragon's head in it," my mother said, pointing to the next box.

The salesman glared at her. "It's a dinosaur," he muttered. "There's no such thing as dragons."

And this continued for the better part of half an hour. Each time the salesman would begin to open another wonder cabinet, my mother divined what was inside, the excitement of watching her father see it over-whelming her. And each time she did this, the salesman's mood grew blacker and blacker.

"Could you let this one be a surprise?" he asked her once.

My mother nodded, then, as he fumbled with the last latch, blurted out, "Phoenix eggs." The salesman roared, jumping up and down like a puppet. My mother laughed, clapped her hands.

Jack didn't notice. He was lost in the contents of the various cabinets. He'd wander through the open aisles and avenues and stare into their insides, reach his hand just far enough to almost touch them.

Seeing that my grandfather was busy, the salesman walked over to my mother. "I've got one more box left," he said. "And I bet you can't guess what's inside that one."

My mother smiled. "Yes I can."

The salesman smiled back. "We'll see." And he took her hand and led her to the back of his stall, to the brick wall that bordered it in the back, and pulled out a large navy-blue steamer trunk from beneath a maroon cloth.

The smile faded from my mother's face as she stared and stared at the box. "What's inside?" she asked, finally.

"You mean you don't know?" the salesman said, gleefully.

"No."

The old man patted the box with his hand. "It's the Future," he said, simply. "I picked it up while I was travelling through Russia a few years ago. Bought it off a count of some description. They have so many titles there."

"Can I see it?" my mother asked.

"Of course you can," the salesman replied, and began to undo the locks.

My mother was dying with anticipation. She glanced over at her father, who was still entranced with the contents of the other boxes a few aisles away. It was the first time in her life up to that point that she had ever been surprised, and while she loved to see that look on her father's face, she wanted it more for herself.

The salesman undid the last latch and opened the trunk. My mother had to step forward to see what was inside. The Future was dark and insubstantial. It occupied the six walls completely and not at all at the same time. The Future, as it turned out, looked exactly like an empty box.

"But there's nothing inside," my mother said, confused.

The salesman grabbed my mother, hard, by the arm, so hard that she yelped in surprise. He pushed her into the box, so that she tumbled inside, hitting her head on the hard, wood interior, and when she was inside, he closed the lid and began doing the latches.

My mother screamed. She beat her hands against the inside of the box. The walls closed in around her. She found it difficult to breathe. She wanted her father, and she kept calling out his name. The old man kicked the box hard on its side, and she could hear his muffled voice tell her to shut up or she'd be sorry. And she was so scared that she did, pushing her hands into her mouth to stifle the sound.

Then she heard her father's voice. She heard him calling out to her, talking to the salesman, asking him if he had seen where she had gone. The salesman said he hadn't, that maybe he should go look for her in one of the other stalls, that maybe she had wandered off. Shaking in the trunk, my mother uttered a small cry.

"Did you hear that?" her father asked.

"No," the salesman said.

So she made the sound again. She called out to her father.

"Emma?"

"Daddy."

"Emma. What the Jesus? Where is she?"

"I don't hear anything."

"Daddy, I'm in the box. I'm in the box."

"Oh my God. Move."

She heard her father shove the salesman, heard him crash into a line of wonder cabinets, their contents spilling out onto the cobblestone floor. He struggled with the locks. "I'm coming," he said. He repeated it over and over. "I'm coming. Don't worry. I'm coming."

He opened the lid and pulled her out, got her standing. My mother burst into tears. He lifted her out and placed her behind another box. Then he turned on the salesman.

After that they didn't go walking on weekends anymore. They returned that night, my mother's face red with crying, her father's knuckles bloodied and cut up. Mary exploded on her husband in between bouts of comforting my mother, getting her changed and running a bath for her.

My mother told me this story only once in her life, two days before she was going to die and I asked her if she had seen everything that was going to happen to us, all the misfortune and change that would occur, when she took to water that chilly summer morning.

"The future is bullshit," she said. "Nobody really knows anything."

BUT CALEB ANSON KNEW. He'd figured it out. During the meeting held in our living room, his family's living room that we had inherited all those years ago with a kiss and a dance.

It all made sense now. The way my father talked about life, about how we tell stories to ourselves to keep moving forward, and how we have to make peace with what we've done, figure out a way to live with those stories, before we can go anywhere new. Caleb saw that new place, and he called it the Future.

"You misunderstood me," my father said the next day, sitting with Caleb in the Two-Stone.

"No," Caleb argued. "I didn't. Don't you see? You did it. You've helped me make sense of my life, of where I need to go, what I need to do."

"That's great, Mr. Anson. Really. But—"

"Call me Cal."

"All right. Fine. Cal. That's great. I'm glad I could help, but looking forward isn't the same as moving forward."

Caleb frowned.

"It's like this," Dad said, holding his hands in front of him as if he were holding a large cup. "What I'm trying to say with the package is that we have to move on from our old stories before we can make new ones."

"And that's what I'm doing, I'm—"

"No. You're not," he interrupted. Firmly. "You're trying to change what happened when you left. You're going for the happy ending."

Caleb's eyes narrowed. "You don't know anything about me."

"I know enough to know that trying to fix what happened in the past isn't a way to live a life. Your mother would have told you the same."

The mention of the first and last matriarch that Garfaxians would ever acknowledge in their whole storied history cast a silence across the table. Both men stared down at their drinks. Caleb gripped the handle of his glass tightly.

"You're wrong," he said, after a spell.

"I don't think I am."

"I'll prove it to you," Caleb said, standing.

"You don't have to prove anything to me, Mr. Anson. Just don't go around filling people's heads with stories that aren't going to come true. It'll only upset them in the long run."

Caleb glared down at my father, then. "I'll show you."

"Like I said, you don't have to show me anything."

But Caleb did. He had to. As he stormed out of the Two-Stone, out of the conversation with my father, he knew it more than he had known anything in his whole life. Dad knew it, too. Everyone in the bar who was listening to their conversation knew it. They could hear it in the man's voice.

"You spoiling for a fight?" Denver asked my father, leaning on the bar.

Cadmus slumped his shoulders, feeling suddenly tired. "I guess so."

AND IT WAS A FIGHT, even though it wasn't much of one. From that moment on, the village was divided, separated between people who had read my father's self-help package and understood what he was trying to say, and those who were taken in by Caleb's promise of the Future.

"The Future is bright," he told the gathered crowds of men at the Two-Stone, the families who invited him over for supper. "We're going to put Garfax back on the map, put our name back in the books, in all official records. We're going to rejoin the rest of the country, be part of things again. We're going to exist again."

"Will we get a new sign?" one of the men asked.

"That," Caleb smiled, "is the first thing that we'll get. The very first thing. You can't have a village without a sign."

Which brought murmurs of agreement and scattered bouts of clapping. Garfaxians have always held a grudge over the theft of that goddamn sign.

"But what's actually going to happen?" one of the women wanted to know.

"We're going to build a hotel," Caleb said.

"A hotel?"

"Don't say it like that," Caleb said. "This isn't just going to be any normal hotel. It'll be the biggest and most impressive hotel that this side of the country has ever seen. We'll advertise it all over the world. Everyone will want to come and see it, will want to come and stay here. The bay is beautiful. We all know that. We've got history all around us. Magnificent scenery. I've been all around the world since I've been gone, and there's not a place like Garfax out there to be found."

Their local pride in the village stoked, more people began to agree.

"And there'll be jobs. Real jobs. Opportunities for our children that we can't provide the way we live now."

More nods. More hand clappings.

"And once enough people come, once this hotel is one of the most famous in the country, perhaps the most famous, a marvel, a celebrated cultural wonder, we'll petition the government to bring us back into their books. They'll have to let us in. Write us back into the histories, include our stories for once."

The clapping and shouting washed through the room like a wave, a tide that swirled and crashed against the walls, pulling everyone along in its wake.

"When we're back on the map, we can finally get proper roads. Safer roads. Wide enough for more than one car to get through. We'll get proper electricity and radio broadcasts. We'll be able to find out what's going on and be able to participate. We won't have to live like criminals. We'll be able bury our dead and marry our spouses legally. We'll be recognized."

The only people who really needed convincing, however, were the Franklins. A few of them attended every impromptu gathering held at the Two-Stone, and more than once the whole clan assembled when they invited Caleb over to explain his plan for the future in greater detail. They were concerned. Since the time when the government historians wiped Garfax off the face of the country's history, it was the Franklins whom the village had depended on. The Franklins were the reason that electricity still came into our homes, that we could still use our phones. They helped manage the worst problems with the roads, fixed broken pipes, and kept us together when the weather threatened to shatter our village against the pines.

To Joseph Franklin, Caleb's vision for the future held little promise for his family.

"What'll become of us?" he asked.

Caleb nodded thoughtfully, looking around in turn at each worried face of the Franklin clan. "I understand your skepticism," he said. "And I can appreciate your concern. But this would not be the end for your family. I don't want you to see it that way at all. You're the most important part of building this new future. Without you none of it can happen."

The patriarch frowned. "How's that?"

"I want you to build this hotel for me. I want you and your family to lead the way. I don't want to bring outside people in. Maybe for the drawing up of the plans, perhaps, but not the actual building. This is about the village making something for itself, about us reclaiming our position."

"But what happens after?"

"What happens if we do nothing?" Caleb asked.

The frown deepened.

"Look, eventually you're going to run out of materials to repair the town with. Eventually there won't be enough pipe or wire or tubing left to keep everything running, and this village will die. It'll rot. And people will start to leave. They'll leave one at a time, or maybe in groups, but they'll never come back. Nobody will remember us. Not our children and not anyone else's children. It'll be like this village never existed at all."

And then there was silence. Joseph Franklin looked over at the faces of his family—his wife, his siblings, their children, his own. They looked back at him, waiting for him to say something, to make a decision, to tell them what to do.

"I'll need to think about it," he said.

Caleb nodded. "Of course. That's perfectly reasonable. Let me know what you decide." He left without being led out, left them all standing or sitting, his words ringing in their ears.

Of course the old man agreed. No one wants to be forgotten. After that, with the public endorsement of the Franklins behind him, Caleb's hold over the village was strong enough that he actually began to make plans. His victory was written in the village newspaper. Despite his claim five years before, Barton Hen was back in the business of reporting the future. We all read it over the kitchen table.

Well, almost all of us.

"Where's Maddie?" Faith asked, after my father had finished reading the article out to us.

Dad folded up the paper and laid it down on the surface of the table, bumping a few lines of dominoes that the dead relatives had left from their afternoon game. "I don't know where your brother is."

Which was a lie. We all knew where he was, but no one wanted to say it. That night, when Maddox came trailing through the front door, more than a little drunk from his performance at the Two-Stone, Mum confronted him in the living room.

"Where have you been?"

"Out."

"Out where?"

"Out with my friends."

She looked down at the floor, then back up at him. "You can't do this to your father," she said.

"I'm not doing anything to Dad."

"Yes you are. Your father worked very hard on that book of his. It means a lot to him. You weren't even at the last meeting. You should be around to support him."

"So I missed one meeting? I am around to support him."

"No. You're not."

Maddox sighed. "Where is he? I'll go talk to him."

"He's upstairs."

"Sleeping?"

Mum shrugged. "Who knows."

Maddox frowned and peeled off his shoes, set them down in a long line with the rest of ours against the wall by the door. "I was just out having some fun," he said.

"I'd really like it if you'd stop going around with Caleb."

"Who said I was?"

Mum held him with her look. "I did."

Maddox laughed. "That's right, and you know everything, right?"

"I know enough," she said.

"No, you don't. Christ, have you read Dad's book? Caleb's actually talking about doing something, making some real changes. And he likes Dad. If it wasn't for Dad, he wouldn't have come up with the idea. He told me. I don't see why there has to be so much fucking drama."

"He's not doing the right thing."

"Who isn't?"

"Caleb."

"And I suppose you know that too, huh?"

Mum nodded.

My brother began to pace, a habit he picked up from our parents whenever he was nervous. "You don't know everything," he said, finally.

"I never said I did."

"You pretend that you do. Come on, Mum. For the first time since you stole that fucking boat, I'm actually a part of things again."

"And I'm glad, but—"

Maddox cut her off. "Do you know how hard it was after you did what you did? Everyone talking about us like that, calling us crazy and fucked up? They laughed at us. At you, at Dad. At me, Oz, and Faith. You don't know what that was like."

"I know it was hard—"

"No you don't. I'm a part of things again, Mum. And I like it."

Mum didn't respond. They both went quiet.

"And now," he said, after a time, slapping his knees with his hands, "I'm going to bed."

Mum didn't stop him.

AFTER THAT, MY BROTHER stopped attending meetings altogether. Some people went with him, followed him to the gatherings Caleb held at the Two-Stone to watch the magic tricks he'd perform. Others left the meetings when they ran out of stories to tell. They'd get to the end of talking about growing up, about problems with their husbands, and just go silent. They'd stare at the floor, and you could tell they were looking at something hundreds of miles away, that they were thinking about something else entirely. Then, almost to a person, they'd purse their lips and nod to themselves.

"Fuck this," they'd say, standing up. They'd excuse themselves, thank my parents for their hospitality, and then promptly stroll down the road to the Two-Stone.

Soon it was down to the nine of us. The four of us in our family, Denver, Tom, Aunt Connie, Lizzie, and her younger brother, Sunny. Sunny was a late addition to the group. He'd hold his sister's remaining hand while she talked about how hard it had been after the accident and how things were better now. She talked about how driving a taxi was the best thing in the world, even though it terrified her at times. She laughed while describing the near misses in the pines, the dancing ghost lights she saw during the night trips.

Cadmus congratulated her. We all did.

Sunny and Faith had been dating for a little while prior to this. Like most Garfaxians, they had known each other all their lives, but only properly met at Quill Lake. It was during the summer when I went up for my first time. Maddox still hadn't made the trip, keeping alive the self-imposed exile that no one remembered but him, so Faith took me.

"You're going to love it," she told me, as we pushed our way through the pines.

Quill Lake is a world unto itself. The pines line the edges of the water so tightly that it's easy to imagine that they don't stop there at all, that they continue down underneath the surface, and that if you were to dive deep enough, you'd touch their tops. The lake gets its name from these trees, its surface perpetually covered by the thousands of cast-off pine needle quills. Garfaxians make their camps along the water's edge. They pitch their tents amidst the pines. At night the boundary between land and water is illuminated by the orange-red of campfires.

Faith took me with her wherever she went for the first few nights, introducing me to people I'd always known but never spent time with. We stopped from fire to fire, joining in for the creation of a song when the instruments came out, or listening to the middle of some long drawn-out argument between old friends that ended in bursts of laughter from the participants and applause from the audience. People danced in and out of the campfire light. A woman might walk into the woods alone, only to emerge hours later hand in hand with a partner. Men left with their girlfriends only to come back empty-handed.

The sense of motion was overwhelming. We drank and we sang and we smoked, then we swam, and always there was somewhere else to go, some new thing to do or story to listen to.

"You're on your own," Faith told me, after the fourth night.

"I can't go with you?"

She frowned. "I'm not your babysitter."

I blushed. "I know, but—"

"Look, you have to do this sometime, Oz. You just can't sit back and expect it to happen. Ask someone to dance, start up a conversation. Kiss someone."

"But I was having fun."

Faith nodded and then pulled me in for a hug. "I know. But I have to go do some stuff by myself."

"All right."

She hooked my chin with her thumb and lifted my head up to look at her. "Don't be so glum. It's really not that hard."

She hugged me once more and then was gone. I watched her go.

I'm not the most spontaneous Brodie. I'm not like my father or my siblings. I've never been able to figure out the trick of taking myself into a crowd the way they do. For the rest of the time up at the Lake I tried, though. I walked up to a fire where a bunch of people were gathered around singing songs, and I sat down next to someone. They turned when I sat and smiled at me. I must have nodded, then stared at the ground, because they turned back and didn't look at me for the rest of the night.

My sister, on the other hand, was busy meeting Sunny Parks.

Sunny was, until he met my sister, one of Garfax's most eligible young bachelors. A likely lad, as the old women would say. He had that quiet kind of confidence that doesn't quite stray into cockiness. A confidence of a man who knew himself. He had his interests, he had his friends, and he didn't seem interested in gossip or troublemaking. He didn't talk about himself much, either, which seemed to add to his appeal tremendously. When you talked to him, he gave you his full attention, he listened, and then he offered his opinion, which always seemed well reasoned and thoughtful.

He was coming back from a night swim when he saw my sister dancing at the fire by his campsite. On the night before they were married, when he and I went down to the pier and shared a drink while looking out at the bay, he told me it was the way she moved that caught his attention.

"She threw herself into it," he told me then. "The most alive part of most people is in their eyes or in their mouth. They either can't talk enough or keep looking around to see if everyone's agreeing. Faith isn't like that. She's alive all over."

Brushing pine needles off his bare arms and chest, Sunny had dried off and approached my sister for a dance.

"I was used to getting a little more of a response," he admitted with a laugh when he related the story to me.

Faith flat-out ignored him. He had simply walked up to her in the middle of a song and interrupted the dance.

"He was rude," she told me.

"I wasn't trying to be rude," he told me later.

After the song ended, Sunny asked her for the next dance, but she refused. She still thought he was rude, and Sunny wasn't used to being turned down. He didn't pester her, but for the rest of that trip, he made a point to bump into her, talk with her, as much as he could.

The night before we left to come back home, he tried to kiss her after they had spent most of that day together. She stopped him.

"In the village," she said.

"What?"

"Kiss me in the village. Not here."

Faith told me all this on the trek back to our car. "Things are always changing at the lake," she told me. "I don't want to come back home and find out it never happened."

Two weeks later, Sunny knocked at our front door. Faith answered.

He reeked of campfire and pine sap from the lake, and when he leaned forward to kiss her forehead, she smelt the rough stink of sand.

"This is me asking you out," he explained.

"All right," she replied.

Sunny came to the meetings at our house largely to support Lizzie, but also to get Dad used to seeing him around places other than the Two-Stone with his friends. Dad didn't seem to notice, though. His mind was on other matters.

Late at night we'd hear him pecking away at the typewriter, adding more pages to his self-help package.

"I thought it was done," I said, finding him in the dining room one evening.

Dad looked over towards me, not at me, but over my shoulder, his eyes half closed. "I don't think it'll ever be done."

I turned to look behind me, but there was no one there, except for Mum, who was leaning on the door frame. "He's sleepwalking again," she told me, before she flicked the lights on and off, causing him to blink.

WHEN CALEB CONSOLIDATED his victory over the hearts and minds of Garfax, when his promise for the future finally took purchase, he left to begin preparations.

"I don't know how long I'll be gone," he told the crowd, who clustered around Lizzie's taxi to see him off. "I have to find an architect, someone we can trust to bring this vision to light. And I'm going to have to find someone to get the business side of things going, get the word out when the time comes for the doors to open. That might take some time."

"We'll wait," the people said.

Caleb nodded, smiled. "Good. I'll be as quick as possible. I'll send word."

Then he was gone, disappearing into Lizzie's cab and then vanishing up the road and into the pines. The crowd of Garfaxians watched him go, standing still for several minutes after just waiting, watching the treeline.

That night my father held the last of his meetings. Only Tom showed up. Faith had taken the opportunity to spend some time with Sunny at the place he shared with Lizzie, now that she was gone for the night. Denver and Aunt Connie were likewise absent, although for no discernable reason.

"They usually call," my father muttered.

Tom nodded.

The mood of that last meeting was funereal, so much so that the dead relatives had abandoned their post in the kitchen to sit with us. Starling fiddled with his trumpet keys. Hugo coughed. Jack and William looked at their respective children.

"Play something," Mum said, looking at Starling.

Starling raised the trumpet to his dead lips and began to play. We all listened. I saw Dad's chin dip down into his chest. Tom hummed along. William began punching his knee.

"I'll be back," I mouthed silently to my mother, who nodded, shooing me away.

I walked out through the living room, through the front door and onto the verandah. Fall was in full swing by then and it was getting dark early. From the verandah, I could see the lights of the village, the bulbs strung up by the pier where the few fishing boats, which get fewer and fewer every year, were finishing up their nightly business. Coughing, I lit a cigarette.

"Hey," a voice said.

I blinked in the dark, squinted, pulling the red tip of the cigarette away to see better. She was sitting on one of the chairs, her feet up on the verandah railing. I could see her shape but nothing definite. It sounds strange, almost like an insult, but I knew who it was by her smell before my eyes adjusted.

She smelled like rain.

"Hey," I replied. "You looking for your dad?"

Sara shook her head. "Just waiting. I needed the car, so I'm picking him up."

"Cool."

I smoked my cigarette. Sara looked out at the bay.

"You been waiting long?"

"Not really."

"Why didn't you come in?"

Sara shrugged. "Didn't want to interrupt."

"You wouldn't have interrupted much. It's pretty miserable in there."

"Dad seems pretty serious about the whole thing."

I nodded. "Mine too."

When I finished my cigarette, I put it out on the ashtray by her arm. "Do you have another one of those?"

"Sure." I handed it to her. When she lit the end, her face sparked into sight for a moment before disappearing again.

"So what do you think's going to happen?" she asked me.

I shrugged. "I don't know. Mum doesn't seem too thrilled."

"I've heard about your mother," she said, matter-of-factly.

"Everyone's heard about my mother."

She took a moment to digest that. "So what do you think?"

I shrugged again, shivered a bit in the cold. "I don't know. Maybe it'll be good. Maybe it'll be bad. You?"

"Maybe it'll be good," she agreed.

Tom came out a little while later and found us there smoking. The open door spilled light out from the house and over us in a harsh rectangle. We blinked it away.

"Hey Dad," Sara said, standing up.

"Hey. You ready to go?" he asked Sara, looking at me.

"Sure. Just waiting for you."

Tom nodded and passed by me, descending the steps to the car.

"See you later, Oz," Sara said, brushing my arm with her hand when she left.

BY THE NEXT TIME that I saw Sara properly, Caleb had already returned. It was the beginning of spring, after a long winter of waiting and speculation. He returned to fanfare, having announced his arrival several days in advance. Lizzie drove him all the way from Benning to the front of the Two-Stone, where a crowd had gathered.

He had all the appearances of a conquering hero.

"But I was not entirely successful," he said. "I always had it in the back of my mind that we could get Ethan Bramble to design the hotel for us." Everyone recognized the name. Bramble was the most famous Canadian architect of the last century.

"Was he busy?"

"Apparently he doesn't design buildings anymore," Caleb said. "He only builds ruins. I spoke to him about it. Briefly. Over dinner at his home. I tried to convey the importance of the project, but he had to decline."

The crowd murmured.

"Not to worry, not to worry. Bramble has many followers in the architectural circles. I went round to some of them. Young men and women working in the same style, the same form. They seemed more than eager. I've got drawings," he said, holding up some rolled-up papers, "that I'll need to go over with you."

Caleb spoke about supplies. He had organized the shipment of building materials, figuring out the logistical nightmare of transporting the disassembled parts of a hotel through the narrow roads leading through the pines. He spoke of Ira Wilson, a businessman he had met in Benning who seemed very interested in helping him market and advertise the hotel far and wide.

"I showed him pictures," Caleb said. "Ira thinks Garfax could be the Banff of the east."

"What's Banff?" the crowd asked.

Caleb shrugged. "Somewhere in Alberta," he said. "Apparently it's quite lovely."

The crowd nodded.

"The important thing is that we're ready to begin. I've got surveyors and the architects coming to stay here within the week to get things ready. With any luck, we can start actual construction, at least the beginning stages of it, by the middle of summer."

Everyone nodded and clapped, cheering the village's prodigal son. Caleb grinned. It was all happening, just as he predicted. Within the week, Ira Wilson, a rail-thin man with spectacles, arrived with a small army of surveyors and architects to look over the village. To a person they each seemed impressed by the surroundings. Garfaxians did their best to make them feel welcome. They cleared out of the village's only motel to make room for the new arrivals; they invited them to dinner and took them for tours of the local surroundings.

Over the next few months, Caleb split his time between Ira, the architects, and the Franklins, who he conferred with on an almost daily basis. Pages and pages of building plans and designs piled up in the hallways of the Franklin home. They blew out the open window and stuck to the side of our houses. You couldn't go for a walk without finding some intricate design of some new and innovative aspect for Caleb's blossoming hotel.

Whole armies of men pushed into the pines, trying to ascertain the best possible location for building. They stomped past the wreckage of cars and rotting furniture. The two remaining sections of Ester Anson's home were of particular interest to the architects, who had heard their mentor talk about it at length during their studies. They walked through the broken rooms, up the terminating staircase, reverently, gently touching the walls that had been so expertly designed and so clumsily torn down. Some of them even stopped by our house, requesting to see what my father had done to the famous man's design.

Once again there were crowds of people in our house, but this time they were strangers. We sat at the kitchen table, waiting for them to finish as they went from room to room, talking amongst themselves about this particular flourish, or that specific stylistic note. They mourned the areas where my father had sewn together the sections of the house into a shape the great man hadn't intended. One of them actually wept, touching with trembling fingers the spot where the floorboards ended, interrupted by another room they were never meant to lead to.

Dad didn't seem to mind. Since the fall, he had resumed his lifelong habit of sleepwalking. We found him in rooms of the house mumbling to himself, talking with the dead relatives or gone altogether, having left in the middle of the night to pursue something that only he could see. My mother had similarly gone silent. She smoked cigarette after cigarette, letting the ashes and ends pile up on the ashtrays strewn about the green checkered tablecloth.

That season was swallowed by the surveyors, by meetings with the Franklins. They finally agreed on a place for the hotel, up the hill and into the pines behind the village itself. With the trees cleared, it would have a spectacular view of the bay and Garfax below. Like a castle on the hill, its towers and walls would rise high above the treeline, as if it had sprung up like that, fully formed, from the earth itself.

"That's what Bramble would have done," one of the architects said. "It's very reminiscent of his earlier work."

"It's perfect," Caleb said.

Caleb and Ira worked in unison with the Franklins to get the village mobilized for the building. There seemed an endless supply of jobs. Diggers and builders and electricians and plumbers. Fishermen who had worked their entire lives on the sea, trying desperately to make ends meet, sold their boats and signed up on the construction crews. Joseph ran the show, of course. He was put in charge. He broke his family apart to lead the different groups, to coordinate the town's efforts. Tom, who had almost begun to enjoy the lull of work over the last few years, suddenly found himself with no spare time to read or do anything else.

"We'll be working like bastards," he told my father over coffee in the kitchen.

Dad nodded.

Mum reached over and touched his hand. "You don't need to work on the hotel," she said. "There's other work you can do."

Dad shook his head. "No. There isn't. And we have to make money somehow."

And he was right. There were no other jobs but the ones that Caleb provided. Everything else was put on the back burner; everything else came second.

The first days of summer were marked by the collapse of pines as workers cut their way up to the location that Caleb and Joseph had selected. They worked tirelessly, into the late evening, to speed up the process. Each morning the landscape changed, as a thick line of empty space moved up from the village and into the dense forest.

From the moment the first tree fell, Garfax seemed to never stop moving. Workers were coming and going at all hours, moving debris, putting it into trucks that disappeared and reappeared at odd hours of the day. There was constant celebration. The Two-Stone never closed. Gregory Peck had to move into a room at his own motel, the only motel in Garfax, to get any real sleep.

"Not that that bothers me," he pointed out, when people asked him about moving into the motel. "I'm making money hand over bloody fist."

I saw Maddox occasionally during those first early weeks before construction began in earnest. We never talked, but we exchanged waves from over crowds. He didn't seem to ever sleep. He certainly never came home. Faith figured he had moved into the motel, or was crashing on the floor of a friend's house.

He had become, my brother, a creature of perpetual motion. His hands never stopped moving. Silver globes and playing cards, dancing sparks and tricks of light, fluttered in and out of his hands. He smiled constantly, and laughed too, which was something that I hadn't seen him do for many years.

"He's working on the hotel," Aunt Connie told Mum one night over a cigar in the kitchen.

"I heard that," Mum replied.

"It's good work."

"I heard that, too."

Aunt Connie looked at her knuckles, took another drag of the cigar.

Despite all the activity, the yearly exodus to Quill Lake was not interrupted. Fewer people went, of course, far fewer than had gone for many years, but we still went. I went up with Faith and Sunny, with the exclusive promise that I would leave them alone after the first night.

"You don't have to keep telling me," I told her as we cleared the pines and came upon the lake.

Sunny smiled. Faith laughed. "Just try and have a good time."

The parties were smaller than the years before, the gatherings more intimate. That first morning there, I woke up early in the dark blue light, before dawn. Shivering out of my sleeping bag, I stifled a yawn and peeled myself out of my tent. The lake was utterly still. Calm. Like a mirror. I looked around the shore at the other campsites. The tents looked unoccupied, even though I knew they weren't. Only one or two fires were still going, but they were almost down to embers. I rubbed my arms and took a breath and held it, listening to the sound of the lake.

The occasional crack of a dying ember. The sounds of ravens moving through the branches. The crunch of sand and dirt beneath my feet.

The air was cool, but I pulled off my sweater and t-shirt, stripped off my pants down to my underwear. When I got to the lake's edge, I looked around again just to check if anyone could see me, but there was no one.

That first step in sent a cold shock through my body, but I didn't pull my toe away. I took another breath, then pressed my foot in entirely. Then the next foot. I stood there for a bit, watched the ripples from my ankles extend outward. Then I went deeper in, wading in until I was waist-deep and shivering.

It took me almost five minutes before I got the guts enough to dive under, pushing my head in and swimming furiously into the middle of the lake. I broke the surface of the water gasping, my whole body shaking. My gasps echoed across the lake, reflected back at me from the walls of pine.

I swam for a bit, then rolled over and floated on my back. Pine needle quills brushed passed me as I floated on by, some of them sticking against my skin, tangling in my hair. With my ears underwater, I listened to my heartbeat and stared up at the sky changing colour as the light hit it. When the last of the dark blue faded, I swam back to shore and dried myself off on the beach. Everyone was still asleep. I pulled on fresh clothes, still shaking from the cold, then collapsed back into my tent, pulling the sleeping blanket tight around me.

In the afternoon I woke up smiling. Sounds of people ambling about drifted past my tent. Occasionally a shadow brushed across the roof. I stretched out, my muscles sore and stiff. That evening, when the fires were lit and the parties started up again, I fished out one of the beers Sunny had left to cool in the lake and joined the group with the largest fire.

I hadn't said anything to anybody for the entire day, and I desperately wanted to tell someone about that morning swim. Because I had never done anything that reckless before, never done anything that even resembled being interesting. I wanted to describe the feeling of being out there and how it was almost like being in the cupped hands of a mountain. But when I sat down, the words didn't come. People were singing and laughing and talking about what had gone on the night before. I tried to speak, to join in, but it all fell short. My smile faded and I nursed the beer in my hand.

Sara sat down beside me. She had just come from one of the other parties. "How's it going?"

"Fine," I said, taking another sip.

"You having a good time?"

I nodded. "Yeah."

"Liar."

I turned and found her smiling. I smiled back. "I'm not very good at this," I said.

"Not very good at what?"

I waved my hand over the party going on in front of us. "This. I'm not very good at it."

"I see."

"What about you? You having a good time?"

"No," she said. "I'm not very good at this, either."

"So why'd you come?"

"Why did you come?"

I shrugged. "It's summer. This is what I do in the summer."

"But you don't like it?"

"I didn't say that. I like it just fine."

"You're just not good at it?"

"Right."

"So the reason you keep coming back is...?"

I took another sip of my beer, thought about it. "I figure if I keep doing this enough, maybe it'll get easier."

"Ah."

"It's very scientific," I said, grinning.

"I see that. And does it? Get easier, I mean."

"Not really," I laughed. "It pretty much stays the same. I think my sister's a little ashamed of me."

"I don't think so. At least I've never heard her mention it. The shame."

"Gotcha."

The music changed. Men came out of the pines carrying a door that they dropped on the ground. Fiddles appeared. People began to chatter, shouting out songs while instruments were tuned, their strings plucked.

"Do you want to?" I asked, turning towards her again.

"Dance?"

"Yeah."

"Sure."

Even though I asked, Sara was the one who grabbed my hand and pulled me up to stand. We moved into the assembled crowd of couples, brushing past friends we'd known all our lives but who seemed strangers in the campfire light. The music began. A fierce scratching of fiddles. One of the fiddlers started, his neck hung low to his instrument. It was a challenge. The other fiddler stood back, nodded his head to the beat, then brought the violin to his chin, the bow to the strings. He replied, and soon both instruments were dancing with each other.

We began to dance. All of us trying to keep up with the music. I tried to imitate the grace of my father, who I'd watched at numerous weddings as he glided across the floor with my mother. We jumped and we twirled. Sara's arms interlocked with mine. Spinning. The musicians began to thump their feet against the solid door they were standing on, trying to pound out a faster beat. We tried to keep up. Couples spun and revolved around each other. Sweat poured down my neck and under my shirt.

When Sara spun, her rain-soaked hair whipped through the air, hitting my neck and my cheek. I laughed and pulled her closer, feeling the heat of her chest pressed up against mine. I slid my hand down the length of her back and then pulled away. Sara looked at me and pulled me back.

One song ended and the next song began, with no gap between them. By the end of the evening, the musicians were exhausted, gulping for air as they sat down on a thick tree stump. I remember their eyes the most. Wild and slightly confused, wondering what had passed through them for the last hour, what sounds. When we asked them what they had played, they couldn't for the life of them remember.

I spent the rest of that trip to the lake with Sara. We met up in the mornings and passed the day going for long walks through the pines, stopping at times when we came to a particular piece of wreckage from decades before. We told each other stories that we had heard. Sitting on the hood of a broken-down pickup truck, I reached out and touched her hair, rubbing a thick strand between my fingers.

"What was your mum like?"

Sara sighed. "She was fine, I think. Beautiful. I was pretty young when she left."

"Do you know where she went?"

She looked at me, her face still, stone-like. "Away. I don't know where."

I was about to ask another question when Sara grabbed my hand and squeezed it.

"Don't."

I tried to hold her gaze but couldn't.

"Not everyone likes to tell stories."

I nodded, embarrassed. "I didn't mean—"

"It's fine," she said, jumping off the hood of the car. "Let's go."

In the evenings, we milled around the various parties, sometimes sitting with Faith and Sunny. Sunny, I found out, told the best jokes. He sat behind my sister and tickled her sides, kissing her neck when she burst out laughing, until she squealed.

Depending on who you ask, I either kissed Sara when we were walking back to her tent or after the end of one of those frantic dances by the lake's edge. Neither is true, because it was actually Sara who kissed me. I was just too nervous. We stood in front of her tent, the conversation dying between us, my fingers playing with hers. I was looking at those hands, saying something, when she leaned over and kissed me. It was a quick kiss, a this-is-what-we're-doing-now kiss. The one after that, initiated by me this time, lasted longer. Then she nodded, pleased with herself. She said good night and crawled back into her tent. I walked back to my own tent on the other side of the lake in a daze.

Sunny drove us all back a few days later, and when I walked Sara to her door, I kissed her again. She looked at me curiously. "What's that for?"

"Just making sure it's real," I said, smiling.

Sara opened the door. "I'll see you soon."

"Yes."

I walked back to Sunny's truck grinning. My sister laughed the moment I closed the door behind me.

FOR ME THE CONSTRUCTION of Caleb's hotel, which came to be known as Anson's Row, is inextricably tied to Sara. The hotel took just a year to build, and during that time we spent most of the time together. We remained at the edge of that delirious chaos that had taken over the village.

I got a job working for Denver Brail down at his movie theatre. It was not my first choice.

"You're not working on that hotel," my mother told me.

"Why not? There's lots of work."

She shook her head emphatically. No. "I've found you something else."

"What?"

"Denver needs help down at his movie theatre. I said you'd be round."

So I went round. He did indeed have work. He'd always had work; it was just that no one seemed interested. With extra workers flooding in from Mantua, the need for something to do when they weren't on the job necessitated Denver into finally giving in and getting someone to help him run the projection booths.

Sara worked at Gregory Peck's motel as a general fixer of all the problems that such an establishment entails. She fixed televisions and heaters. She changed out locks when keys went missing. She replaced windows after a party had gotten out of hand and a telephone had been thrown in protest.

We spent a lot of time out of Garfax, driving around the narrow roads, exploring the paths that were all degrading from lack of upkeep, the pines slowly closing them off through their ceaseless seasonal creep. Sometimes we'd take a couple of days and drive up the coast, following old maps from before the government historians came. We'd arrive at villages that no longer existed, the only signs being a crumbled-down dock or ruined houses with their roofs torn off, left standing alone in front of the ocean.

One time we parked in the small shadow of one of these broken-down ruins during a rainstorm coming off the ocean. We sat in the back seat, our bodies curled around each other, listening to the drumming of the rain on the roof overhead. I ran my hand through her hair and wet my forehead with the moisture. When we pulled off our clothes, the rain got inside the car, dripping drops on naked skin, forcing laughter and shivers simultaneously.

Each time we passed by the hotel, it grew. The framed skeleton continued to form until, almost overnight, it was complete and beginning to be skinned. Caleb invited everyone to come and see the progress. We'd take tours of the half-finished rooms that he filled out with a complete description of what it would all look like after they were done.

The image was so precise in his mind, so solid.

"It's going to be beautiful," Sara whispered to me, as we stood in what would eventually be the grand banquet hall.

"Yeah," I said, squeezing her hand.

Maddox was always around the hotel. He never stopped. He got a job with the Franklins, and when Dad went to work for them too, he switched so that they could work together. My brother nailed beams together in the heights of the skeleton and then laid boards to seal the frame. He balanced on the edge of precarious ledges to secure joists. He was even prone, it was said, to dance on the roof as it was being completed.

Dad continued to work more and more until we were never sure if he was awake or asleep when he talked to us. I was rarely home as it was, but when I was, I made a point to always try to talk to him. I flicked on the lights in the room he was in and asked him how his day was.

"Building," he said.

"Sara and I went down the other day," I'd tell him. "It looks beautiful." He nodded, not really paying attention.

I had heard from my mother that she had taken to tying him to the bed at night with a length of rope so that he wouldn't wander off and get struck by one of the trucks constantly coming in and out carrying more supplies.

My mother hardly left the house. I don't know what she did during the day. I'd come home and find her watching a game of dominoes going on with the dead relatives or reading books.

"What did you do today?" I'd ask.

"Nothing," she'd reply.

She never seemed bored. She was waiting, and waiting is something my mother had a gift for. Maybe I waited for a bit as well, but as the completion of the hotel grew closer and I spent more time at work or with Sara, I lost my patience for it. The Future was right around the corner. It was set to arrive any day now.

"WHAT HAS HE BEEN DOING in that place?" Cadmus asked, sitting on the verandah, his feet resting on the railing. "It's been almost a month now."

He was referring to Caleb. We didn't even have to ask. It had been just under a month since the last of the construction had finished up at the hotel. The craftsmen and workers had completed their final tours, tying up all the loose ends, making sure all the fixtures and furnishings were perfect. Everyone was back in their homes now. After a year of frantic building, of ceaseless motion, the world had stopped. Garfax was holding its breath.

"Maddox knows," Faith said.

Cadmus looked over at his middle child, who was sitting next to Sunny. They had come to join us all for dinner. Sara had come as well. We were all together, sitting and smoking, drinking our coffee, enjoying the last hours of the late summer evening.

"He's with him?" Dad asked.

Faith nodded.

Dad frowned, looked back at the hotel that rose out from the pines at the mouth of the bay behind the village, just like the castle Caleb had promised it would be. "So what are they doing?"

Sunny coughed. "I've heard there's cars that come and go in the middle of the night. Lots of cars."

"Where'd you hear that?" Faith asked, playing with his fingers.

"Just around," he shrugged.

"It's damn odd."

We all nodded along, then went quiet again. Mentioning Maddox often resulted in silence. In the whole year of building, we had only seen him a handful of times.

"I just hate this waiting," Cadmus murmured.

We wouldn't have to wait long. After the month passed, Caleb appeared in the village again. He stopped at each and every house, at each business, and invited them to come up to the hotel that evening. "The Future has arrived," he explained in a hushed voice, as if he were afraid that if he spoke any louder, it would vanish.

He walked up the hill and up our driveway and up our stairs to our front door. He knocked three times and then waited until my father came to the door.

"Mr. Anson," he said.

"Cadmus," Caleb nodded. "I'd like for you and your family to come and join us all at the hotel tonight."

"What for?"

"I'm unveiling the hotel. Everyone is welcome."

Cadmus nodded.

Caleb extended his hand. "It would mean a lot to me if you'd come, Cadmus. I know we had a bit of difficulty at the beginning, but I'm telling you the truth when I say that none of this could have happened without you. You inspired me."

"You did this all by yourself, Mr. Anson. You don't need to thank me."

Still, my father took Caleb's hand and shook it.

"It would still mean a lot if you'd come."

"We'll be there," he promised.

And we were all there. All of us. Every single last member of the village came out that evening. The air was warm enough that we could walk about without jackets. We left our house and walked down the hill and into the village. We met up with other families and joined the growing stream of people heading up through the pines, on the new road that Caleb had built, up to the hotel.

It was late evening. The sun was setting.

I remember that the lawn surrounding the hotel was immaculately manicured, as if it had been trimmed to precision with a pair of sharp scissors. We stepped on that grass and the green blades were solid beneath our feet. We hovered around the edges, fishermen and craftsmen, husbands and wives, whole families. Even the dead were curious to see what all the fuss was about, all dressed up in their finest funereal wear. They stayed at the edges, just inside the treeline of pines that circled the massive structure. Timothy Franklin was there, his neck still broken, his skin still white. I saw him once, then looked away. The living Franklins were there too, walking through the crowd, shaking hands, smiling like idiots. Everywhere there was laughter and nervous anticipation, the gentle buzz of wonder as we gazed at the great house that we had built together.

Caleb appeared on the massive verandah, stepping out through the large double doors that led into the lobby. People started to quiet down until the entire crowd was completely silent, waiting anxiously for the village's prodigal son to speak.

Joseph Franklin joined Caleb on the verandah. He hobbled up the steps. I realized then just how old he was and how quickly the years had caught up to him. When he reached the top step, Caleb bent to help him, holding him gently at the elbows, smiling down at the suddenly aged man.

He held up his hand.

"Friends," Caleb said. "We are standing on the threshold of a dream. A vision of the future that we have made real through our own efforts."

I stood beside my parents with Sara, holding her hand. I didn't notice until his hands were on my shoulders that Maddox was there.

"Hey, little brother," he whispered.

Our parents turned. Maddox nodded. "Mum. Dad."

"You haven't been around in awhile," Mum said.

"I've been busy," Maddox said. "With the hotel."

"So I see."

"Isn't it wonderful?"

Mum nodded, swallowing hard. Sad. "Yes, Maddie. It's beautiful."

I missed the rest of Caleb's speech; the weight of Maddox's hands on my shoulders was too great. Sara squeezed my hand and I looked over at her. She smiled at me, reassuringly, and I tried to smile back.

Then the crowd applauded. There were shouts and cheers. Maddox's hands left me, but I could hardly tell. I had to look to make sure. Out on the verandah, Caleb handed Joseph a box connected to a long cable leading into the lobby of the hotel. He shook the older man's hand as he gave it to him. The old man bowed.

He held up the box and the cheers intensified. Then he pressed a button, flipped a switch, turned a lever, I couldn't tell from so far away. The result was the same. The sky exploded into a thousand halos of candle-warm orange and yellow lights. I hadn't seen them before, so expertly hidden were they in the pines and over the hotel, the thin lines of cable and clear glass bulbs virtually invisible in the night sky.

The hotel, the crowd, the pines themselves, bathed in the light as if we were in the middle of a dream populated by a cloud of fireflies. The cables turned and bent in the wind, giving the illusion that the lights floated above us. We all stared, our mouths open in wonder. Some people cried, their hands going to their mouths and the tears sliding slowly, cleanly, down their cheeks.

Cadmus and Emma looked up at the sky, holding hands. My father leaned close to my mother, but not close enough so that I couldn't hear what he said next.

"Am I dreaming?"

"No," she whispered, a tear rolling down her face. "This is happening."

"Good."

Music started as if from nowhere. But not nowhere. From inside. Musicians walked out from the lobby, appeared at the windows, and began to play. Fiddle music. Pianos and trumpets. We all found our voices and the crowd began to move inside, shaking the hands of Caleb and Joseph as they passed.

The dead relatives emerged cautiously from the treeline, stepping out into the open, their eyes cast at the lights around them. Bewildered, they looked to each other. William Wilson, my father's father, wept openly, his hands balled into tight fists. His hollow frame shook he was so moved.

The quality of light was just so perfect that night.

It soon became clear to all of us what Caleb and my brother had been doing for that last month and what secret cargo those strange cars had transported. For in every room, from the lobby up to landing of every floor, there was some beautiful statue or priceless artifact that held some significance to the Anson house. Transported all the way from Alberta, where Ester Anson had passed away so peacefully years before, all of Caleb's family heirlooms that had not been inherited by my father were put on display around the hotel. There were paintings and murals that the industrialist Simon had purchased in auctions following the Great War. At the bottom of the staircase stood a complete and fully restored suit of armour from the fourteenth century.

And it wasn't just Anson artifacts on display. Within the great collection were local pieces. Photographs cluttered the walls, wonderfully framed, chronicling the many faces of Garfax's past. There we were, rendered in black and white, jumping into the bay during the summer or heading out in the boats when we had a full armada to plumb the once fertile depths of the ocean for fish. Here were pictures of Ester and Simon Anson, the building of their house, the death of the man, and finally, the dismantling of their dream. Here were pictures my father had taken of that house, that moveable hearth, broken into sections and placed on long trucks, moving slowly through the dense pine. And there were stranger pictures. Pictures I didn't recognize. Pictures of a wedding between a tall, thin man in a suit too small for him and a young woman in snug-fitting jeans and blue hair. A piano that almost defied description stood in the grand hall. It seemed half machine, as if built out of the shell of a car. A sign accompanied the instrument-engine, explaining its unique history in saving the village from the government sponsored historians.

There were maps, too. Old maps. Maps that dated back from before the historical purges of the seventies. Older Garfaxians clambered around the framed glass, pointing with sure and steady hands at the name of their village, their home, in its proper place within the province's domain.

We wandered through the halls, Sara and I, moving through the rooms that lined up perfectly one after the other, each time more and more surprised by what we saw. Sara pointed out a photograph of her father,

Thomas, sitting at his desk at home surrounded by towers of books he had borrowed from my parents. We found him later in the crowd and pulled him to his picture so that he could see.

"I don't look like that," he mumbled, more than a little drunk.

Sara teased him, poking his sides. "That is exactly what you look like."

Drinks and food were provided and soon everyone was happy, drunk, and dancing. They filled up the grand hall and spilled out onto the verandah to smoke, pulling musicians with them to carry on their dance. Garfaxian couples, young and old, stole away from the crowd and climbed the staircase to the empty rooms, pushing open the doors to reveal naked, unlit beds. In the dark they christened these with abandon.

Sara and I moved through the halls, went exploring. We pushed our way into rooms only to be pushed back out again by naked friends, giggling to get back to their own discoveries. We laughed back, and moved quicker down the halls, our hands roaming over each other.

I don't remember everything that happened that night. I don't remember the passing of time or feeling tired. If I try and put it all together in my head, it plays out in sections. I remember certain rooms, meeting certain people, but nothing that brings it into one evening. It couldn't possibly fit into one night. Everything I did, everything we did, it couldn't possibly. It could have been a week in that night. A month. Maybe years.

When it ended, when the light bulbs dimmed and the sky brought down a dark blue crush that summoned dew from the manicured grass, I found myself lying beside Sara on the lawn, her head on my chest. I smelled her hair, that rainwater scent mixed in with the grass. All around us people in small groups, or one by one, were heading away from the house. They moved quietly. No one spoke. They held onto each other, keeping each other standing as they made their way down the road and back into the village.

I stroked Sara's face until she stretched and opened her eyes.

"Good morning," I said.

"Is it morning?"

"Almost. Come on, let's get you home."

She grumbled. "Come home with me," she said.

As we made our way across the lawn and away from the hotel, I turned back and looked at the lights flicking off in the windows of that great building. In the morning blue, I saw Caleb standing by the verandah, watching his long night pass from dreaming into waking. There were people already at work, a whole army of them. Garfaxians who had gone through that night and had woken up to change their regular clothes for uniforms and duties. They moved quickly, putting right and cleaning up the mess we had made.

The hotel was now officially open for the whole world. Caleb waited for it.

BUT THE NEXT DAY nobody came. They didn't come the day after that, either. Or the day after that.

We all waited.

By the end of the week, people were asking questions, talking amongst themselves. We asked those of us who worked at the Row, but they had no answers either. One afternoon, while walking through the village to see Sara, I ran across Maddox walking down from the hill.

"Hey."

He stopped short. "Hey. How's it going?"

"Fine. You still up at the hotel?"

"Yeah. I've got a job there."

"I heard that."

Silence.

"So when are the people going to start showing up?"

Maddox shook his head, shrugged. "Don't know. Soon, I think. Caleb's been talking to Ira. Apparently there's busloads of people about to head off from Benning. Soon we'll be swamped."

But no busloads showed up. He wasn't lying, though, my brother. There had been buses planned. People had purchased tickets. But they never showed up. They never arrived.

"Where are they?" Caleb hissed into the telephone, pushing his frustration over stuttering static all the way to Ira, who sat at his desk in Benning.

"They got turned around," Ira said. "Misdirected. Did you know there's no signs that lead to Garfax?"

"Yes. But—"

"It's not even on any maps."

"You already knew that."

166

"I know, I know. There's just been a bit of a mix-up. People are getting angry, here."

"I'll send my own drivers," Caleb said, slamming down the phone.

Rounding up his own drivers from his army of workers, he paid for Lizzie to ferry them all to Benning in her cab. But by the time they arrived, all the guests had left, furious, believing they had been tricked.

"You have to clear this up," Caleb shrieked into the phone. "That's your job."

"We're getting a lot of really bad press," Ira said. In the background he heard yelling, the banging of doors. "They think the whole thing's a fraud. They want a return on their money."

"There is no money left," Caleb said. "I've put everything I am into this place."

"I'll see what I can do. But it's not looking good."

Another week passed. More angry phone calls. Until one day Caleb called and no one on the other end answered. And then the next time he called, the line was disconnected.

The future had not arrived. Not only that, it didn't look like it would ever arrive.

When it came time for the army of workers at the hotel to get paid Caleb gave a speech explaining the situation, asking them for their patience. He used large words, describing in laborious detail the solidity of his money, and the difficulty he had in making it liquid.

"This sounds like bullshit," one man said to another.

"That does sound like bullshit."

Some of the workers stayed on, believing in Caleb, but many left. Then more left. Until two more weeks had passed and there was hardly anyone in the hotel at all. Maddox was there, though. We heard about that. He was always at the man's side. Listening to him, taking his orders, passing them along.

One night, after a night of drinking at the Two-Stone, five former workers went up the hill to the hotel and broke two of the large windows at the grand hall that looked out at the bay, then ran away into the black. The next night, a few more people showed up and broke more windows.

There is something intensely satisfying about the breaking of glass. The sound it makes, the feeling of power as it breaks into a hundred pieces.

Two months later, the trucks started to show up. At first, when we saw them come over the hill, we thought that they were the promised buses, and we all came out to see them. But these trucks were empty. They had come from the bank. And they knew exactly where they were going. They drove right onto the well-manicured lawn.

With all the commotion, a number of Garfaxians walked up to see what was going on.

Caleb was livid. He ranted and raved at the bank men, at the burly moving men who accompanied them on all sides. They presented papers and then gave the nod to their workers, who moved, row on row, into the hotel, coming out minutes later carrying furniture and fixture, artifact and photograph. They boxed them all up, carefully, and loaded up their trucks.

"What's happening?" Garfaxians asked Caleb.

But Caleb didn't answer. So they asked the bank men, who told them. The money was gone. Debts had accrued. They were coming to repossess what was no longer his.

"But it's ours," Garfaxians said. "These things are ours. They're our history."

"Not our problem," the bank men replied.

So Garfaxians went into the hotel along with the workers and took what they could. The bank men didn't care. They pulled photographs off the wall and sheets off the bed. They ripped curtains off their rails. Anything that they could get their hands on, just to have something to come away with. More people showed up. There was screaming and cursing. Hurt feelings and harsh words.

Someone saw Maddox in the melee. He was trying to calm down Caleb, who was shouting at the top of his lungs, tears streaming down his face. Caleb pulled him into the grand hall. The crowd followed. With maddened eyes, the prodigal son searched for something that he could put his own hands to, make his own. He saw the strange piano, that instrument-engine.

"Grab it," he said, pointing to Maddox. "We're taking it with us."

"I'll need help," Maddox said.

"Just do it," the prodigal screamed.

Maddox tried. He strained and managed to drag the piano all the way to the verandah, pushing past the river of people coming and going, everyone carrying something with them. The piano was heavy, though. He would need help on the stairs. He asked Caleb but he wasn't listening. He got help from a couple of the fishermen.

They got the piano down three stairs when it slipped, spilling out from their fingers.

Maddox was in front; he pushed against the weight, tried to stabilize it, but it was too heavy, too unwieldy. The piano toppled. It tippled. Then it came crashing down, its metal hull splitting, the gears and strings inside exploding into a cacophonic smash on the stairs, broken melodies trickling down onto the grass.

The crowd stopped. No one said a thing. Caleb hit him. Caleb hit my brother and he hit him hard across the face. Stunned, my brother tumbled onto the grass. The older man was on him then, kicking him in the side, yelling at him, calling him all manner of names. Blaming him. Blaming my stupid bitch mother. My senile drunk of a father. Blaming all of us. His own parents. This whole damned village. Everything in this nonexistent village that didn't have enough respectability to have its own sign, to belong to any book or map or sensible record.

And when he was done, when Caleb was finished beating my brother, he went back inside the hotel and ran to his own room, now devoid of all furnishings, and locked the door behind him. My brother lay on the grass, bruised, and looked at the crowd looking down at him.

"Don't," he said, tears in his own eyes now. "Please, don't. Stop looking at me."

But they couldn't. They couldn't stop. Maddox got to his feet, stumbled. He couldn't stop himself from crying, from sniffling. He held his arm and walked away, away from the hotel and the village. He walked into the pines.

When he was gone, the crowd moved again, going back into the house to see what there was to be got. They moved slowly, though.

It took three days of back and forth before the last of the trucks disappeared entirely. Everything was gone. The floorboards, the walls, everything lay bare. The windows, every single last one of them, were broken. Glass cluttered the grounds. Wind whistled through the halls, but no one recognized the tune.

VII

Losing Faith

ABOUT A WEEK OR SO after the trucks brought in by the bank men had come and gone, a group of men stumbled out of Garfax's only motel after a night of drinking to find themselves at the end of a chilly blue morning. The sun was rising but wasn't visible yet. They could see its traces in the tips of the pines, making the woods around Garfax look as if they were burning from the top down. Bleary eyed and shivering from the cold, they staggered out and away from the motel and began the long walk through the village.

No one knows who these men were. They were only ever seen at a distance. A few dedicated fishermen spied them from the docks when the group stopped to take a collective piss off the pier. Gregory Peck, whose side business apart from the Two-Stone was running the motel, told me that he didn't know who the men were either, that there was so much back and forth between workers in that day that it became necessary to take the locks off the doors. Workers slept wherever they could find room.

After passing the pier, the men began their clumsy ascent up the hill, wobbling at moments when the incline jostled against their equilibrium. It must have taken them a half-hour walking at that pace, making constant stops for cigarettes or to let one of their number scramble to the side of the road to vomit. By the time they reached the town's outskirts, the sun had fully risen, and whatever fog had rolled in that morning had been dissipated by the heat.

Their destination was the town sign, the one that Caleb had promised Garfax when he first proposed his dream for the future. The men left the road and strode out onto the grass, and stood there in silence underneath the sign for long minutes.

How many were there? It's hard to say. Accounts vary. But eight strikes me as likely.

The original village sign was carved out of wood and repainted regularly by various people in town. It didn't resemble in any way the new sign, which was larger and made of metal, sporting the same colours as all the signs you'll find on the highways criss-crossing the province. It was a perfectly suitable sign. One that suggested that this place, this village, was just the same as any other place you'd find on any legitimate roadmap.

One of the men picked up a rock. He bent down, squinting against the sunrise to find one heavy enough. He hefted it in his hand, felt his head spin a bit, then, when he had righted himself, threw it as hard as he could at the sign. The metal clanged. It echoed in the pines. Another man picked up a rock, this one larger than the last, and threw it. This one left a dent. Then everyone began picking up rocks until there were none left to throw. Then they picked up sticks and began bashing away at the sign.

I heard them shouting. I heard them shouting as I woke up, because it was that sound, coupled with the striking of the sign, that made me stir. I crept over to the window and leaned out but couldn't see them. I couldn't make out what they were saying, either. They were animal sounds. Senseless. Five minutes later, I heard the signposts break and the metal crash to the ground. I heard them stomp up and down on it. You might think that the sound they made was celebratory. The delighted scream of an act of destruction. But it wasn't. There were tears and rage and all kinds of pain in those screams.

CALEB LOCKED HIMSELF AWAY in the bowels of his hotel. No one saw him for days. So after the village recovered from its initial shock, we turned once more to the Franklins to tell us what to do.

I wasn't there, but not because I didn't want to be. I was in the kitchen when Faith picked up the phone and passed it to Sunny, who was filling in for William Wilson in a game of dominoes with the dead relatives. Sunny took the phone, nodded respectfully to the dead, then spoke into the receiver, figuring it was his sister. It wasn't. It was one of his friends. People were moving, he was told. They were all going over to the Franklin house to see what was to be done.

Sunny and Faith got their coats on, and I was just about to do the same when my mother stopped me at the door.

"I need you to do something for me," she said.

"Do what? There's a meeting at the Franklins."

She waved the comment away. "Don't worry about that. There's something I need you to do."

"What?" I looked over at Sunny and Faith, who were already at the open door and looking back at me, waiting.

"I need you to get me apples," my mother said.

And despite my arguments against the fruitlessness of getting apples at a time like this, Mum stood resolute on their utmost necessity, as well as the timeliness of their arrival. So when Faith and Sunny broke off down the road leading through the village to walk up to the Franklin house, I had to keep walking to the grocery store.

Everyone went to that meeting. On my way to the store, I was the only one heading the other way. Everyone passed me by, pulling at their coats, talking amongst themselves. Some friends from school tried to get me to come along, but each time I had to beg off. There was no one in the grocery store, either. Not even a clerk behind the till. On the counter there was just a sign saying that they would be back after the meeting, and a basket with assorted change in it next to a pad of paper and pen to figure out totals.

I figured out the price of six apples, factored in the provincial tax that Garfaxians still take into account but never pay, fished through my pockets, made change, and then left, slamming the door on my way out even though there was no one there but me to appreciate it.

EXCEPT THERE WAS SOMEONE there to appreciate it. The slamming of the door, I mean. I didn't see him. He had just passed the store as I was coming out, heading the other way. He turned at the sound, the hard crash and rattle of glass, and stopped in his tracks. He watched me go, noted the slump in my shoulders, the sullen way I carried myself, and then, satisfied and mystified at the same time, he turned and continued on his way.

If I had seen him, I would have remembered. He's a hard man to forget. For one thing, and it's the first thing that you'll notice when you see him, it'll be the thing that will keep him forever in your mind, the man had only shaved one side of his face in the last year. The other side was shaggy, unkempt, wild. So if you saw him in profile from the right side, you might think that he was some kind of vagrant, and if you saw him likewise from the left, you'd imagine him a saint.

I asked him, later of course, when I knew who he was, why he had done such a thing, why he had chosen to shave only one side of his face.

And he responded, in that strong and confident voice of his, that it forced him to remember at all times that he was a man.

"Which side?" I asked.

"Which side what?"

"Which side makes you remember?"

The man whose name, I would come to learn, was Sebastian Catafalk, thought about this for a moment, then replied, "Both of them."

Catafalk watched me go, then turned back to where he was headed. He was headed, quite simply, to Caleb's hotel. A month before he had heard some workers in Mantua mention it in the same breath as the name of our village, a village he had been trying to find for almost ten years.

A man who shaves only one side of his face to remind himself of his essential humanity views the world in a completely different way than most of his brethren. For one, he didn't take into consideration when he approached the hotel that it was uncommonly quiet. He took no pause when he discovered that every single window had been smashed in. The only thing that bothered him was that the door was locked.

Catafalk frowned. He rang the bell, or rather he pushed his finger to where the bell should have been, only to find an empty hole in the wall exposing loose wires. The front doors to Caleb's hotel were almost entirely made out of glass, so while it played against his expectations for a door, Catafalk stepped through the opening as if he were invited.

He went to the front desk and looked for a bell. He didn't find one. He waited the appropriate amount of time, then called out for service. When none came he began to wander the halls. He marvelled at the woodwork and the design, swearing that if Ethan Bramble himself hadn't designed such a hotel, then a great admirer of his work must have.

Catafalk found Caleb hours later, on the second to highest floor.

Caleb descended the stairway, having heard the man's voice calling out from below. He held in his hand an iron poker, one of the only things he had managed to save from the bank men and their trucks. He brandished it like a weapon.

"Who are you?" Caleb hissed.

Catafalk turned, took in the older man, who wore a cape of curtains around him like a blanket and was waving a poker in the air. He frowned again. "I'm looking for a room," he replied, simply.

Caleb's eyes must have widened at that. "You're lying."

"I most certainly am not. I just got into the village and I need a place to stay."

"We're closed."

"Really? I didn't see a sign."

Caleb struck the poker on the ground, breaking off a thick splinter of bare floor. "There doesn't need to be a blasted sign. You just need to have eyes to see we're closed."

"I can pay," Catafalk said.

"I don't want your money," Caleb said, advancing on him, grabbing Catafalk by the shirt. He started to lead him down the stairs and out. "I know what you're doing here. You're here to make fun. You're here to laugh and point and to take what you can get. Well, sorry. There's nothing left to take. It's all gone. And I'm not going to let you stand there and laugh at me."

Catafalk stumbled down the stairs, steadying himself on the railing, utterly confused. "I'm not laughing at you."

"Of course you are. Everyone laughs at me."

"I don't know what you're—"

"Just get out. Leave me alone."

When they reached the ground floor, Caleb unlocked the front door and pushed Catafalk onto the verandah before slamming the door shut and locking it again. Through the empty space where the glass used to be, he pointed his poker at him. "Don't come back. There's nothing left for you to take, and if I see you again, I'll bust your goddamn head open."

"But—" Catafalk began.

Caleb turned away and ran back upstairs, practically bursting into tears, his cape of salvaged curtain trailing behind him.

The man stood there for a time, stunned. He looked around him, the way many of us do when confronted by something truly bizarre, and then slowly descended the front steps. It was then that Catafalk saw a tall man come out from the pines. He too, Catafalk noted, looked a little bit confused, as if his original intention was to emerge someplace else.

"Hello," Catafalk said.

"DON'T SULK," my mother told me. "There hasn't been a single instance in human history where sulking has been considered attractive."

"I'm not sulking," I said, sitting at the kitchen table, watching the domino game.

"Right."

While the smell of apple pie baking in the oven wafted through the house, I paced back and forth, occasionally looking out the window for Faith and Sunny to arrive. "Stop it," my mother finally said. "Do something useful."

"Like what?"

"Try setting the table."

"We just had lunch."

"Set the table."

I sighed. "Fine."

After shooing the dead relatives away and cleaning out their ashtray, I started to set the table, just as Faith and Sunny walked in, talking quietly to themselves.

"Well?"

It hadn't been much of a meeting, but what there had been of one didn't do anything to allay any of the village's fears. The crowd stood on the front lawn of the Franklin house for over an hour, waiting for Joseph to emerge, to come out and tell them what to do.

"The lawn was covered in wires," Faith told me.

They were the wires taken from the hotel, wires that the Franklins as a family had stripped as best they could so as to better salvage them for the village's use. There were pipes in piles as well. Anything that they could use, that they had taken from other projects to help Caleb build his dream for the future, now lay in piles on their front lawn, waiting to be stored away.

The whole family was out on the verandah. Sometimes they went into the crowd or held up their hands when people started shouting, demanding the appearance of the patriarch. The crowd so desperately wanted to hear it. Whatever it was, whatever the solution, they needed to hear it. They didn't know what it was, but they would know it when he said it. They would know it was it because it would be Joseph who said it.

When Joseph appeared, the crowd went silent. Like air going out of a room. He looked old. That's how Faith described it. So very, very old. The years had caught up with him so quickly that he hunched under the strain. He wore a Hudson's Bay blanket around his shoulders. It wasn't cold, but he shivered anyway.

Joseph stood on the verandah and looked out at the crowd. The crowd looked back. For three minutes he stood like that, looking and being looked at. Then, with no more ceremony than the flicking of a switch, he turned and walked back into his house.

The crowd erupted.

"We're fucked," someone said. "We're absolutely fucked."

And it was true. Everyone felt it. What everyone had feared to say, what had kept them up at night, their guts all torn up in knots, had been said.

The rest of the Franklin clan tried to fill in the gap by explaining that things weren't so bad, but that for the next few years things would be difficult. The building of the hotel had been a massive undertaking, but eventually things would get back to normal. That everything would be all right.

But it was difficult to listen to that, difficult to hold out hope when the entire inventory of tubing, pipes, and wire the village had left to patch up any future problems with lay in piles on the ground, utterly finite.

After Faith had finished the story, we sat at the table, the four of us, quietly listening to the dripping of the tap in the sink, the smell of apple pie baking in the oven.

"So what happens now?" Faith asked Mum.

Mum looked up, her lips pursed. She looked at Faith, then at Sunny, then back to Faith again before shrugging her shoulders.

The timer of the oven went off just as the front door opened.

"Emma," Cadmus called up, kicking off his shoes. "We have a guest."

I must have frowned.

We all stood up and went out to the living room, where Cadmus was hanging up the coat of a man whose face was half beard, half clean-shaven. "This is Sebastian," Cadmus explained. "I ran into him while I was out walking."

Catafalk nodded a hello to us. We nodded back. "It's a pleasure to meet you all," he said.

"I'm so glad you finally arrived," Mum said, walking over to shake the man's hand.

Catafalk smiled, slightly confused. "I was expected?" He looked over to my father, but he was just as perplexed.

Mum nodded. "Of course you were. Do you like apple pie, Father?"

THERE WAS NOTHING Father Catafalk liked more than a steaming slice of apple pie, except perhaps one that was smothered in cream. When all of us were seated, Mum placed a bowl with a particularly large slice in front of the man, as well as a container of cream beside it. His eyes drank in the sight. The crumbling walls of the crust. The trail of steam coming off the apples. The energy required to wait for the rest of us to be served and seated was visible, and even after that, when we were all ready, he pushed off the moment a little while longer to say grace.

He prayed quietly to himself, his lips mouthing the words. We all looked at each other. None of us being religious, we looked at each other, looked at him. With our fingers, we traced the squares of the green checkered table cloth.

"Amen," he said, finally, with a nod. He picked up his spoon, held it there quivering in mid-air for a moment, then plunged it into the pie, allowing it to mix with the cream, then brought it to his lips. He was practically shaking.

We ate in silence. No one wanted to interrupt him, distract him from this holy experience. Sunny hardly touched his pie at all, he was so busy watching the man enjoy the food my mother had made.

When he was done, Catafalk thanked my mother and we started to talk. He explained to us that he hadn't had a genuine slice of apple pie in almost ten years, ever since he had been sent out from Benning to minister in Garfax.

"Your village," he told us, "is very difficult to find."

He detailed the route he took to Dad, who in turn brought out the various road maps he had collected since he arrived in the village. Each new edition featured fewer and fewer of the villages that he knew to exist along the coast. Catafalk traced the road he had taken with his finger, and it forced my father to frown. "You went in completely the wrong direction," he said.

Catafalk nodded. "I was just following the signs."

During his travels, he walked along roads that continued on for days, only to arrive at a dead end, the concrete disappearing into a wall of pine trees, the forest having swallowed it up over the decades. He spotted patches of railroad tracks that seemed to have been dropped down from overhead; there was no evidence they had ever been connected to a longer line. For over ten years, Catafalk had travelled up and down the coast and through the pines, stopping at the remnants of villages that no longer existed, save for the people living there. No one seemed to know where Garfax was. Some of them seemed to be surprised in what century they were living.

"You don't have radios out here, do you?" he asked.

"We used to," Faith said. "But not anymore, no."

Catafalk shrugged. After the first year, he started to spend more and more time with the people he ran across, the criminal communities that appeared on no official government document. He married couples who had been together for decades but wanted it to be official. He baptized the elderly and the young alike. He walked through graveyards and said last rites for bodies already turned to dust and bone.

"That first year was the hardest," Catafalk confessed, taking the bowl with the second slice of pie my mother handed him. "By far the worst. I was at the ends of my ability. Nothing made sense and I couldn't seem to find my way back."

It was a crisis of faith, lost and wandering like that in the pines for so long. Catafalk was only twenty-seven when he started the long walk towards Garfax. Hardly experienced, he was not prepared for the reception he received wherever he went. People clung to him. Asked him all sorts of questions. Demanded spiritual services from him that he had never been trained to perform. The young priest found himself talking to dead men in the pines, comforting them as they wept dry tears of dust on his collar. He stumbled across communities utterly separated from civilization, where families lived more like animals than men, running through the trees and jumping into the cold Atlantic water naked, howling

179

at the moon like wolves. He followed the dancing ghost lights off the road and came across the hulls of buses and buildings long left abandoned and broken, open to the ravages of the elements. And one time he saved a young girl who had the habit of floating away if not weighed down by heavy stones sewn into her clothing.

"I've seen more in the last ten years than most men in my profession will see in two lifetimes," Catafalk concluded, putting his spoon down. "And I've finally arrived where I set out to." The priest smiled then, although with a face only half shaven, it had all the appearance of a smirk. "It's been a good day."

NEWS OF CATAFALK'S ARRIVAL in the village was well received. It was the first good bit of news we'd had in weeks. After listening to Catafalk's story about finding a room at Caleb's hotel, Mum insisted that he stay with us until he was more settled. Catafalk blushed at the generosity and mumbled a sincere thank you.

"But where's he going to stay?" Faith asked.

"He'll sleep in Maddie's room."

It was the first time since the bank men came that she had uttered his name. It was the first time that any of us had mentioned him, even though he was constantly in our thoughts. We didn't need to ask where Dad went on his long walks. We all knew, without asking, that he was out searching for his son.

"But what if he comes back?" I asked.

Mum sighed. "Then we'll figure something else out."

"He is coming back, isn't he?"

Mum didn't have an answer to that.

With the priest staying with us, Garfaxians made the daily pilgrimage up the hill to our house to ask for his help in all manner of spiritual affair. Right after finishing breakfast, he'd be off, visiting people in their homes, walking with them through the tombstones of the graveyard that looked over the bay, counselling them in their confusion, or checking on our local church.

Catafalk spent little time in the church. After a decade of ministering on the hoods of abandoned cars, in the living rooms of families, he found the building too restrictive. He found it difficult to breathe. This suited the local parishioners just fine, as they had gotten used to leaning on each other through the hard times with their own reading of scripture.

Despite all this, the problem facing the village didn't go away. Even though the Franklins removed the piles of pipes, tubing, and wire from their lawn, squirrelling them away in shacks and storage rooms, everyone knew that it would only be a matter of time before things ran out. In the Two-Stone, men huddled around tables, around their drinks, and tried to figure out what to do next. A few brought out my father's book in hopes that it would shed some light on the subject, but it only made them feel worse.

"Maybe we should leave," someone said.

But no one wanted to hear that.

Garfaxians began going to the movies again in droves, and I was busy running the projection booth at Denver's theatre. It got so busy that Denver set up a cot for me to sleep between reels and an alarm clock beside me to make sure I didn't miss a single one. We played the same films that we had for the last thirty years. Sometimes I'd go down into the theatre and watch people holding hands and mouthing along to the words.

As for Denver, he was around less and less. He was often seen walking through the village to call on Aunt Connie. When I asked him about it, trying hard to hide my smile, he smiled back and shook his finger at me. "You mind your own damn business," he said. "You only have to worry about keeping the movies going."

"So what are you going to do?" Sara asked me during one film, the two of us curled up together in the cot. She meant to whisper, but it came out as a shout. The noise from the projector was fierce, and we both had to yell to be heard.

"Everything's going to be fine," I shouted. "The Franklins will figure something out."

And I meant it. I really, really meant it.

We listened to the infernal rattling of the projector. Sara wrapped her hands over my own. "And if they don't?"

But I didn't hear that. I'm not even sure now that she said it. Beside us the alarm clock went off, signalling the need to change to the final reel of the film. I got up.

IT'S AMAZING SOMETIMES what some people see and others don't.

Despite her ability to occasionally remember the future, my mother was a bit surprised when my father said to her, one night during the middle of the construction of Caleb's hotel, that Faith and Sunny would get married.

My parents were in the living room, sitting together on the couch that looks into the kitchen. Faith and Sunny were doing the dishes, with Faith washing and Sunny drying before putting them away. That was pretty much all they were doing. A few words passed between them, just stories about what had gone on that day, plans they had for the weekend, but that was enough for Cadmus.

"You're a romantic," my mother said, poking him in the ribs. "All men are."

Dad nodded. "That's true. But they'll end up together, I think."

"And what makes you say that?"

My father pointed at his daughter and her boyfriend doing dishes. "That."

"They're just cleaning up."

Dad shook his head. "Yeah, but it's the way they're doing it."

Mum looked closer. "They don't have a lot in common," she said.

"We don't have a lot in common either, if you'll remember."

"All right, fine. I just don't see it."

Dad pointed again. "You see how they talk to each other? How they work together?"

"Yeah."

"Other people might do it differently. If they were friends, they'd talk more, maybe. But they're a couple. Like they're already married."

And Mum looked at him then. She slid her hand across her lap, across his and held his hand. "You know, sometimes I wish I could see things the way you see things."

Dad grinned. "I wish that, too. But you're all right."

"I'm all right?" Mum asked, smiling now.

"Yup. Perfectly serviceable. There's not another woman like you."

Mum leaned into my father's shoulder and he brought his arm around her. Together they watched the couple finish up the dishes. When Sunny put the last dish away and Faith drained the sink, they turned and sort of just stood there on the linoleum, looking at each other, saying very little.

"Fine, you've convinced me," my mother said.

WHEN YOU THINK of marriage proposals, you think about stories you've heard, movies you've seen. You conjure up the image of an expensive meal at a nice restaurant, the rise of violins, the getting down on one knee, and the opening of a small box. Attention flickers between eyes and ring. Tears form. Hands go to one's mouth. Smiles all around and then a large hug. A crushing of two bodies. Blushing. Yes. Oh, of course, yes. And if there are any witnesses, all eyes are on you. The two of you. Everybody's grinning, and they'll go home that night and tell the story of being party to your proposal. There will be clapping, and for years afterwards you'll remember that clapping.

Which is a really nice moment. The kind of moment you look forward to and in some way expect for yourself for a very long time.

To his credit, Sunny tried his best.

Not that they hadn't discussed marriage before. During the building of Caleb Anson's hotel, it became clear to them that there was something solid between them, a mutual respect and affection that they could build a life on. They never said it, of course. Faith has never been the kind of person to gush about her feelings. Neither has Sunny. Part of that confident air that I talked about before, that air that engenders feelings of admiration amongst those around you, is not talking about what's on your mind so much.

They had talked about marriage over the course of a few months. Neither of them posed it as a question. If Faith visited Sunny at the hotel and Sunny showed her one of the completed rooms, or a staircase that he had worked on that he was particularly proud of, he might say to her, "When we're married, I'd like to have a staircase like this in our house. You can build a good house around a staircase like this."

And she'd look at him and nod. "It's a very nice staircase."

Or when they were out at the Two-Stone with their friends, or maybe down at Quill Lake for the summer, and watching a couple hang off each other, tell out loud the stories of how they had met and all the other stories couples tell and retell about themselves, Faith would lean over to Sunny and say, "We're never going to be like that. Not even when we're fifty and old."

And Sunny in response would move his hand to place it on her breast.

But a proposal is different. There are rules. Or, at least, there seem to be. And Sunny tried to follow those rules. One day, when Faith was busy, he came over and sat down with my father and told him about his plans to ask Faith to marry him.

Dad listened to the whole speech, and there was a speech. When he was finished, Dad waited for him to keep talking, but he didn't. He just finished.

"And?" Cadmus asked.

Sunny frowned. "And what?"

"Why are you telling me this?"

"Um, well, I was kind of asking for your permission."

"Oh." Dad said, surprised. He looked around him for a moment, suddenly perplexed by the situation he found himself in. "I didn't realize that was what you were going for."

"Sorry," Sunny blurted. "I thought I mentioned that when I talked about respecting you and everything. Not wanting to step over my bounds."

"Yeah. I remember. I just didn't think you were asking me."

"I was."

"Oh."

"Yeah."

Dad looked at the floor, then at Sunny, who was waiting on his next word. Then he looked at the floor again, and sighed. "I still don't see what this has to do with me."

Sunny explained it again. Word for word, he repeated the speech. Dad interrupted him in the middle. "No, I understand that. That's great. But, it's not me you have to ask."

"I don't have to talk to Mrs. Brodie, do I?" Sunny winced.

Dad laughed. "No. I wouldn't put you through that. Although I'm sure she'd have a lot of fun with you, Sun. She does like to make nervous people sweat."

"I've noticed."

"It's an attractive quality in a woman."

"Yes."

"But not for someone in your position, I'd imagine?"

"No."

"Right. Look. I like you. I like your family. I like how you treat my daughter. But when it comes down to it, it doesn't matter what I think.

You have to ask her."

Sunny nodded. "Right."

"Do you have a ring?"

Sunny did have a ring. It had been his mother's. Lizzie gave it to him when he confided in her his plan. She hugged him, then. Held him close. "I love this," she cackled.

"Thanks."

"You're so nervous. It's great."

Sunny's plan was simple. In Garfax there are no expensive meals. No nice restaurants. There are violins and people who play them, but he knew Faith wouldn't appreciate a crowd. He thought that he might propose to her at Quill Lake, until he remembered how they met and got together and figured that wasn't the best place.

Saturday mornings were sacred times for the two of them during that period of construction. They both had the day off work and would lie in bed through the morning and into the afternoon. If one woke up before the other, they'd wait for the other to wake up, enjoying the warmth shared between their two bodies. They had signals to show when they were awake or not, although they weren't really necessary.

"She smells different when she sleeps," Sunny told me once, just before the wedding. "I can always tell when she wakes up, because the smell disappears."

"What smell?"

"It's kind of like cinnamon," he explained.

The Saturday morning that Sunny proposed marriage to my sister, he hadn't slept for the entire night. He lay behind her, his arms around her, waiting for her to stir. They'd often talk for hours during the morning, lying together like that, catching up after having spent the week working. He stared at the clock, willing the minutes to pass quicker. He watched the light change in the room. The black of night turn to the dark blue of early morning before it got broken up by all kinds of whites, yellows, and oranges from the sun coming through the window.

He had the ring in a box in the space between the mattress and the headboard, so that he could reach for it at the right moment and have it appear in front of her face, emerging in his hand from beneath a pillow.

Faith eventually woke up, stretched beside him. And they talked. For the life of them, neither can tell me what they talked about. When the time came, Sunny recited yet another speech that he had prepared for the occasion.

"What are you doing?" Faith interrupted, in the middle of hearing a recitation of all the things Sunny found attractive about her.

"Let me finish," Sunny said.

And then, when he was describing how he felt when he first saw her, first kissed her, she interrupted again. "What's wrong? You never talk like this."

"There's nothing wrong. Be quiet."

Faith sighed and went back to listening. Sunny, a little irritated now, continued. Until the moment arrived and he grabbed the box and pulled it out from under the pillow.

"Faith Brodie," he said. "Will you marry me?" And he opened the lid of the box.

Faith didn't say anything. Sunny didn't say anything.

There was nothing in the box.

"Is this a joke?" Faith asked.

Sunny dropped the box and jumped over Faith, digging behind the mattress for the ring. "It was there," he said. "Right there. It must have fallen."

Faith sat up, giving him space for his search. "Is this my proposal?"

"Give me a second," Sunny said. But he couldn't find it. "It must be under the bed. Get up." Both of them got out of bed. Sunny lifted the mattress up off the frame. "Can you turn on the light?" he asked, stepping into the frame, getting down on his knees.

Faith turned on the lamp.

A few seconds later, having searched through the dark carpet, Sunny stood up holding his mother's wedding ring in his hand. Without ceremony, he pushed that hand towards Faith. "Sorry about that."

Faith took it from him, brushed off a bit of carpet hair.

"So?"

"You're ridiculous, you know that?" Faith said, stepping into the bed frame and next to Sunny. She pulled him towards her and hugged him. "What am I going to do with you?"

Sunny relaxed. Then he frowned. "That was a yes, right?"

Faith tapped him gently on the head with the palm of her hand.

"Pay attention," she said.

My sister left on the last bus ever to pass through Garfax.

For years the company that ran the buses threatened to cut off service if the village didn't widen the roads. More accidents, they argued, occurred within ten miles of Garfax than on any other stretch of highway in the province. Roads narrowed at random intervals, producing sharp corners and blind spots. High beams from abandoned cars disappeared into the mess of pines, reflecting back distracting ghost lights.

Not to mention the lack of business the company did when it came to Garfax. What few tourists we had were accidental. They were on their way to somewhere else and ended up getting turned around in the maze of deteriorating roads with contradictory signs. Training new bus drivers was an exercise in futility. The only man who knew how to drive them with any accuracy was Jamie Felps. When my mother went to water, it was he who drove the bus the night my father returned.

Jamie lived in the village. Over the years he had become more of a gas station attendant than a driver of buses. The only trips he ever made were the biweekly jaunts for more gasoline, which he brought back to the small company hut located next to a company gas pump that locals made use of. Selling and pumping gas had been the only thing keeping him there until Caleb Anson's hotel failed and the future began to look infinitely finite and bleak.

A couple of months after the bank men left, Jamie announced in the middle of the Two-Stone that his location had been cancelled by his company and he would be returning to his hometown of Benning the following week. Within hours he was swarmed by Garfaxians, none more worried than the Franklins, who depended on the services he provided as gas man.

"I'm sorry," he mumbled through a drink. "But who you are you kidding anyway?"

When Faith heard the news, she threw on her coat and ran down the hill to see if she could catch Jamie at his office.

Faith has always wanted to leave Garfax. In this she was a bit of an oddity. Few people ever leave Garfax, and many who do often return. But for Faith there was no argument, no getting around it. She wanted to leave Garfax. She wanted to see the world. One of the most attractive things about Sunny was that he didn't want to stay in the village either.

The day Faith agreed to marry Sunny, they walked down to the small bus station and bought two open tickets out of Garfax and into Benning.

"After we're married," Faith said that afternoon, while telling us the good news, "we're leaving on the bus."

"So when are you getting married?" Cadmus asked, beaming.

"When we have enough money. We want to get enough saved so we can start somewhere properly."

"Where were you thinking of going?" Mum asked.

"Alberta," Sunny said. "I'm always hearing there's lots of work there."

Faith found Jamie in his hut, in the office that occupied most of the space, going through boxes of papers, receipts, and company paraphernalia. Lifting up the door that separated customer from clerk, she pushed the two tickets she had bought with Sunny into the older man's face.

"What about my tickets?" she demanded.

Jamie, still drunk from the Two-Stone, gazed for a moment at the tickets. "I can refund them now, if you'd like?"

"I don't want a refund," she screamed. "I want the bus. I have the right to have a bus when I want one."

"I'm sorry," Jamie mumbled. "But I'm leaving in a week. There'll be no more buses after that."

Faith clenched her fist around the tickets, crumpling the paper. She opened and closed her mouth, then, turning, walked back up the hill, in through the front door, and into the kitchen.

"You should have told me," she said to Mum, who was speaking with me at the time.

"I don't know everything, Faith."

Faith opened and closed her mouth again. Then she sat down, defeated, at the kitchen table. "What am I supposed to do now?"

"You don't leave on a bus," I pointed out. "When you get married, you can just get someone to drive you to Benning. You could ask Lizzie."

But Faith wasn't listening. She was thinking of the piles of tubing, pipes, and wires on the lawn of the Franklin lawn. She was thinking that she didn't have to be our mother to see Garfax eventually becoming a place filled with vehicles without gasoline, a place few cars ever passed through anyway.

"I have to leave," she said, in a small voice.

Mum walked over to her, behind her, and put a hand on her shoulder. "Then you should leave."

"But we don't have enough money yet. We're not even married yet."

Mum nodded. "Your father and I can help you with the money."

"No," Faith said, shaking her head. "You can't do that."

"Don't you tell me what I can and cannot do."

Faith sighed. "But what about getting married. I wanted to—"

"Faith," Mum said, squeezing her shoulder. "If you want to leave, you should leave. If you want to get married, we can see what we can do. When does the last bus leave?"

"A week."

Mum coughed. "A week? Well, more has been done in less time before, I suppose."

FOR THE SECOND TIME in my life, our house began to move again. As soon as the decision had been made that Faith and Sunny would be on that last bus out of the village, and that they would get married before they did so, Faith was on the phone. By the end of the first hour, there were people in our house. Dad, Sunny, and I were entrusted with several pages of lists, errands to perform. The older women set up camp in our living room and delegated the work down to their Canadian daughters-in-law, who scurried through the village on their own missions.

It got so busy that the dead relatives had to give up the ghost of their game altogether, and move out into the privacy of the pines to get some peace and quiet.

Suddenly it was as if the last two years hadn't happened. Men who had wept bitterly about the failure of Caleb's hotel laughed with Sunny as they rounded up the necessary supplies and tried on their best clothes from a hundred years ago, delighting if they fit and blushing if they didn't. Women began talking to my mother again, joking with her, telling her gossip and all the old stories from before she went to water. She moved through the house the way she once did, going from person to person, story to story, and then moving on before the telling got stale.

Dad took me out on his walks into the pines to look for Maddox. That was the only thing that hadn't changed. He didn't tell me that was what we were doing. We weren't to mention it. He just told me that he needed my help and off we'd go. For the better part of three days, we walked up and down the hills that surround the bay, coming across all sorts of wreckage that we sometimes recognized and other times didn't. I made sure we checked the old cars where Maddox used to show me magic tricks, the sections of Ester Anson's house where he used to tell me stories, but we never found him.

We didn't talk much during the walks. When he did talk, Dad often said things that didn't make a lot of sense. For an hour, we wouldn't have said a word and then he'd start in the middle of a story, telling it as if I had listened to the whole thing before. He didn't look at me when he spoke. He looked away into the pines. I pulled a lighter out of my pocket and struck it in front of him. He'd blink a bit, gather himself, then continue walking as if nothing had happened.

Two days before the wedding, in the morning when I expected Dad to come down the stairs and for us to go out into the pines again, he surprised me by handing me a kilt. "Try it on," he said.

"Why?" I asked.

"Because you need to have something proper to wear for the wedding."

"But I have a kilt."

Dad shook his head. "That won't fit. You haven't worn that since you were a child. Try that one on. It was your brother's."

"But what is he going to wear?"

Dad looked at me. "Just try it on."

After I tried on the kilt and found that it fit, Dad handed me the rest of the clothes to go with it. The formal shirt and black jacket. The sporran and the dress shoes. That evening I took them round to Sara's to show her.

"You have nice legs," she pointed out, watching from her vantage point on the couch.

I looked down at my legs. "Thanks."

Sara stood up and straightened my black bow tie. "You look really nice, Oz."

"Thanks. It feels kind of strange, though."

"I know. But it looks good on you."

"So what are you going to wear?" I asked, brushing a rain-soaked length of hair away from her face.

Sara smiled. "That's something I'm going to leave for a surprise."

HERE'S A PICTURE. It's the last picture I have here with me, and that's fitting because it's the last professional photograph my father ever took. It's a group photo. We're all in it.

Faith and Sunny are centre, of course. Sunny is wearing his father's tuxedo, a suit that the elder Parks only wore twice in his life before he died. It fits Sunny well, and there were many times that night when Lizzie came up to me, cradling a bottle of beer against her neck, looking out across our front lawn at my sister and her brother twirling around each other in the fading light, and told me with a break in her voice that he looked just like their father when he was that age.

"I've seen pictures," she told me.

Faith is wearing a wedding dress that is far too formal and frilly for her liking. She's grinning in the photo like an idiot. It's a self-deprecating grin. One that, to me, seems like it acknowledges the absurdity of the whole event. It's a grin that says, "Look at what these crazy people have me doing now. I must be insane." But it's a happy grin, too. She can be as sarcastic about it as she wants, but in the picture my sister is having the time of her life.

Behind them is Catafalk. In most of the wedding photos Dad took during his career, he would usually have the priest stand to one side or another.

"A wedding photograph is about the couple. About the family. Not the priest. But with him I couldn't resist having him in the middle."

I can see what he means. One side of his face shaved, the other not, he parts the two families perfectly. He isn't smiling. His lips are together. A straight line. He looks very much like a man waiting for the next strange thing to happen.

My parents stand behind Faith. Like everyone else, they are wearing their best. Dad is wearing his kilt, and wearing it always makes him stand up straighter. He is the tallest man in the group and is smiling proudly. His arm is linked with my mother's, who is also smiling.

Lizzie stands for her parents beside her brother. Her face is red from already having had too much to drink and from crying just before this picture was taken. She is dressed the simplest of the group. A plain light blue dress that falls nicely on her. Her hands are clasped, one plastic and one flesh, holding each other. You can't tell from the picture, but her legs are shaking.

Sara and I are standing next to my parents. I'm dressed in my brother's clothes and she is wearing a green dress that is stunning. It doesn't have any shoulders to it.

"So it wouldn't get stained in the picture," she explained to me later, as we walked back through the village to her house. In most of the pictures she has of herself, there is a damp spot that shows around her shoulders from her permanently rain-soaked hair.

"You have nice shoulders," I said.

"Thanks."

And we bumped against each other, more than a little drunk.

I kept thinking Maddox would show up, but he didn't. When the phone rang in the middle of the night, I'd pick it up, thinking it was him only to find it was one of the Canadian daughters-in-law asking their mothers-in-law about some esoteric detail in the mission they had been sent on. I passed the phone on to the small circle of old women in the living room, talking and smoking like a bunch of conspirators.

After the ceremony and after the pictures, after the dancing and after the drinking, when it was time for the bus to go, we all went down, the whole village, to see Faith and Sunny off. They weren't the only ones leaving. Along with Jamie Felps and all his belongings, a number of other Garfaxians took the opportunity to leave. We said our long goodbyes, promising visits and bursting into tears and hugs.

The bus left later than expected, delayed from all the sudden confessions and praises. Jamie didn't seem to mind, thrilled to finally be a part of the village.

"This is what a bus driver's life should always be like," he mused.

It's a nice photograph. There are little details in it that you'd have to know the people to catch. Aunt Connie and Denver are in there as well. They're standing a respectful distance apart, but you can see them holding hands in the space between my parents. If you didn't know any better, if you were just seeing this photograph on its own, without the story, you'd think that this was it. You wouldn't notice that my brother isn't there. You wouldn't pick up on the suddenness of it all. You would only think that it was wonderful.

VIII

Wonderfull

THINGS BEGAN TO FALL APART within a year of my sister's wedding.

In the beginning it was little things. A few houses lost power, or maybe lost telephone reception. Nothing large. Nobody drove as much as they used to. The Franklins figured out a way around the gasoline problem, taking over the shipment and refuelling of the pump themselves. But still, we drove less. We didn't know how long they would be able to keep that up.

Then people started to leave. First it was one at a time. Young people, mostly. They'd pack in the evening and leave in the morning, taking their car, or if they didn't drive, get Lizzie to take them all the way to Benning. We'd knock on their doors when they didn't show up for work. We'd look through their windows or maybe walk into their rooms, only to find everything gone.

No one left notes.

Dad continued his long walks through the pines, and over time those walks grew longer. We didn't talk about it, but we didn't need to. It made no difference that Maddox wouldn't be there, that there would be no reason he would stay out in the trees for a whole year. That was the last place Dad heard he was, though. That's the last time anyone saw his eldest. So until he heard someone say different, he kept up his walks.

But they started to take a toll. Like I said, they were getting longer and longer. Once or twice I went with him, but for the most part he went by himself, after he was finished with whatever patchwork job he had going with Tom. Despite an overabundance of work, work that had been neglected during the construction of the hotel, Tom and Dad had trouble getting the materials. The Franklins, and I say the Franklins because no one saw Joseph after that, held a complete monopoly over the wires, pipes, tubing, and other materials needed.

Like he had done for most of his life, Dad began to drift back and forth between sleeping and waking without noticing very much. Sometimes he'd go walking for the better part of a day and into a night, and he'd come back without a real account of where he had been and what he had seen. When asked by Mum, he'd say he spoke with people who had left Garfax months or years before, or who never lived here in the first place.

Mum asked Catafalk to speak to him, and the priest did his best, accompanying my father on some of these walks. After a few weeks of spending time with him, Catafalk returned and told my mother that there was nothing he could do for him. "He's lost," Catafalk said, sadly. "And there isn't a one who can help him until he finds what he's looking for."

Listening to this, Mum nodded and thanked Catafalk for all his help.

One time Dad disappeared for almost three days. We went searching on the morning of the second day, and only found him that evening when Denver Brail almost hit him with his bus coming back from Mantua.

"He was just wandering out there," he told me. "I flicked my headlights at him and then he collapsed."

Back home, we nursed him through the water his body desperately needed and the food he craved. Mum and I spoke later out on the verandah.

"We're going to have to do something about this," I told her.

"There's nothing we can do."

"What happens if he doesn't find his way back one of these days?"

But she didn't have an answer to that.

WITHIN THE FIRST SIX MONTHS, Sara started to talk about leaving as well. Through Lizzie, she had managed to get her hands on some university applications. And while it was tricky for an actual university to acknowledge the grades of a high school located in a village that doesn't exist on paper, she seemed confident that with her marks, she would be able to get in.

"There's no future for me here," she told me once as we lay in bed.

I looked over at her, saw her silhouette in red off the alarm clock numbers. "I'm here," I said.

She rolled over and looked at me. "There's no future for you here, either. You can come with me. You can get a job. Or go to school."

I shook my head. "I can't. Not with Dad the way he is. Not until Maddox comes back home."

"You could always tie him to the bed," Sara said. "Isn't that what your mother used to do sometimes?"

"No," I replied. "We couldn't do that to him. Not permanently. Look, when Maddox comes back, it won't be my responsibility anymore. I'll be able to leave."

Sara sighed. "Maddox isn't coming back, Oz."

"Yes, he is. You don't know that he isn't."

By some strange twist of luck, aided in ways that I never discovered by Aunt Connie, Sara gained acceptance into university. At the end of the first year since my sister left, I helped Sara pack her things into the back of Lizzie's cab.

"So when will you come and see me?" Sara asked.

"As soon as I can," I promised.

She gave me this sad look then, reached over, grabbed my hand, and squeezed. "I don't want you to end up staying here," she said. "I want you to come with me. As soon as you can."

"As soon as I can," I said. "I will."

I watched her drive away in Lizzie's cab, watched her go up and over the hill and disappear into that mess of pines that makes the roads narrower and narrower with every passing year, and then I turned and walked back home.

AND DAD CONTINUED TO DRIFT.

Sometimes, when I was in the living room, half-asleep and watching some static on the television, volume turned all the way down, I'd hear the phone ring. A minor heart attack later, I'd have the receiver in my hand, pressed up against my ear, and listen to the sound on the other end.

And I'd say, "Maddie?"

But the person on the other end never said anything. I only heard breathing. The connections in Garfax have always been weak. We hear static, the sound of wind over the wires, whenever we pick up the phone. So I listened to that sound. I said his name again. I told him that we missed him and loved him and wanted him to come home.

A few minutes later, the phone would go dead and for the rest of that night, I'd wonder if I'd dreamt it all. I wouldn't be able to sleep. My head was just full of all these thoughts. I imagined my brother standing on the verandah, looking in at me through the window. The image was so strong that the hairs on the back of my neck stood on end.

Where would he be staying? Would he be at Quill Lake, making a living by the water's edge, partying it up with the few who still made the yearly pilgrimage, showing them magic tricks? Would he have moved to Mantua, that colony of former Garfaxians and other people from all the disappeared villages, where there was at least some steady work? Or maybe he slept in cars in the middle of the pines? It wasn't that uncommon. That thought scared me the most. Thinking of him out there in the dark, amidst the trees, stretched out in the back seat of a car with its windshield broke and some blood on the dashboard.

When I went for my own walks through the pines, everything I saw turned into evidence of his passing. I came across a metal ladder propped up against a tree, all rusted from being left out exposed. There were nests in the tree overhead. Empty nests that had been abandoned. I remembered the story he told me about raven eggs and pictured him climbing trees all over the pines, looking for the right one.

I thought of Timothy Franklin.

And all these thoughts distracted me so constantly, with no barrier between waking and sleeping, that I'd wonder if I was becoming more and more like my father, whose appearance in rooms at odd times now occurred with startling regularity.

Often I found myself in a bedroom, or walking down to the basement carrying boxes, thinking I was alone only to find Dad standing there, swaying back and forth, humming to himself. The only thing that made the room feel full except for me were the sounds he made.

We took, Mum and I, to carrying flashlights with us wherever we went, so if we found him in a state of somnambulance, we could wake him, take his hand, and lead him back upstairs.

As more and more of the young people left, some families started to migrate as well. Families are harder to move quietly and quickly than individuals. They never seemed to get away without us seeing them or hearing about it. If pushed, they'd say that they'd just had enough. That they saw the way the wind was blowing and they didn't want to be there when it all came down.

"Don't you make any mistake," they'd say, hanging their heads out the driver's side window. "This can't last for much longer."

And for the people who stayed, the auld ones like Aunt Connie and Denver Brail, Thomas Lonnie and Gregory Peck, Hen Barton and even Catafalk, each passing brought on a wave of fierce nostalgia. When no one showed up for a film, and fewer and fewer came each week, Denver would pull me into the theatre and tell me stories about Garfax that I'd never heard before. Suddenly, stories abounded. More so than in any other time before. And I'd listen. People would invite me round so that I'd listen. I asked about my mother often, because since everything that happened that summer morning, I wondered how it fit with everything else that followed. I tried to put the pieces together like some sort of mystery, hoping it would give me an answer.

THREE MONTHS INTO THE SECOND YEAR, Mum and I were having breakfast at the kitchen table when she looked over at me and said, in the simplest voice, "I'm going to die soon, Oswald."

I put my fork down.

"What do you mean you're going to die?"

She shrugged. "I mean what I mean."

"You've seen it?"

"I know it."

"When's it going to happen?"

"I don't know specifically. But probably soon."

It was like it was nothing to her. She was so calm and collected about the whole affair.

"Have you told Dad yet?"

"No."

"Are you going to?"

Mum considered it. "No. I don't think so."

I called Faith in Calgary. She answered the phone laughing.

"Hello."

"Hey."

"Hey, stranger. How's it going?"

"Are you busy?"

Sunny yelled something in the background. "Yeah, a little. What's up?"

I sighed. "Mum. She says she's going to die."

"What?"

I repeated myself. "She says she saw it."

"Are you fucking with me?"

"No."

"I'm going to call her."

Mum stopped talking to me for weeks after that. If she passed me on the stairs, she ignored me. Plates of food were left in the fridge wrapped in plastic.

Faith didn't return my calls either. I moved boxes of my stuff over to an empty room in the motel, where they sat unopened in towers. When the silence got too much, when I was done listening to stories and just wanted to talk, I called Sara.

"I can't talk to anyone," I told her.

"What's wrong?"

I relayed to her the story with my mother. Informed her of how things were going in the village. How more people were leaving all the time.

"You need to leave," she said.

"I can't. You know I can't."

And that would be the end of that phone call.

Dad stopped coming home altogether. He'd sleepwalk through whatever work he had, then disappear into the pines. I'd find him on the side of the road, and even when I flashed lights in his eyes, he didn't want to come back with me. His eyes were red, almost dusty from not having closed in so long. I brought him sweaters, blankets, anything to keep dry. I brought him food. I spent time with him.

The only thing he ever noticed was the food.

The weather began to turn toward the beginning of the fall. People in the village, even those up on the hill, started to wear sweaters, even indoors. I watched from the concession stand as families tilted forward and trudged their way against the winds. One night, after my last showing, I went into the theatre to clean out the aisles and found Mum staring at the screen. She wore her housecoat and the rubber boots she used to do gardening with.

"Mum?"

She turned. "Hey."

I left the industrial-sized black garbage bag in the aisle and went over to sit beside her. "What's going on?"

"The seventeenth," she said. "'I'm going to fall down the basement stairs on the seventeenth."

She even gave me a time.

I DREAMED another conversation with Maddox, except this time he spoke.

"Oswald," he croaked. "I swallowed it. I swallowed the egg."

I rubbed sleep out of my eyes and checked the clock. "Maddie, it's 11:30."

The line went silent for a moment. "Oh."

"What time is it with you?"

"8:30."

"Where are you?"

And he started crying. My shoulders dropped. I had called Faith the day before and told her what Mum said in the theatre. But I had been awake then.

"Maddox?"

"I swallowed it, Oz. I can't get it out. I've tried making myself sick. It doesn't work."

In the dark, I thought about all the ghost stories he told me growing up. Poltergeists that pushed people down stairs and rattled chains. I heard the click-clacking of domino tiles on wood. "Where are you?"

"You're not listening."

I couldn't speak. I lay back on the sofa, set the cradle to rest against my ear. He breathed heavy across distance. He cried and I watched the numbers tick off the clock on the VCR.

He hung up seven minutes after midnight. I lay down on the couch and woke up to Mum asking me if I wanted hash browns.

"Sure."

I waited at the house for Faith to arrive. I picked up the phone and called Denver.

"I won't be able to come in for the next couple of days," I told him. "There's some stuff at home I've got to deal with."

"Everything all right?"

"Everything's wonderful."

Aunt Connie dropped by in the afternoon and asked Mum if she wanted to come to the movie theatre with her. Mum looked at me. "I think I've got plans with my son tonight."

I shook my head, waved them both off. "Don't worry about it. Have fun."

When they left, I picked up Dad's toolbox from the shed and opened the door to the basement stairs. I pulled the string light and started looking for problems. I wobbled the banister to see if it had any give. Not much. I tightened the screws as far as I could without stripping them. I tested each stair by bouncing up and down. They creaked. Sliding out the blade of the exacto knife, I peeled the layer of shag carpet off in strips, tossing them in a pile at the foot of the stairs.

The work took a few hours. I hammered down the staples that held the carpet so they lay flush with the wood. I sanded the frayed edges. The shredded shag material filled two garbage bags. I double bagged them and left them at the foot of the driveway with the trash cans. After that, I walked down into the village and bought a brighter light bulb, shoe-laces, and a small screw-in coat hook. When I got home, I cleaned up with a broom and returned Dad's old toolbox to the shed.

I was drinking milk and playing solitaire dominoes when Mum came back.

"How was it?"

She smiled. "Fine."

I had left the door to the basement open. Seeing this, Mum moved to close it. "What did you do?"

I told her.

Mum sighed. "You can't save me," she said.

"Yes I can."

Mum turned off the light and closed the door. "Thanks."

"Do you want to play a set?"

"No," she said, shaking her head. "I think I'm just going to go to bed."

We walked on eggshells for the rest of the week. Faith drove up in a rental car she picked up in Benning. "How do you feel?" she asked Mum, before she even took off her shoes.

"I feel fine."

"Have you been to see a doctor?"

"I'm not sick."

"So you haven't?"

"Faith. Take off your shoes."

"She looks fine," Faith said later, after Mum went upstairs to bed.

"That's because she's not sick. She says she's going to fall down the basement stairs."

"What happens if we don't let her near them?"

I shrugged. "I don't think it works like that."

Faith visited Dad in the pines. She came home red-faced. "He's not coming back," she said.

"Did he talk to you?"

"No."

We sat Mum down in the morning. "What do you want to do today? We'll do anything."

"You don't have to do this."

"Mum," Faith said. "What do you want to do?"

We took walks down to the village and played an improvised mini-golf on the beach. We went to the wharf and looked out at the abandoned, derelict fishing boats. From the cabinet beneath the shelves in the living room, Mum pulled out old videotapes and we watched them, the three of us, curled up on the couch, eating popcorn.

I forgot that we had taken so many videos growing up. When I think about childhood, I tend to think about it in photographs my father took, or ones Mum took at special occasions. But for a time there was a video camera. We saw Lizzie Parks dwelling at the periphery before Mum put her in our house before going to water. We saw birthday parties for all three of us. Denver Brail came over to the house and played dominoes with Dad. Mum had some of her friends over, including Aunt Connie. They drank and smoked and laughed. There's one video of the three of us, Maddox, Faith, and me, sitting on the middle landing of the stairs in our pajamas listening to the noise downstairs, desperate to go down and join the fun but scared that if we moved we'd be sent up to bed.

And sometimes there were just the two of us. Mum and I. And we'd talk. I'd ask her questions. Push her for answers about going to water, about what all of it meant. I asked her about seeing the future, and she told me it was more like remembering than actually seeing.

I asked about the Franklin boy. I asked about Dad.

And she told me story after story after story, so that it all started to wash over me in waves. I tried to find my place in that sea.

ON THE SEVENTEENTH, Mum wouldn't leave the house. "I know what you're trying to do," she said.

"What?"

"That's not the way this works."

"Let's just go and see one movie."

She came for one, then left with Faith. I ran one more, then asked Denver to take over. For dinner we had a feast in the living room. We crashed out on the couch, watching the rest of the home videos, and when those were finished, we simply talked.

"'Should I get Dad?" I asked, looking over at Mum.

She shook her head. "No."

"I could. I could just drive down there and bring him back."

"No." Mum ran her hand through Faith's hair, who slept next to her on the couch.

"Can I get you anything?"

Mum smiled. "It's not going to happen for a little while."

But we both knew what time it was.

Five minutes left.

She slapped her hands against her knees and moved to stand up.

"Where are you going?"

"To get my cigarettes."

"Don't," I said. "Please."

Mum sighed and looked at me.

"Just give me ten more minutes."

And suddenly, just saying it like that, got me more scared than I had ever been since she told me. I grabbed her hand and squeezed. "Please, Mum."

You see, a part of me didn't believe her. Despite all that had happened before. Because she was my Mum. And she was still so young. And beautiful. And she wasn't sick at all. And because I fixed the stairs and if she didn't go near the stairs for another five minutes, everything would be all right. She would be all right and then things could be different. There wouldn't be any of this bullshit. Because. Because I would have saved her. And if I saved her, then anything was possible. Because my mother remembered the future, and if I changed that, if I saved her and changed that, then anything was possible. Maddox could come home. Dad would wake up. Sara would come back. And we'd live here together. In Garfax. And no one would ever die, or leave, and we'd be all right. We'd all just be all right. Like it used to be. And none of us would ever have to leave. Because we were all so healthy and young. Because there was just so much more wonder left to see.

"All right," Mum said, seeing the tears in my eyes. Ten more minutes.

And we didn't talk. We just sat there, my mother, who I've always been the most alike but never really understood, and I. I stroked her knuckles with my thumb and she did the same.

It must have been fifteen minutes when she said something. "When you were born," she told me. "I was very sick. I wasn't sick with Maddox, and I wasn't sick with Faith. But I was sick with you. And that had nothing to do with you. That wasn't your fault. It was the medicine the doctors put me on."

"You've told me before."

"I know. So for the first few days I couldn't really move or hold you or do anything with you. But as soon as I could, as soon as they let me out, your father and I took you to the ocean. You were born in Benning, but we took you home with us here. We took you to the bay, onto the beach. It was morning. Very early morning. I was still a bit drugged up with the medicine they'd given me, but I wanted very much to take you to see the ocean. I wanted you to see that as soon as possible."

"I know."

Mum looked at the clock. "Twenty minutes."

I could barely breathe.

"I'm going for those cigarettes now."

Stepping over my legs, Mum walked into the kitchen. I leaned forward and grabbed the remote, rewound the tape. It was a birthday party. I couldn't remember which one. In reverse, the kids moved faster. They jumped up and down quickly, smiling every few seconds. I checked the time on the VCR and smiled when I saw that we had beat the time.

I smiled, and then heard my mother fall down the stairs.

It wasn't until much later that I realized what had happened. That she had systematically changed the time on all the clocks in the house, speeding it up by half an hour.

"She had a stroke," the doctor told us at the hospital. I stood there looking at the doctor, watching his mouth move, and I imagined Mum standing in the kitchen. She pulled a cigarette from her purse and lit it. Outside the kitchen window, she could see the treeline of the pines. She smiled.

Faith didn't want to go to the funeral. I convinced her. I had to drag Dad. He stood there and didn't move. Catafalk held the service. It was his first actual burial where the person had just recently died in years. When I got him home, Dad walked upstairs to his bedroom and closed the door behind him. The next morning he was gone. The front door swung open and I found him ten minutes later in the middle of the road, walking along in his pajamas. We drove home and I put him back in his bed.

The very next day, it started to rain. Lightly at first, but it didn't stop throughout all of the morning and into the afternoon. And by evening it was pouring down. I watched it from my bedroom window.

"I'm heading back," Faith said, when I came down. Her bags were stacked by the door.

"You can't stay for a little bit more?"

She shook her head. We hugged stiffly.

"You shouldn't stay," she told me. "There's plenty of jobs in Calgary. You could live with us for a bit. Get settled."

"I can't," I said. "Dad's alone now. Until Maddox comes home."

When she heard me say my brother's name, Faith nodded, gave me a sad look. She hugged me again. "Take care," she whispered into my ear. Then she was gone.

I tied Dad's door shut with a length of rope that I attached from the door knob to Maddox's old bedroom across the hall. He shuffled around at all hours, banging on the walls.

Sara called. "I heard about your Mum."

"Yeah."

"I'm sorry."

"I know."

"I would have come up. No one—"

"It's all right."

She didn't speak for a minute, then said: "Will you be coming now?"

IT CONTINUED to rain. The rain never stopped. As it went on, it intensified. After the first week, I started to worry. I walked down to the Two-Stone to see what everyone else was saying. I slipped three or four times on my way down, so that when I walked through the front doors, my clothes were covered in mud.

No one said it directly. I heard the story later through Denver. What people were saying, that is. That, being that the storm coincided with my mother's death, it was her doing. They called it Emma Brodie's storm.

The Franklins scrambled desperately to try and keep up with the demand, but more and more houses succumbed to the elements. Roofs caved in, or were torn off by winds. The one time I walked up the hill to Caleb Anson's hotel, I saw walls bulging and a few of the floors already shattered. I stepped in, called out for Caleb, but got no response.

Winds grew in intensity, and the fishermen had to abandon their boats. By the end of that week, the boats were little more than kindling, having been smashed over and over again in succession against the rocks. The ocean dragged away the wreckage, pulling it out and away to where we couldn't see it anymore.

Garfax's graveyard disappeared during one night of a particularly heavy downpour. The tombstones and grave markers were uprooted by the wind and water and carried, tumbling and smashing against each other, into the sea. The earth eroded away and more than one Garfaxian confessed to seeing coffins sail down the hill and into the water. When I went down the next morning to see the devastation, it looked as if there had never been anything there. I couldn't tell where anyone was buried, not even my mother. The ground was that smooth.

Catafalk was there. So was Denver.

"That was a fucking act of God," Denver said, looking at the smooth trail the graveyard had made in the slope on its way into the ocean.

"That seems pretty much par for the course," Catafalk responded, not the least bit surprised. I shoved my hands in my pockets and shivered in the downpour.

The roads were the next to go. Having never been properly serviced since the government historians came, they dissolved overnight and became rivers of dirt, stone, and mud. Electricity continued to flutter, until one night all of the lights in our house died altogether.

While Dad was still in a bad way during that time, it was the losing of the lights that pushed him completely over the edge. He stopped assuming he was awake at any hour of the day. For when he went to flick a light switch to check and see where he was, in dreams or in reality, he began to assume he was always in dreams.

I found us some old miners' helmets with headlamps and we wore these as we went about our daily business. We didn't bump into each other much. I let him out of his room after the storm intensified to such an extreme that even his sleepwalking did its best to avoid it. I found him having conversations with people who weren't there, crying over my mother's death, or telling the ends to stories he hadn't finished years ago.

One night I woke up to the sound of a baseball bat smashing into a wooden frame and breaking glass. I ran downstairs to find Dad breaking each and every clock in the house. Methodically moving from one to the next. I grabbed the bat from him and held him until he fell asleep again.

"Those clocks," he wept. "Those fucking clocks."

MY MOTHER'S STORM lasted for four months, and during that time most of Garfax was destroyed and washed out to sea. Bit by bit the pines seemed to draw closer, finally doing what they had been threatening to do since Townsend and Garfax discovered this bay so many years ago, pushing us all to water.

When I couldn't handle my father, I went into the village and spoke to the few people who remained or helped those who were leaving pack what they could and get them to Lizzie's cab. It seemed that no matter what the weather was, Lizzie made it through. Her cab was a beast. A warrior. Road or no road, she made it back and forth between Benning consistently.

"What's your secret?" I asked once, quaking in the cold.

She smiled, opening the trunk and showing me a chainsaw and several small cans of gas. "Lots of trees fallen between here and Benning," she said. "Sometimes you just have to cut your way through."

"What am I going to do?" I asked Denver. I was sitting with him and Aunt Connie in the theatre. The two of them were holding hands, sitting next to each other, regarding me as a couple might regard a stray.

"I think it's time for you to leave," they said.

"But my father," I said.

"You're not responsible. And Maddox isn't coming home."

And finally I started to believe that.

One afternoon, although it was hard to tell with all the rain when it was day and when it was night, I went and spoke to Catafalk. I told him I was leaving, and asked him if he wanted to come with me.

He shook his head.

"That's crazy," I told him.

He nodded. "I have to stay," he replied. "It took ten years for me to get here. It makes sense that I should be here to see the rest of it through."

"And then what?"

The priest smiled. He raised his hands to the heavens in a shrug. "Who knows? I want to see how it ends."

RAIN POUNDED against the roofs and the walls of the village for so long that we almost stopped noticing altogether. At home, my father and I stayed away from the rooms closest to the outside, retreating deeper and deeper into the house with our miners' helmets on till the sound dulled away to a gentle drumming.

And we waited.

Cadmus Brodie has always been a man of many stories. When I was growing up and he told me about his own family, where he had come from and what he had done before having children of his own, he described his life as one bound up in forces larger than himself. He fell into things. His sleepwalking took him into all kinds of situations, meeting all kinds of people, seeing all kinds of wonder he couldn't have imagined while awake.

Although when I was growing up, he never finished any of these stories.

Faith pointed it out to me once, while I helped with the dishes after a meal when Denver was over. The two older men were sitting at the kitchen table, smoking cigarettes, playing a friendly game of dominoes and telling stories. Dad was talking about his adventures as a photographer in the territories.

"He doesn't finish stories," Faith said. "Had you noticed that?"

I looked over at him, thought about it, then shook my head.

Faith nodded, smiled knowingly. "He just jumps from one to the next. He never finishes anything."

That didn't seem right to me, but when I tried to remember, I couldn't come across any time when my father had actually finished one of his stories. All of the endings I remember were supplied by other people at the table as they struggled to tie up the loose ends before Cadmus lept forward into the next yarn.

"That can't be right," I said.

Faith nodded again, plunged her hands into the dishwater. "He only finishes stories when he's asleep. When he's awake, he just starts them. Listen to him sometimes, when you see him walking."

And from then on I did.

HOPELESSLY LOST in a constant state of slumber, unable to tell the difference between waking and sleeping, Dad started to tell the ends of all his stories. At first I didn't know what he was doing. He just seemed to be babbling. I'd be feeding him dinner and he'd look up at me, suddenly, and start talking about seeing his long-lost stepsister that night he first met his employer, Fetch. Then, after that story was done, like it was gone forever, he'd finish a story about cans of peaches that he had plundered as a child and the time he had accidentally knocked his mother's eye loose while he ran around the living room as a child, arms stretched wide, pretending to be an airplane.

He wasn't talking to me. I know that. I don't think he even knew I was in the room. He was just talking, telling stories.

One day, when we were deep in the living room, all of us, dead relatives and all, huddled around the table playing dominoes, he started talking about Samuel Townsend and Alexander Garfax.

Everyone in the village has heard this story before. Everyone knows about Garfax's mad quest to discover that great lost city of Scotland, Bennogonium, and how he hoped to find it in the New World. They know about Townsend, the captain whose luck ran dry and whose ships were destined to sink. They know about the game of dominoes, of the trick that Garfax employed to keep him alive. They know about the fishermen who heard tales of that nameless little bay, of the bountiful schools of fish that lived there.

But that wasn't the story my father told.

"There were three of them," he told me, without meaning to speak to me, click-clacking his tiles on the board.

"Three what?" I asked.

"There were three."

The game never ended. Garfax and Townsend played until they both died, within days of each other. When the fishermen came and set up the village that Townsend had named after the man who had doomed him to end his days there, they brought their families and their friends. This new community took pity on the two madmen playing dominoes on the beach. They viewed them as the town patriarchs, the founding fathers. Respected and humoured but not listened to.

So when it rained or when winter came, they took the two men into their homes. They even tried, at times, to separate them from their game, but this never took. For each and every day of their lives spent on that bay, the two men came together and played.

"Today's the day I'm going to win," Townsend would say at the beginning of each day, placing his loaded pistol next to the board.

"Maybe," Garfax said. And when it looked like Townsend might win, Garfax changed the tiles when he wasn't looking.

The two men married women from the village. These women, whose names have never been recorded, should be noted as being two of the most understanding women of the nineteenth century. They loved these madmen out of, I think, a sense of obligation, but they loved them all the same. I would like to believe that this love was reciprocated.

The men grew old and they had children. One each. Both boys. And these boys took the names of their fathers. After the funeral for Alexander Garfax, for he died first, Samuel Townsend retired to his bedroom, never to return under his own power. He would be carried out a week later by his wife and son.

The very next day after the funeral, the second Samuel Townsend came to the house of the second Alexander Garfax, his father's pistol in his hand, and said to him, "Today's the day I'm going to win."

And so the game continued, almost as if they original men had never died. The second Samuel Townsend wore the uniform of his father, patched up and repaired by his mother and then, when she passed, his own wife. He read the log book that his father had kept as if it were a holy book, as if he had written it himself. He became an expert on all subjects nautical, even though he would never step a foot off solid ground. The second Alexander Garfax did likewise. He spent the rest of his days when he was not playing that deadly game taking long walks through the pines, looking for that great lost city mentioned only in passing by Herodotus, and quizzed travellers endlessly about what they had seen in the hopes of discovering more clues.

They ignored completely the village's passing into the twentieth century.

"But there were three?" I asked, watching my father trail off a bit in the middle of a play.

"Yes," he said, blinking away layers of dust from his eyes. "Three."

The third Samuel Townsend born was a girl. And while you might think that this would have caused a change in the game, it didn't for the longest time. She was freakish. That was how her father explained it to her. Many things happened at sea, and one of those things that worked its way into her own personal mythology was that the third Townsend had been horribly deformed during a trip to the Orient, where she had contracted some exotic malady that had robbed her of her manhood and created cancerous lumps on her chest. Like the original Townsend, who often complained about coughing up blood, this last descendant bled as well. Reading deeply, almost diving, into the space between the lines, the last captain found a place where she could fit. She became an expert of the sea and took with her always her grandfather's pistol, claiming it to be her own.

In the beginning, the hatred toward Garfax that her forefathers had passed down to her also made sense. But during the nightly game over the years, Townsend discovered that she hated the eccentric Garfax less and less. She enjoyed his stories, his strange theories and wonderful discoveries that could never be proven outside of his ability to tell them.

They slept together once, six months before Garfax left the village. It was awkward and clumsy, provoking so much confusion that Townsend once more returned to the refuge of her grandfather's book, whereupon she found a story about his one-time homosexual encounter with a sailor. Justifiably ashamed, the original Townsend had framed this event in vague language, but it was enough for the third Townsend to latch onto. The next night, when Garfax returned and wanted to resume their previous activities, she stopped him, informed him of their transgression, and said that she could never be with someone of an inferior rank.

Arguments proved pointless, flowery words even more useless. Townsend ripped them up, all these dangerously new words and sentiments. When Garfax finally left the village that bore his name, ashamed and broken-hearted, he took all meaning out of Townsend's life.

I listened to my father's story, the end of the village's history that I'd never heard, without moving for several minutes. The dead relatives, likewise, didn't move. The only sounds in the room were the occasional cough from Hugo, a memory from his time in the gas brigades of the First World War, and the click-clacking of domino tiles on the wood of the table.

"What happened next?" I asked.

No one knows this story anymore, but it's true. Even the people who were there barely recall it with any accuracy. There are no records anymore. No official accounts written down to make it solid in our minds. But once there was an explosion of history in this country, a torrent of stories that was so large that it terrified people.

"After the war," Dad explained, looking at his great-uncles, Hugo and Starling, "the government changed the way the schools taught history."

A commission was organized. They went around the world collecting all the great stories, all the histories, and brought them back. The idea was that by knowing all the histories, that this new country would be able to avoid the tragedies that had befallen the world. They did not want history to repeat.

But there was too much. Too many stories. They had to split them up. So during the time after the war and before the purges, schools all across the country learned completely different sets of stories. Children in Edmonton learned about duelling practices among the French nobles, while at the same time studying stories of Australian Aboriginal Dream Time and the construction of China's Great Wall. They learned their own stories, too. Local stories. Students in Montreal learned about the various revolutions of Europe, coupled with ancient Norse legend. Children from Middle, Saskatchewan, wrote tests on the various occupying forces of Jerusalem and the One Hundred Million Suicide in Japan.

The problem came when these children went on to university, when they met up over long distances and tried to share their stories. There was just too much confusion.

"Nobody knew how to speak to anybody," Dad said.

So the government sponsored a cadre of historians to simplify the history, bring it all together into a single tome they could publish and release across the whole country. There was some resistance. Suddenly empowered by studying their own histories and those from across the world, people from less renowned villages rallied against the changes. The purges followed. In an effort to make a single story out of the country, the historians edited out those villages and townships that had never contributed a notable footnote or had any real economic resource. There were massive book burnings that spawned paper storms, showering the country with fragments of words and pages that tasted like ash on the tongue. In response, renegade historians went across the country trying to save libraries and villages, secreting them away from the relentless gaze of the government-sponsored historians.

Which is what happened to Garfax.

IF YOU CHECK, you'll never find this village on any map or in any record. It doesn't exist as far as the rest of the country is concerned. The government historians came and went, taking with them our sign and all evidence that we were ever here. The only thing they didn't take was the people.

"They hid," Dad told me. "One of the renegade historians came and got everyone to move the village into the pines, so that when the government men came, there was no one there to greet them but the captain."

The third Samuel Townsend stayed, despite the protests of the other villagers. She knew what it would mean, that they would take her away, finally getting her away from the bay and the life that she had inherited from a man long dead two generations back. And that's exactly what happened. The men came and took her away. They took away her grandfather's book and took her off, never to be seen again. They probably thought she was crazy.

I imagine that scene. I can see it in my mind, even though I've never seen a photograph. A middle-aged woman, her hair cut short, wearing her grandfather's naval uniform, a uniform that is barely hanging on her body, it's so old and worn. I can see them pulling her into the car, refusing to call her captain. She keeps telling them that she's a member of the British Navy, that she's a captain, that she's male.

Maybe they laugh.

But compared to losing Garfax, losing that inherited game and the one person who actually saw her, if only briefly, for someone other than a long-dead ancestor, would that last indignity really have stung as badly as I imagine it would have?

THERE ARE SO MANY STORIES that won't make it in here. Stories that Denver and Aunt Connie told me, while I sat with them in the empty movie theatre, trying not to smile as they held hands. Stories about the train out in the woods, about the two-dollar fortune, about the identity of that renegade historian who saved the villagers but not the village, and why since that time there hasn't been a single fish in Garfax Bay, a water once brimming with resource.

Dad told me other stories. I couldn't stop him. I had to walk away, out into the pines and through the rain, just to stop them from coming. Soaked to the bone and shivering, passing furniture turned to mulch and crumbling architecture and rusting cars, I couldn't keep anything straight.

All the stories washed over me. I thought of my mother, who went to water one summer day and changed the way the village looked at us. I will never know why she did it other than the reason she gave me, one that I still don't understand. I thought of my sleepwalking father, of the pictures he took. I thought of my siblings, both disappeared and gone, never to return. I thought of Caleb and his parents. Of that first great house that was split into five sections and the second that never held a single guest. I thought of Timothy Franklin, of the day the radios started speaking. And the game. I thought of that game. The insanity of it all. That first grudge carried down that ended in a frustrated one-night stand. And I kept thinking. I kept thinking because I couldn't stop, couldn't stem the flow or force any way for it to make sense.

I tried calling Sara, but the phones no longer worked anywhere in the village. On my way back home from the theatre one night, cradling a rapidly dissolving paper sack of groceries, I saw Catafalk standing at the water's edge, staring out into the bay, his hands in his pockets.

Back home I watched the rain get into the library. I tried to save it, but there were just too many books. The rain ruined whole sections at a time, liquefying all the pages until they lumped together in one large mass of white and incomprehensible black, separated from their covers. I found my father's self-help package and read it again. I read it to him, trying to spark some light of recognition in his eyes. Instead he told me a story about how he had lost his virginity to a Glasgow girl who took up with him because one night she found him sleeping in a tree, with no knowledge of how he had gotten there.

WHAT HAPPENS NEXT?

I WALKED INTO my father's bedroom and woke him up. It took the better part of an hour. I flashed lights in his eyes, sparked lights. He blinked. I took a wet washcloth and lay it over his face. He gasped from the cold.

"Oz?" he said, pulling the cloth away from his face. He looked surprised to see me, as if he hadn't seen me in weeks.

"Hey, Dad."

"What's going on?"

I smiled at him. I tried to smile. But Cadmus Brodie has always been a good judge of people. He knows them too well. He saw the strain on my face, the wear around my eyes. He saw where they were red and then when he looked down, he saw the length of rope in my hand.

"I'm sorry," I said.

He sat up, straightened his back. It was the most awake I had seen him in months. "What do you have to be sorry about?"

I brought up the length of rope, squeezed it in my hands. "Dad, I have to leave."

He looked at me, looked at the rope. "All right. When are you coming back?"

"I'm not."

"Oh."

We both sat there for a time.

I tried to say that I wanted to save him, that he should come with me. That we could escape this place together and start somewhere new. But I didn't. There was only so far my father was willing to compromise.

We talked for hours. He asked me about what had been going on and seemed surprised when I talked about the storm.

"Do you know about Mum?" I asked.

"Yes," he said, looking down at his hands. "I know."

And when it was time, I told him that I needed to tie him to the bed.

"I don't want to be tied up," he said, a touch of fear in his voice.

"I know."

"I don't want to be tied up."

"I know."

"I need to be able to move."

"Dad," I said. "If you sleepwalk, you might end up hurting yourself."

He looked at me.

"If you don't tie yourself to the bed," I said. "I can't leave."

There are many stories about my father, about how he is loved by people. When my mother went to water, there were other stories, though. About how his marriage to my mother was on the breaking point, about how they were divorced already and keeping it quiet, or that he had moved us to a country that wasn't our own and that he was selfish in only thinking of himself. And maybe he was selfish. Maybe he was, but he was never cold. He loved us, all four of us, to the best of his ability.

The bravest thing my father ever did was take that rope away from me and tie himself to that bed.

"I'm sorry," I said, as I reached for the doorknob.

He shook his head. He had been crying himself. "Nothing to be sorry about," he said. "You take care. I love you."

"I love you, too."

AND I RAN. I ran through the pines as fast as I could, even though it was dark from the storm and difficult to see. Branches whipped at my face and I held up my hands to keep from being blinded.

I brought a flashlight with me, but even that didn't help. The arc of light caught the hulls of long-abandoned cars, windows broken and smashed from impacts with trees. There were buses, too. Their long, stretched-out wrecks looking like the carcasses of great whales. And there were buildings. So many buildings. Towers and walls. Rooms without doors, without roofs. I don't know where they all came from. Picture frames hanging in the treetops. Oak tables furnished with plates, and bowls collecting nothing but rainwater.

I came across a car. I came across several. Eventually I found one with the keys left inside that started when I turned the ignition. The headlights came on, and when they did, the pines in front of me burst into illumination. I was at the bottom of a small hill, so only the bottom trunks of the pines in front could be seen through the storm.

There were people out there. White legs, moving through the branches. Some of them standing still. I heard the song of Starling's silver trumpet and when I got myself free of the rut the car was in, I started driving. And when I realized that there was a radio inside, I began to talk.

I hope you can hear me. Can you hear me? Are you still with me?

I'VE BEEN DRIVING for hours and it's still not light. I'm almost out of gas.

I know what I'm going to do next. When I run out of gas, I'm going to get out of this car and start walking. Up ahead the hill slopes upward, and I am going to climb it. Hopefully there will be a road at the top of that hill.

If there is, then I will walk along the road until I see a car. I will hold out my thumb as it passes me. I will do that for each car until someone picks me up. I will run up to the passenger side window. I hope it will be Lizzie.

If so, then she'll lean over across the passenger side and roll down the window. She will ask me where I'm going. And when she asks, I will tell her.

WE'RE ALMOST THERE.

Acknowledgements

A BOOK IS LIKE ANYTHING ELSE—it takes a village to raise. And while this one was family born, it was raised primarily by strangers, the most important of these being Aritha van Herk. I don't think there would have ever been a book if it weren't for her. She spent three years trying to teach me to be brave in my work and finally, when I still wasn't ready, tricked me into it. For that and everything else, I owe her immensely. Many thanks to Sean Stewart, who answered an angst-ridden e-mail eight years ago and taught me that the most important thing for a writer to have is an acute sense of dissatisfaction. To Christian Bok, who told me about the importance of endurance. I am deeply indebted to the Board and everyone else involved in the production of this book at NeWest Press. It's been a long stretch, with people coming in and out of the process, and I appreciate everyone's dedicated attention and affection for this novel. Special thanks go out to Tiffany Regaudie and Virginia Penny, who ran the last leg of the race with me and in a nice twist were instrumental in a small but pivotal change that was made to the last few lines. I also want to put it out there that Thomas Wharton, my editor, has the patience of a saint. I am incredibly grateful for all the latitude he allowed me in making the changes I wanted to make, as well as pointing out the times when I was actually being quite silly. Thank you, Tom.

And of course, I'd like to give a shout out to all the usual suspects. James Holiday-Scott, the brother I never had, who went through the shit first and then had the kindness to show me all the shortcuts. Natalie Z. Walschots, that littlest adult who dreams with electricity, introduced me to wunderkammers and is genuinely excellent company; this novel would have looked completely different without her input. Ed Schmutz, who helped save Garfax from the historians, taught me the sheer necessity of dance and was the first to play for me the works of Franz Emerick. Thanks also to Rene Froetscher, who corrected my spelling of that most famous German composer you've never heard of. Tara Drouillard, who said four magic words when I needed to hear them the most and made a point to show me that history doesn't always repeat. Crystal Munroe, who still tells the best stories and is the only passenger I will ever need; without her there would be no Lizzie Parks, and the novel would be poorer for it. derek beaulieu, a man who was avidly supportive of my writing when he really had no business being so generous. Thanks to Garth McEwen, who told me so many years ago a story of horses and shotguns and gave me the seed that would eventually become this book—I miss your company. Finally, I'd like to single out my family one last time. To Diana Mary Cranstoun, William Allen Scott, and Victoria Fiona Jordan Scott; without the three of you, I'd have no stories worth telling.

Everyone who is important to me is in this book, in one form or another. Thanks for sharing your stories, insights, and company with me over the last few years. Any and all mistakes contained within are mine.

About the author

WILLIAM NEIL SCOTT was born in Aberdeen, Scotland, but spent the majority of his life in Calgary, Alberta. Scott completed a BA Honours Degree in English with a Concentration in Creative Writing, at the University of Calgary. *Wonderfull* is his first novel.

A note on the type

This book is set in Quadraat, a contemporary typeface that was developed with digital reproduction in mind, yet has a strong calligraphic sensibility. Designed by Fred Smeijers for Fontshop International beginning in 1992, Quadraat has developed into an extensive font family that seemed just right for this story.

Library and Archives Canada Cataloguing in Publication

Scott, William Neil, 1980–
Wonderfull / William Neil Scott.
(Nunatak fiction)

ISBN: 978-1-897126-19-6

I. Title. II. Series.
PS8637.C695W66 2007 C813'.6 C2007-902160-3

Editor for the Board: Tom Wharton
Cover and interior design: Virginia Penny
Cover image: Virginia Penny
Author photo: Diana Scott

NeWest Press acknowledges the support of the Canada Council for the Arts
and the Alberta Foundation for the Arts, and the Edmonton Arts Council for
our publishing program. We also acknowledge the financial support of the
Government of Canada through the Book Publishing Industry Development
Program (BPIDP) for our publishing activities.

NeWest Press
201–8540–109 Street
Edmonton, Alberta T6G 1E6
780–432–9427

www.newestpress.com

NeWest Press is committed to protecting the environment and to the
responsible use of natural resources. This book is printed on recycled and
ancient-forest-friendly paper.

No bison were harmed in the making of this book.

1 2 3 4 5 10 09 08 07

printed and bound in Canada